Lost Men

Also by

Brian Leung

WORLD FAMOUS LOVE ACTS

Lost Men

A Novel

Brian Leung

THREE RIVERS PRESS · NEW YORK

Copyright © 2007 by Brian Leung
Reader's Group Guide copyright © 2008 by Three Rivers Press, an imprint of the Crown Publishing Group, a division of Random House, Inc., New York

Published in the United States by Three Rivers Press, an imprint of the Crown Publishing Group, a division of Random House, Inc., New York.
www.crownpublishing.com

Three Rivers Press and the Tugboat design are registered trademarks of Random House, Inc.

Originally published in hardcover in slightly different form in the United States by Shaye Areheart Books, an imprint of the Crown Publishing Group, a division of Random House, Inc., New York, in 2007.

Library of Congress Cataloging-in-Publication Data
Leung, Brian.
Lost men : a novel / Brian Leung.—1st ed.
1. Fathers and sons—Fiction. 2. China—Fiction. I. Title.
PS3612.E92L67   2006
813'.6—dc22   2006028803

ISBN: 978-0-307-35165-4

Printed in the United States of America

Design by Lynne Amft

10 9 8 7 6 5 4 3 2 1

First Paperback Edition

For Vernilee, Emmogene, Barbara Jo, Audra Fern,
Willie Catherine, and always, for giant squid
and kids on the lam.

The Age of Regret, years ago, far away from the now. Westen Chan has not seen his father for months, will not see him for decades. He is still not used to being around his great-uncle Cane. The two of them sit in the cab of the idling pickup. His uncle pats him hard on the head. "Your aunt Catherine thinks this is a good idea." She has sent them off to meet the only other Chinese in the county so Westen will know he isn't alone.

The pair step out of the truck. Westen is small, even for eight. He is dark-haired and olive-skinned; people guess that he's a mix, perhaps even Spanish or Black Irish, but never Chinese. His uncle Cane is tall with heaped shoulders, a lumbering walk, and a bristly head of white hair. His face and arms are pink and splotchy from too many years of sun.

Westen and his uncle walk between long, tin-sided buildings, the clucking hum of chickens sifting over them. It is the egg ranch of Parker Cheung. The late morning is damp, misty, and the pair head toward the covered loading dock where Parker and other men are stacking egg flats on racks. Parker's face is obscured by the bill of his sweat-stained cap, but when he turns to say hello, he reveals his Chinese face, the broad roundness of it anchored by a wide but compressed nose. Westen is both cautious and pleased to see a Chinese, someone who shares the features of his father.

"Cheung," Westen's uncle says.

"Cane," Parker returns, lifting his cap to wipe a plaid sleeve across his brow.

"This little fella is my great-nephew Westen. What do you think about that?"

Parker reaches out his hand, and Westen steps forward, returning a hopeful smile while taking the man's palm. He is surprised at how rough it is, and then, in an instant, is taken back by the sourness of Parker's odor. He lets go of the man's hand and stands again next to his uncle.

"What can I do you for?"

"Catherine thought we ought to come by and see if you might give Westen a tour of your operation."

"If you like eggs and chicken shit, I've got plenty to show you."

The two men shake with laughter, but Westen remains still. This man is not like his father at all. Not like any Chinese he's ever met. This man, in fact, is exactly like his uncle Cane. Suddenly there is a woman's voice, and the three turn toward a house not too far off, a gray vacancy of smoke rising from its chimney. "Pak. Pak," the woman calls. She is leaning out of the window, and Westen notices she is Chinese too. "Bring me dead chicken," she yells.

Parker looks at Westen and his uncle. "You two want to stay for lunch?" While the men laugh again, Westen thinks he definitely does not want to eat here. Holding up a cracked index finger bent slightly above the last knuckle as if broken years ago, Parker continues. "Give me a minute," he says, stepping away and into one of the chicken houses. The ranch is busy with other men walking between the buildings; it gurgles with the sound of hundreds of hens, then a roused clucking that Westen recognizes as the sound of fear. A dull *thwack* stills the clamor and Parker returns holding a white, beheaded chicken by its feet. It hangs at his side oozing a beaded drool of blood, which drips to the dark ground like glowing red candle wax.

"Say," Parker begins, extending the chicken toward Westen, "how about running this up to the wife, little man?" The bird smells and doesn't look nearly as white close up. Westen checks his uncle for direction because he does not want to touch this dead thing.

"Go about it," his uncle says. "Cheung and me got a meeting with Mr. Daniels for a few minutes."

Parker offers a conspiratorial chuckle. "It's Mr. Beam that's waiting on us." He looks at Westen. "Just carry it on up to the wife and tell her I promised you a cookie." Westen takes the chicken by its leathery feet, holding it as far away from his body as possible.

"Go on now," his uncle prods. "And best not to tell Mrs. Cheung about the meeting." He winks at Parker and the pair head inside the egg building.

Alone, Westen is aware of the sound of water falling. He looks up the hill where he is to deliver the chicken. The white house stares back at him from two red-curtained windows. To one side, half a football field away and through a stand of pine, he spots the wide lip of a waterfall, the dimension revealing itself as an unbroken expanse. The constancy of sound is nearly overwhelming. In front of this wall of falling water a thick, dark bridge extends itself, dead-ending at a cliff. The scene gives him the odd sensation of being distant and present all at once. A person in blue, a woman he guesses, sits on the railing, dangling her feet over the side. Her body gestures forward and back, clearly at ease with the precarious height. Westen has the impulse to call out to tell her to be careful, but she is much too far away to hear him.

Once at the house, Westen stands in front of the door thinking he might just drop the chicken and run. Before he can make a decision the door swings open. Inside, a plump woman with dyed hair and narrow black eyes brings her hand to her face in mock surprise. She is the one who called down to Parker for the chicken. "Your auntie say you come today," she offers without introduction, looking Westen up and down, nodding while she takes the bird. "Okay. I guess you *Quang Dong Wa*?"

Westen grins. He knows the meaning. "My father is."

"No. Say *you* Cantonese."

Sensing this is not a rhetorical command, he complies and accepts Mrs. Cheung's invitation to enter the house. She is the kind of Chinese he remembers, her assertive manner and broken English acting as a temporary balm, though he wonders how it's possible she and Parker are married. The house is surprisingly bright, filled with books and chicken-shaped knickknacks of all sorts. Westen and Mrs. Cheung pass a sliding glass door offering a view through the trees of the bridge and waterfall.

"You sit here," Mrs. Cheung says as they reach the kitchen. She taps a chrome chair with yellow vinyl upholstery that matches the Formica tabletop. The chicken is flopped into the sink. "I clean outside in a minute." She sits opposite Westen, hands folded in front of her, embroidered orange maple leaves on her sweater vest, each surrounded by small beveled rhinestones that could be rain or sunlight breaking through a fall canopy. "Your auntie ask me talk to you. Why you not a happy boy?"

"I'm happy," Westen says, but he knows there is no conviction in it.

Mrs. Cheung places her hands flat on the table and stands. "Wait," she says, exiting the kitchen. When she returns she is holding a pad of paper and a large red book with gold Chinese lettering. She asks Westen a series of questions: his birth date, the time he was born, how to spell his first name. With each query she consults the book and writes on the pad of paper. Her work is certain and officious, as if she is interviewing a job applicant, her lips thinned in tight concentration. Westen watches her blunt fingers press the pencil, embedding dense Chinese characters into the paper. Mrs. Cheung makes a single nod with each notation. In a quiet moment when she is double-checking her work Westen watches a drop of water collect at the lip of the kitchen faucet until it relents to gravity. "Maybe I should go find Uncle Cane," he says when the drop falls.

Mrs. Cheung looks up from her pad. "They drinking. Don't worry. I take you home."

Westen knows he will not see his uncle for the rest of the day.

"You will visit China," Mrs. Cheung says, pointing to her math. "But I think you will be an unhappy boy and an unhappy man until then."

Westen cannot comprehend the forecast, but he makes an attempt. "China will make me happy?"

"No," she says emphatically. "Nothing *make* anyone happy. But I going to help." She reaches into her pocket and retrieves four items: a thin red ribbon, matches, a candle, and a palm-sized box covered in worn blue velvet. She ties the ribbon around the box, leaving a bow the size and shape of a small butterfly. "My mother give me before I come to U.S. I give you now."

There is something about this gesture that comforts Westen as he watches Mrs. Cheung light the candle and drip dense wax onto the knot of the bow. "My mother do this too. She tell me I'm unhappy girl after my father die." The pair sit quietly looking at this new red-winged creation sitting atop the blue box. "Now you open in China only at right moment," Mrs. Cheung continues. "Maybe you be happy. Before that, no good. You tell someone, no good. This only *your* box."

"When will this happen?"

"Wait for your father like I wait for Mr. Cheung," she says. "He come back. You put away until then. Be a good boy and remember to listen to your auntie. She love you."

Westen feels a flush of heat and hope at the prospect of his father's return, but he wonders just how long he is going to have to wait. Picking up Mrs. Cheung's box, he carefully feels its weight. "Is it magic?" he asks.

"No," Mrs. Cheung says firmly. "It hope."

1

The son receives a letter from his father;
he considers his home and how to respond.

A letter from my father has arrived, and I don't want to open it. I found it with the other mail as I walked up my gravel drive looking through furniture ads, bills, and inquiries about my pigeons. Among these was an envelope in my father's handwriting, posted from Los Angeles. Part of me wants to put the letter back in the mailbox. He has written *Westen Chan* on the outside, a last name I haven't used since I was eight, when they changed it to Gray. The morning mist rolls past me, reaching around my body like a slow hand as I open the envelope. There is not much to read, a few lines. The second-to-last one says, "I want to take you to China."

I sit on the stump of an old pine I cut down last year, and reread the letter.

Dear Westen:

Yes, it has been too long. And yes, I have paid a big price for leaving you. I am sure it has cost you as well. I have been in contact with your aunt and she tells me, among many things, you have chosen to remain alone. If I have caused this, I'm sorry. There are some important things about your mother you should know. I have a debt to you I have not paid and I want to take you to China. Please, I would like to explain myself and I hope you can forgive me.

Your Father

How can I forgive a man I have not seen in decades? And he says I have chosen to be alone. Aunt Catherine has kept my confidence, then, because it is only true that I'm alone *now*. I was in love for a long time, but I learned I am not meant for relationships. Being left is a pattern in my life that began with my father and I choose not to invite the opportunity again. Now he returns with an offer of a trip to China, which sounds like a word I shouldn't know, something without meaning. But it comes to my voice and I whisper it into the Northwest air, where I imagine it hanging for a moment, white and fragile and foreign.

I think of a woman from years ago who lived on an egg ranch, Mrs. Cheung, who drove me home when my uncle was getting drunk with her husband. She left me with a gift, and before letting me out of the car reminded me that the blue box she'd given me was between the two of us. Even now I know where it is hidden and I think I should leave it there.

I look up from the letter and standing in front of me is the neighbor boy, Marky, and his friend Claire. They are both nine years old and round as balloons. Sometimes I let them tag along when I go fishing. Claire reminds me of a very old woman in very young skin. She wears her hair in a tight crown of braids. Her family is Methodist. Whenever she gets a chance, she chastises me for not being married. "Don't you want children and someone to love?" she likes to ask.

"Yes," I always respond, even though, for me, I don't think either is possible.

"Oscar's dying," Marky says now. He sounds resigned and sad. Oscar is his yappy, swaybacked dachshund that likes the cheese crackers I slip him when I walk by Marky's house. In fact, I've known Oscar longer than I've known Marky. The dog is old, so I'm not surprised, though I act otherwise.

"That's awful," I say. "What's wrong with him?"

Slightly agitated, Marky scratches his bristly head. "He's got tumors. And my dad says we can't bury him in the yard when he dies."

"Why not?"

"Because," Claire chimes in, rolling her eyes, "his dad's cuckoo in the noggin."

I stifle a response. I've met Marky's father, and Claire's diagnosis isn't far off. Once he made the entire family sleep outside because he had a dream their house was going to burn down. He's not a bad man, but I understand a father's power to disappoint, which is probably why Marky and I get along so well.

"Dad says he don't want diseases in his yard. We even have to keep Oscar in the garage till he dies."

I look at the farthest part of my property and then back at Marky and Claire's plump faces. "I'm sorry about Oscar," I say. "But when he dies, you can bury him here."

"Really?" Marky reveals his gapped front teeth. "You don't care about tumors?"

"As long as they don't grow into tumor bushes, of course not."

Claire pats me on the hand in her overly mature manner. "You're a dear," she says, looking at my father's letter, which is still in my hand. She grabs Marky's elbow to pull him away, as if she knows that this piece of paper contains something weighty. On some unspoken cue they both run up the street, though they start walking after fifty yards or so.

So I'm thinking about getting a piece of oak for a headstone and somewhere I still have the wood-burning kit Uncle Cane gave me when I was a child. If I think about these things, maybe I won't have to think about my father and the intrusion of his letter into my life. The Columbia River is where I've carved out a place for myself: the dark blush of heather at the edge of the lawn, wild lupine I brought down from the mountains. I coax each plant from hard seed soaked in warm water. This is how I discovered patience. I have always been calmed by the pine tree at the edge of the property, the last of the old trees in Blue Falls. I have stood beneath it in the rain—the needles capturing the drops, altering their speed and course. Sometimes in a downpour, the base of the tree, with its broad branches above, feels like an open shower.

My father has never been here, never seen my home. Locals call it the Lighthouse because the second floor has a ruby-colored oval pane of glass. Flecks of gold mixed into the glass help to create its color. Early travelers on the river used the red glow of the window in the evening hours as a landmark. I have always wondered at this touch of extravagance in such a basic wooden house. The roof leaks in a new place every few years, and some of the pine siding has split. Still, not bad really for having gone through nearly a century of snow and warm, humid summers.

This used to be my great-aunt Catherine's home. When my father gave me up as a child, it became my home too. Now my aunt has moved permanently to San Diego, and I have stayed. After I was done repainting the white siding and green trim, I bought it from her. I pick up odd jobs in town, and in good weather I get yard work. Between that and selling my racing and show pigeons, it's enough.

I am part of life here in the Columbia River Gorge, its constant green slope terminating in a blue artery of water. I live on a steep grade, always on the verge of stumbling. The ponderosa and hemlock and the spring flowers mask volcanic rock. In the fall, the feathery yellow of the aspen will crack across the mountains like hatching chicks. Each season offers a new identity. When you live here long enough, you learn to do the same. It seemed like a way of life until now, as I hold a letter that's calling me by my old name.

2

The son considers a letter to his father;
he recalls his childhood bond.

I have carried my father's letter for three days. His stationery gets increasingly worn with each reading. He wants to take me to China when I spent so much of my life wanting him to take me home.

I sit in the brightest room on the top floor of my house, preparing to write my father that I will not go to China with him, something I wish I could tell him in Chinese. I have lost nearly all the words I used to know. When I was very young my father mostly spoke to me in Cantonese and Mandarin until he was certain English would not overtake my voice. Even my blond mother, with all her hard Caucasian syllables, got through breakfast and dinner in broken Chinese until I was two or three. Please—*m-goy*—was the only word she pronounced truly well. Before I fully learned English, she often used this word, followed by a number of hand signals that completed her sentences.

The early language barrier with my mother brought me and my father close. He wanted me to be Chinese. When I was in kindergarten, I came home one day and complained that the other Chinese children were calling me white. He took off his black-framed glasses and pinched the faint bridge of his nose.

"No. No. You are Chinese," he said, firmly. Though it is not lost on me now that he chose to convey this in English.

He walked me to the large mirror on my closet door. We stood side by side, holding hands as he spoke. "This is what your classmates see," he said. "You have the same olive skin as they do, the same dark hair. They also see that some things are different." He ran his finger down the line of my nose. "This is your mother's. Yes, and your eyes, too. But someday you will also have a voice just like mine. They don't understand that you're lucky to have some of both of us." We looked at each other in the mirror. He held his black hair in place with oil, and his glasses were tinted, giving his cheeks a faint amber tone.

He must have realized I wasn't satisfied. "What no one can see is that you are Chinese inside," he said. I almost asked what that meant to him.

"*Wo xian zai ming bai le,*" I said instead. I knew that when I spoke Chinese it made him happy. "Now I understand." It is one of the few phrases that has stayed with me, along with his promise that I would someday have a voice just like his, something from the inside. I have always wondered if that came true.

After the talk with my father, I woke every morning to a plate with three large dates on my bedstand, placed there by him to remind me of our heritage and prosperity. It was the one gift he looked forward to as a small boy in China, he explained to me once. Every year on his grandmother's birthday he received a small tin of dates. From his descriptions I can even picture it: the gold metal sealed around the edges with red wax. He counted each date, and calculated how small his bites must be for the gift to last a year.

Along with this daily offering, my father and I had another morning ritual. After I finished the last of the dates, the pits neatly piled on the plate, my father lay facedown on the floor without his shirt. I hopped out of bed and walked the length of his back several times. His vertebrae pressed into the arches of my small feet, sometimes giving with a sharp pop. Above his left shoulder blade were two evenly spaced round scars the size of marbles. He told me very little about these except that they were caused by bullets when he and his family were escaping from the Communists. The man who would have been my uncle did not survive.

Unable to start my letter, I open the window. The morning light comes to the gorge like a vapor, thin and speculative. The trees are warming and the scent of pine is as elemental as oxygen or hydrogen. I spent much of my childhood here at the edge of the Columbia. A hundred years ago this property was the center of a working farm, sheep and chickens for loggers and fishermen. Now it's reduced to a few acres, overtaken at the edges by young trees. This is a land of enclosure. The forest wants to return and I have decided to let it.

The apple tree behind the house has gone wild. Its spray of thin branches hangs over the part of the building where I keep my pigeons. Every winter I think this tree has died and every spring it surprises me, first with white blossoms, then budding out in green. When I was eight, Aunt Catherine lifted me on her shoulders so I could reach past the hornets and bees and bird-pecked fruit and pick the highest apples.

Beneath the tree is Uncle Cane's whetstone, rusted in place. This is where he sharpened our ax blades every few weeks. A tin can hangs at the side by a wire. I kept it full of water while he pedal-pumped the round stone, dribbling water to reduce the white sparks. "Sharpening will be your job when you get older," he told me. I have never used it.

Now I sit at my desk trying to write to this man who brought me dates and whose skin was soft and moist under my feet. The paper in front of me is blank, except for the words "Dear Father." This greeting strikes me as odd now, but there was a time when I would have meant it.

I am skeptical. My father has not written since I asked him to stop his annual correspondence, the dispatches from Hong Kong or Los Angeles every year on my birthday. Always a check and an apology, but never an opportunity to open the blue box that was supposed to give me hope. What could he want now, in my thirty-second year? I am not the Caucasian-looking boy with the bowl-cut hair that he left after my mother died.

I have never understood why my father gave up after she was gone. Before my mother was struck by a car, they playfully argued over names for a daughter when we went out to eat dim sum. They considered Wuhan, or Beatrice for her mother. After my mother died, my father's eyes looked scooped and waxy and he barely spoke to me. I was waist-high to the people at the funeral, all of them in dark suits, as if I stood in a forest of black trees. I remember the green grass beyond my mother's mahogany casket, and, after the service, my father's words. "You're going to stay with your great-aunt Catherine for a while." And then, as if this mattered to me, "They have two nice homes." In a couple of sentences, my life was rerouted. Instead of studying Chinese characters and painting on rice paper on Saturdays, I learned to train racing pigeons and to pull salmon out of the Columbia.

From my open window I see Claire walking up the drive in a black wool coat, her braids a perfect nest on her head. Marky follows in a white shirt and a red tie, pushing a wheelbarrow containing a small cardboard box that must hold Oscar.

When they arrive in front of the house, I am waiting and ready, though the timing is not planned. Claire steps forward, her formality palpable. "It's so very good of you to do this," she says, shaking my hand.

I show them the wood headstone I've made, all the letters capitalized—OSCAR. Marky is silent, his soft brown eyes regarding the wooden marker. "I think it should say his whole name."

"Oscar Kobelentz?" I ask, presuming Marky's last name is his dog's.

"No," Claire says, exasperated. "It's Oscar Mayer Wiener."

"Of course it is," I say, wanting to laugh that this detail escaped me all these years. And so we spend a few minutes burning Oscar's full name into the oak headstone before we take the box down into the yard, where the grave is already dug. Claire, of course, presides over the service. Marky stands close to me, placing a hand on my arm and leaning in slightly. I feel his weight and sadness, and I wish for him that his father were standing in my place.

Claire quotes a few Bible verses and eulogizes Oscar in a firm tone, as if there were an entire yard full of mourners. She tells us the expected things of his loyalty, his happy little bark, the way he got furiously agitated by roman candles and sparklers on the Fourth of July. Then Claire's voice changes, softens, and she looks directly at Marky, her somber tone lifting, a kindness coming across her eyes meant solely for him. "Of course," she says, "there are no dogs in heaven. But in Oscar's case, I'm sure God will make an exception."

It's the perfect thing to say, and all three of us feel satisfied before we lower Oscar into his grave. Claire snaps her fingers and Marky pulls a blue velveteen box from his pocket. "Oscar's tag," Claire says, placing it on the casket. An image flashes in my mind, Mrs. Cheung returning me to my great-aunt's house, *this* house, in my hands her blue velvet box secured with red ribbon. I had rushed upstairs and into the attic, where I wrapped my future in a doily, tucking it in the dark joint of an exposed beam. To this day it is retrievable, and in this moment I understand that the answer to my father's letter is inescapable.

We cover the rectangular hole, after which Claire claps her

hands together and says, "I believe you're serving tea and cookies to the bereaved?"

So that's what we do, walk to the house and have tea and cookies. "It was a lovely service, Claire," I say, rocking on the porch swing.

"Oh yes," she says, sitting up straight, two gingersnaps in her left hand. "God's spirit was with us." She looks around and, perhaps reacting to an extended silence, turns to me. "Why do you like being alone?"

"I just prefer it."

"No," she says, closing one eye as if she's looking into a microscope. "No, you don't."

I do not want to explain to Claire, or my father for that matter, that I have crapped out in love, that it has found its way to me but circumstances thwarted it each time. There are some, like me, who are better off alone. At least this is what I tell myself.

Marky is clearly still angry that Oscar was not allowed a final resting place in his own yard. He washes down half a chocolate-chip cookie, and with blackened teeth abruptly says, "I'm never going to talk to my father again."

"That's a horrible idea," I say instinctively. And just as quickly I'm certain that when they leave I will retrieve Mrs. Cheung's box. I must go to China. All these years I have done just as Marky, stomped my foot and given my father the silent treatment, held my breath for years to prove a point. I don't know if I *can* talk to him anymore, but I want to try, to be able to say the word *father* and have it mean something. He says he wants to tell me something about my mother I do not know. Maybe it will be a beginning. Maybe I can breathe again.

After Claire and Marky say good-bye, I walk into the house and go upstairs toward the attic, remembering Mrs. Cheung's words to me years ago. Nothing can *make* me happy. Yet she gave me that box, which holds out some hope, however moldering. I wonder what my father wants to accomplish with me now, and I consider this trip he proposes as if I'm watching one of my pigeons, beginning a journey with only an internal bearing. Other racers look at the return time, but for me the game is imagining the territory covered. Even in the air, all routes are not equal. There are currents, updrafts, and wind shears like hurdles and walls. When the birds return, it is not so much the time I assess as the damage done.

3

No matter how many times you reread your own writing, make these notes, the events with your son will never change. No. And yet you come back to your own words as if they will transform. Why do you waste your time? Who except you cares about what happens to a father and son? And yet, here you are, perhaps for the final time, an old man writing notes in his own journal.

Yes, yes. I must record the truth on every line, for my conscience and penance if nothing else. I write as if someone is listening, though I think now this is not possible for me. My son, Westen, was problematic from day one. Not at all how I imagined. In all my businesses, I have survived on the instinctual knowledge of success and failure. My investment in the trip appeared troubled from the start. In the back of my mind I expected to meet my eight-year-old son. I saw it as *di er ci jihui,* a second chance. Instead, at the airport, I was greeted by a thirty-two-year-old man. He looked so much like his mother. He had her small rounded nose, and lips that curved up slightly at the ends even though he wasn't smiling. I used to think he looked like me. "You're late," he said. These were our first face-to-face words in almost twenty-five years.

There we were, not a father and son really. Two men going on a trip together. Two strangers. A transaction.

"So upset already?" I asked him.

"I'm sorry," he said. "It just came out. I guess it's not going to happen like I hoped. Like it would all feel natural. Like I knew you. I guess that's what we have to learn again."

No, we did not talk much on the plane. At times it seemed Westen almost stopped himself from speaking. Would half-turn to me and then not advance what he'd planned to say. An hour into the flight, the attendants passed out shaving kits. Then Westen spoke. "I wonder if any of this is usable," he said. His voice was nearly uninflected, another quality of his mother's when she was concealing emotion.

"Perhaps," I said. "Not the razor."

"Uncle Cane taught me to shave, you know."

The point was clear, unmistakable. A fatherly duty I had not fulfilled. I wondered how many of them there were, and thought perhaps I should start keeping a tally. "That makes sense," I said. "He was your father figure." Those were words I did not want to say, but I knew they were true. I did not leave my son. I abandoned him. *Yes, you knew there would be such concessions and consequences on this trip.*

"When I was fifteen he took me to the drugstore and we bought a can of shaving cream and a bag of disposables. He made me pay for them myself. At home, he told me about lathering in circles, keeping the water hot, and dipping the blade after every two strokes. And to always shave with the grain so you don't get ingrown hairs. Which sounds funny now since I probably had about five hairs worth shaving at the time."

Westen looked at me with a tight, economical smile. I counted the years backward. "I was in Mexico City then," I said. As it came out, it sounded even to me like an inadequate excuse.

"In Mexico City?" He sounded surprised, as if he had been there too. "Is there anywhere you *haven't* been?"

"I've done a great deal of business in many places."

"Except Washington State," Westen said.

"True," I said. "Not there." I closed my eyes, listening to the efficient roar of the jet engines. "What are your last good memories of us?" I couldn't help but ask.

Westen was quiet for a long time, but I knew he'd heard me. "Before Mom died. You and I went to Griffith Park Observatory and looked at the Moon. You told me a story about a monkey that lived in one of the craters. Do you remember? You said he was bored all the time on Earth. The keepers brought toys and fruit for his cage, but he never looked at them. Every day they gave him new toys and different fruit, but the monkey was still bored. He never noticed anything. The keepers finally gave up and shot him into a Moon crater, where there was just the darkness and rocks. Do you remember telling me that story? It was pretty good."

"No, no. Not exactly, but your mother and I figured out quite soon you responded better to stories than spankings."

"That's one thing you gave me," he said. "I can tell a story just like you."

Yes, Westen grew up on stories. He himself was a story created by his mother and me, but it was a story he didn't yet know.

I wanted to offer an excuse why it seemed so easy to give Westen up, why I wanted him with me on this final trip to China. I thought if we reconnected, then it might not be so difficult to tell him these things. Maybe I erred. No, not maybe. I could have told him everything in one painful gesture and let it go. Cut my losses.

Maybe it was wrong from the beginning. Westen's mother and I had been dating only six or seven months when we took our first vacation. New Orleans. It was July and I had been in the U.S. just over a year. From the moment we stepped off the plane, Celia complained about the heat and humidity. But it did not bother me at all. In fact, it made me homesick for Hong Kong. Even in the French Quarter, with its sagging balconies and thickly painted cast iron, so different from the vertical steel and glass of Hong Kong. Yet the weather made me think of home.

Celia and I mainly stayed inside drinking, listening to live music. At night, not even waiting to get back to the hotel, we had sex in doorways as if we had a monopoly on every dark place. Half of it I don't remember, except Celia prodding me to relax. "You have to stay young. You're in America now," she said more than once. The vacation was an unofficial celebration of Celia's graduation from nursing school and my first year with a student visa. On our last night, Celia wore a matching white miniskirt and halter top. She was beautiful. Blond, blue-eyed, with wonderfully pale skin. Yes, my first American girlfriend. My first real asset. That is, she made me feel worth something. She held my hand, always walking faster than me. We wanted to find a bar that did not have someone outside trying to hustle us in. She kept saying, "I've got to get out of this heat."

I can finally write this part down. We arrived at a dark building a few blocks off Bourbon Street. There was a curtain drawn across the open doorway. A small sign on the wall said FINAL WEEK, ELVA CARTRANE. We couldn't hear anyone singing, but there were the low sounds of a piano, stand-up bass, and saxophone. As we walked through the curtain, a woman began to sing. She nodded to us when we took a table near the stage—a slightly raised, dim platform crowded with shadowed musicians. Elva Cartrane. The rest of the room was dark as well, except for the bar and orange candles on the tables.

Celia ordered us two Battering Rams. For about an hour we listened to the music. Singing without a microphone, Elva had a low and throaty voice. Her left hand dabbed sweat from her brown skin. She sang about men. She sang about God. Sometimes it seemed she was singing about her own life and she forgot we were there.

"This is more like it," Celia said, taking a sip from her drink. The room was hot and smoky, but she was right. That was when the U.S. still seemed exotic to me. Yes, I was trying hard to be American. Maybe to be Caucasian. Papá's warnings when I left Hong Kong were barely echoes. And there Celia and I were, in a room that was dark and damp and smelled like sex. I felt as if we were at the core of something like success, as if I'd almost arrived. I felt prosperous, yet didn't know how wrong I was.

SO EARLY IN our trip and my son sat next to me brooding, and this is what I thought of: two men related by blood and corrupted by different vocabularies. "What's the difference between a story and a lie?" Westen asked.

"It depends on who's listening."

"I'm all ears. Which will I get?"

I thought about this for a few seconds. "History," I told him.

"Which brings us back to my original question."

These were our semantics. If I told Westen about his mother and me, if I told him about my final illness, which words would he replace to create his own meaning? Under the best of circumstances a father tells his son he is dying and sees love manifest itself instantly. I had no right to expect such a reception to my news, and yet revelation was inevitable. Improbably, I thought somehow China would fix everything.

4

The father and son arrive in China;
they get their first view of Shanghai.

My father and I arrive in Shanghai at midnight. I am already searching for the right moment to open Mrs. Cheung's box. It is nested under layers of tissue paper in my backpack, the bow flattened, wax darkened and cracked but intact. I don't kid myself that anything much will happen when it's opened, but there is something comforting about bringing it. In this way I'm reminded that Mrs. Cheung was practical, did the books for the egg ranch and raised a family. She didn't go in for potions, poultices, or prayer. But she knew to give me this box. This act of preservation and made-up ritual is all unlikely, and yet survives under the very reason I still pick up parking-lot pennies and recite the phrase "Find a penny, pick it up, and all day long you'll have good luck."

The taxi stand in front of the airport is singed with halogen and neon light. The air is warm and humid and smells of fatty foods. For the last fifteen hours we've hardly found anything to say to each other except *passport, tickets, customs.* On the plane, when he wasn't sleeping, my father kept his earphones on and read a photography magazine, wrote now and then on a pad of paper.

"Let me tell you," my father says, "beware of cars when you cross the road. This is not like the U.S."

"I'm more worried about the mosquitoes." I point at the insects darting around us, red and green sparks lit by the neon light.

"Your mother was allergic," he says. "Did you know that?"

"She was a lot of things I don't know." I pretend to turn my attention to our suitcases next to me.

My father walks the short distance to the terminal to get the last of our bags while I watch the rest. I'm thinking of my mother and wishing she were here too. I miss her. I miss us. Of course, this is not new, but it is different. I had always located this emptiness at home, but now that I'm halfway across the world I realize we carry loss with us.

And so I'm wondering already how this trip can be of any use to my father and me when neither of us has the power to rewind the clock and make himself whole again. That time was before I was eight years old. I call it "the other life," when my mother and father and I lived together in Los Angeles. Our apartment was always hot, camphored by nearby eucalyptus and oleander. Once a month the three of us walked down the steep concrete banks of the Los Angeles River to gather algae growing in the lethargic water. It was part of my father's treatment for asthma. The last time we did this, we went to a new place on the river. My father chose this spot because it was more natural. The concrete bed was almost completely covered by sand and large river stones. In the center of the channel a stretch of cottonwoods had taken root and thrived. A group of mallards swam in one of the wider parts of the water. It was easy to forget that there were miles of concrete on either side of us.

We found a section deep enough for the kind of algae my father preferred. Mosquitoes and gnats gathered in small clouds above the pools where the algae swayed in thick strands. We waded into the water, pantlegs rolled up to our knees. Pulling at the algae that was soft like green cotton candy, we carried it to my mother and dropped it into the plastic bag she held. I could tell she didn't believe in my father's remedies, but she merely explained, "He would never do anything to hurt you."

We saved the algae for the humidifier when I slept. Sometimes when I am in bed and I hear the faint movement of the Columbia, I think of those nights we brought the river home, when I felt the current cleansing my lungs of asthma, taking the weight off my chest like a form of gentle erosion. I wonder who I might have become, had that family remained together.

My father arrives with the last bag and stares at me blankly as a small red taxi pulls up. Inside, we are cramped, separated by the luggage we can't fit in the trunk. He immediately begins speaking to the driver in Chinese. He turns to me. "We'll drop our bags at the hotel and get something to eat. It's late, but I know a restaurant that will be open."

I'm more tired than hungry, but I shrug and look out the window. Everything at this level is cast in a dull yellow. There aren't as many bikes as I expected, but perhaps this is because of the late hour. The geometry of the city suprises me, the tall, bright lines of high-rises contrasting with the curving, narrow avenues.

"All these streets used to be canals," my father says.

"Recently?" I ask.

"No, no. Don't be dumb." He stops himself abruptly and tries again. "Not for a very long time."

The taxi pauses at an intersection. On the corner, just a few feet from us, a woman sells noodles and wonton from a dented metal cart. Her gray hair is pinned back tightly near her ears, angling off her forehead sharp as tent flaps. A greasy white bulb lights her age-spotted hands as she stirs the noodles. "Why not just have that?" I ask. My father speaks to the driver, who replies and laughs.

"He says that if you eat from a cart tonight, you'll spend the next two weeks touring the bathrooms of China."

Both of us chuckle just as the taxi moves through the intersection, the friendly high pitch of my father's amusement melding with my own sound. I remember a version of this from my childhood and I cut myself off. Right now there are fathers and sons across the world sharing a laugh together, and we have not earned the right to be among them.

5

The son describes their first day;
he discovers they will not be alone.

Though neither of us is hungry, we eat a late dinner of fish covered in a brown, peppery sauce on a bed of steamed romaine lettuce. The restaurant is dark, almost closed for the night. The tables are stacked with upturned chairs, and an old man is mopping on the other side of the room.

"Did they stay open for us?" I ask.

"Maybe," my father says. "I've sent them a little business over the years." He reaches into his coat pocket and sets a dull white envelope on the table next to him, yuan for the bill, I imagine.

"If I'd known they were going out of their way, I'd have just skipped dinner. I'm not really hungry."

"Look," my father says, sounding irritated. "It's fish and lettuce. That's not asking much. The sooner you eat, the sooner they go home." He looks at the envelope and brushes it with his fingers. "I told you there was something about your mother I need to share with you." His nervous tone makes me unsure I'm prepared to hear what he's about to say, but I listen. "No, no. I guess I am sharing something about myself too," he says.

The old man with the mop approaches the table smiling and speaking in Chinese. My father looks relieved and gestures for the man to sit with us. They talk for a moment and look at my untouched food. The thick section of fish is a dark, oily glow on the white plate. "I'm done," I say.

"I'm done too," my father says, slipping the envelope off the table and back into his pocket.

"What's in that envelope?" I ask.

"Documenation," he says. "Nothing for you to be concerned with."

IN THE MORNING, my father takes me to Yu Yuan Garden in East Shanghai. He doesn't bring up my mother and I don't ask because I'm not going to make it easy for him. The streets are crowded with bicycles, the sidewalks full of people cooking noodles and wonton. Above, the windows are strung with drying, faded clothes and wood birdcages. I mention that it doesn't seem a likely place for a garden.

"Not anymore," my father says, leading me forward. "Mostly for tourists. Not much to see."

"Then why bother?"

My father stops and looks at me through thick lenses enlarging his Chinese eyes. "Nothing is all good or all bad," he says. "And there is a great deal in between." He continues on, a conspicuous tourist in a light blue shirt, khaki pants, and white tennis shoes. One thing I recognize already: He's changed since I was a boy, has gotten abrupt, as if he's afraid to say too much. We turn a corner into a hazy square filled with souvenir vendors selling cheap handheld fans and small carp-shaped lanterns. The square is crowded. For some reason my eyes catch a woman in a simple yellow dress. Her hair is pulled back in a ponytail that falls between her shoulder blades. Her skin is light, except on her face, where she has dusted a hint of cheekbone with blush. She's lovely.

The woman opens her white handbag, fishes around inside,

and then reclasps it with her small fingers. I watch until she disappears into the crowd, another Chinese face among hundreds. I think she's lucky.

We walk to the center of the square, where there is a rectangular pond with dusty green water, yellow and orange fish shifting slowly beneath the murk. It's not long before I feel as if I'm being followed and I quickly turn around. I'm confronted by three oversized Chinese characters, people in dirty, limp costumes with grotesquely large plastic heads. One of them is saying something to me and pointing at my camera. My father intervenes. "No. No," he says. "You have to pay to have your picture taken with them."

I appreciate the cleverness of the ambush. "They look like rejected mascots from a Chinese football team," I say. My father agrees and we look around the square. It is hazy, hung with colorful flags and lanterns that can't hide the fact that the buildings themselves are deteriorating. "This is it?" I ask.

"No, no. A little further. We're meeting them at the gate."

"Meeting who?"

"The tour."

"A tour? You didn't tell me about a tour." I had imagined my father taking me through China alone. Pictured, somehow, a moment when I would spring open Mrs. Cheung's box and know how to speak to him again. Though maybe I'm better off not being alone with my father for an entire trip.

"Just for the first part," he says. "I thought it would be easier on both of us. And besides, I am an entrepreneur, not a scholar."

The rest of the tour group is waiting at the gate of Yu Yuan Garden, and my father introduces us to the guide. The others are all Chinese, cameras dangling from their necks, water bottles clutched in their hands. One T-shirt reads YMCA WALKATHON! American Chinese, I decide.

"How'd you get stuck with us?" one of them asks me. She's

short and plump, with obviously dyed black hair that's so thin it rests on her head like a hairnet.

"That's my father." I point to him. He's still speaking to the guide.

"My goodness. You two don't look a thing alike." She reaches out her hand. "I'm Ellen and this is my husband, Phong." She shakes her head, giving me a thorough look.

"Biological," I say.

"My goodness."

Yu Yuan Garden is a series of walkways and brackish ponds shaded by willows and low-slung pines. Each water place is presided over by a separate building—living quarters and ceremonial offices with the original furniture. The guide describes selected points in broken English, and my father always asks questions. I'm not really listening to either and walk ahead.

"Bored already?" my father asks, catching up to me. The guide is behind us talking about rock formations taken from Lake Taihu and placed in one of the ponds.

"Lion. They look like lion. You see?" the guide asks as the group murmurs in confirmation.

"Just underwhelmed," I say to my father. "But it's only our first day and I didn't think sightseeing would really be our priority." As I say this, I realize how true it is and at the same time, how difficult. I *want* to talk to him. I wonder if it's occurring to both of us right now, what an extravagant gesture this trip is between two men who only want to say "I'm sorry," something that might have been handled on the phone, or over hamburgers in an all-night diner. What are we seeking in this ritual of our own design that couldn't have been accomplished more simply? The answer, I think, is precisely the unknown thing that has launched us on this voyage.

"The sights might be more interesting than what I have to say," my father says. In one sense I'm okay with the fact we have not opened up our regrets. I do not know him well enough to offer up my life, much less forgiveness. So where is this trip going? Not the physical one with its itinerary of cities, but the one between my father and me? I am not a boy. He is not a young father. Yet here we are, both trying out roles we haven't played in twenty-five years.

We turn back toward the group. They're still searching for the lions. "There, there, and there," I say, pointing to each lion. It hardly seems like a puzzle to me. "Think of that bit as an open jaw and you'll see it. Up there are two ears. See? And to the right, the third one, the holes and the outcropping are eyes and a nose." I look at the guide. "Right?"

He pauses and stares at the rocks. "Just right," he says hesitantly. I'm not convinced that before now he's ever seen the lions himself.

6

*The son recalls an evening with his mother;
the memory of a death occurs.*

I am awake in the darkness of our hotel room, my father's puffy breaths the only sound. I turn Mrs. Cheung's box over in my hands. It is both solid and soft. My fingers play along the bow, follow its loops down to the loose ends that I could so easily pull. Perhaps inside is merely a wise Chinese saying on a scrap of paper. I prefer to imagine a bright light expanding into the room when I pull off the lid, maybe the voice of a god booming a new direction for my life.

When I was a boy, my father sometimes played this kind of game with me. One of us closed our eyes while the other placed an object in his hands, leaving him to guess what the object was or to make up some fantastic story about it if he was stumped. My mother, though, wouldn't indulge in playing such childish games with me. My old maid cards were mostly untouched and Chutes and Ladders sat ignored in the back of my closet. Instead, when I turned four, and we were alone, she cleared the kitchen table of its egg-shaped shakers and plastic napkin holder and got out playing cards. We sat across from each other and she shuffled—she always shuffled first. The cards pattered against each other, flipping rapidly between her fingers. She taught me gin, and later, when I started coming within two or three cards of going out, she showed me how to play rummy.

What I remember most, though, are the jigsaw puzzles my mother kept in her mahogany-stained rolltop desk and on the card table in our living room, where she put them together. It was a mystery to me that my mother could assemble these fragmented pictures. I didn't understand how she conjured the images of red barns bordered by yellow fields, of gumball machines and harbor scenes—whatever she wanted from the pieces, it seemed. As far as I was concerned, my mother was an artist, a magician.

She worked on these puzzles late at night mostly, when my father and I were long in bed. Once I woke up and heard the muffled rattle of the little cardboard pieces. I understood my mother was opening a new box and I got up to see what she was working on. The living room smelled faintly of bleach and I knew she was soaking her nurse's uniform. My mother sat in her folding chair, sifting through pieces in the box. She wore her faded blue terrycloth robe, and her blond hair was down, still kinked from the bobby pins she wore at work. She looked up, holding her arm out to me. "Can't sleep, Love?" she asked. I shrugged and scooted in close to her.

"What are you making this time?" I pointed to the gray up-ended pieces in the box.

"Marbles." She held up the cover. From edge to edge, marbles of all colors filled the photo.

"Do a truck."

My mother laughed and squeezed me. "It doesn't work that way. I have to put together the picture on the box." I had never considered this rule before, and it bothered me.

"Some people start with the edge pieces." She fished around the box and pulled out a piece that was flat on one side. She explained how one could find all these and create the border of the picture. "But that's too easy. I like to find a specific point and build out from there." She pushed her chair back and lifted me onto her lap. "People are fun to start with. Not too many puzzles have them, but when they do, I find their tiny heads or pieces of their bodies and try to put them together first. Then I build the world around them."

My mother held up the cover of the box again. "Where should we start?" I considered the different marbles. Most of them shone brightly, solid blues and reds and greens, and clear ones with twisted candy-cane ribbons of color inside. Finally, I pointed to one that was mostly hidden. Was it yellow? Or was it clear and refracting that color from a marble beneath it?

"Tough one," my mother said. She poured half the pieces onto the table and gave me the box containing the rest. "Let's find it."

I don't know what time it was or how long this took, the process of finding that exact, obscure marble, but the world was dark and quiet, except for the single light we used and the heavy tick of our kitchen clock. At some point my mother brought another chair to the table and made herself coffee. I appreciated the smell because it always meant she was settled in, relaxed. She never made a pot before work or if she had an appointment. It was her way of winding down, the percolator announcing in its gurgly way that all was well.

My mother finished looking through her half of the puzzle well before me. Her search had come up empty and we both stared at my curvy pile of pieces. Buried in there was a fragment, an image of something itself buried. I couldn't help feeling that it was a lost thing, huddled and waiting for me. I continued, more intently now, but my mother didn't intrude. She sat quietly and watched as I inspected each piece. Sometimes I held the more promising ones up to the box.

After I had gone through every piece, I looked at my mother. How had I missed the one we were looking for? "What do we do now?" I asked.

"We try again, Love." She was tired, awake simply for me. She picked up the box lid and put it between us. "What should we look for exactly?"

I considered the picture for a moment, the field of round glass and the tiny spot we were focusing on. "Maybe it's not all on one piece," I said.

My mother smiled at me as if this was a surprise to her, as if this wasn't something she'd probably known from the outset. "So now we look for the marbles that touch ours and I bet we can put it together." She got up and poured another cup of coffee while I began sorting through the pieces once again. After an hour we had our start. We looked together at our minuscule progress as if we'd built the Eiffel Tower. My mother ran her fingers through my hair and yawned. "That's a good night's work, Love."

When I think of the life that followed, I often consider the last puzzle my mother and I worked on together. I was eight when she brought home the big box containing a two-thousand-piece puzzle. It was too large to set up on the card table, so we used our wide kitchen table instead.

Our challenge was a boy in the foreground flying a red box kite. My mother wanted to begin with him, but I preferred a different route. We decided to make our starting point the string, a vague white curve diminishing in the blue sky. I worked on it after school and my mother sat down to it after her shift at the hospital. Sometimes in the evening, if my father was out, we sat across from each other at the table and worked together. Our chosen path led us down the string, after days, to the improbably neat boy wearing a white shirt and red cardigan. Then there was the green hill on which he stood. Everything beyond and above was blue, as if he were perched on the precipice of some attainable horizon.

When we were nearing the end, we intentionally waited for

each other. On the final evening, after dinner, we sat down to the last hundred pieces of blue, some flecked with red. There was a chunk of sky left to create in the upper-right-hand corner and, somewhere in there, a boy's kite. Both of us shared the familiar mixed feelings about finishing a puzzle, approaching the closure of it.

"We've been keeping that boy waiting a long time," my mother said. "I wonder if he knows what he's got on the end of that string?"

I followed the white line from his small hands up into the shiny, wood-grained hole in his universe. What would be the consequence if we decided to leave it this way? In Sunday school they told us that God had taken six days to create the Earth. What if he had left something out—decided, perhaps, not to bring forth light? I asked my mother this. She looked at me calmly and thought for a moment, tucking her hair behind her ears. She leaned forward, shadowing our puzzle. "He did leave something out," she said quietly.

My father walked in just then with an offer to take us out to dinner. We left the puzzle for the night, nearly complete, not knowing it would stay that way. The next morning my mother was struck by a car on her way to work. A few days later the kitchen table was stacked with casserole dishes and baked goods from relatives. Losing my mother was hard, but I managed by being helpful to my father and sitting with the relatives who came to visit us, listening quietly to their grief. I cannot recall what they said. All I really remember is watching that final jigsaw puzzle being crumpled off the table and into its box. My mother and I could have finished it in just a few minutes. A boy connected to an incomplete sky by a thin white string.

7

The father finds a distraction;
he translates the Dragon and Frog.

From the time Westen and I got on the plane until we met the tour at Yu Yuan Garden I felt as if he and I should be more productive. But mainly there was awkward silence. *Ta taoyan wo.* Yes, there were things I hoped to say, but the moment never seemed right. On the first night I thought to tell him about his mother, open the envelope she left for both of us, but I couldn't face it. No, I also understood I was less prepared than I thought. This is partly because I had no idea Westen would be so sullen. I couldn't seem to say the correct thing. And maybe also there were those things I did not want to tell myself. The surgery in the U.S. had not worked. This was my first trip to China with my son, and a final trip to China for me. Maybe a year, the doctors told me, certainly not more. Because I could not say what I needed to, everything was awkward. When I told Westen I'd wished that he would be happily married by now, he shook his head at me, frustrated. "You and Claire," he said.

Yes I asked, of course. "Is that your girlfriend?" *Just one of the questions that proved you knew nothing about your son.*

"We're religiously incompatible," he said, chuckling without humor. "And she's nine."

I could hardly bear even this smallest tension. How could I

broach the reasons I'd brought him to China? I knew I had a reprieve when I met Mr. Wang, our tour guide, and the rest of the group. There were many friendly people. Talkers. They were Chinese-Americans who spoke hardly any Chinese. When the tour guide could not explain something in English, he turned to me. I translated his descriptions for the rest of the tour.

"*Wo yuanyi ba zhezhong yuyan shuo de geng hao,*" I said to Mr. Wang on our first meeting.

He shook his head kindly. "Your Mandarin as good as my English," he said.

At the end of our visit at Yu Yuan Garden, Mr. Wang pointed to a pair of stone figures. One was a dragon whose tail looped along the entire garden wall. The other was a frog just beneath the dragon's chin. Mr. Wang told the legend. I translated.

"This dragon can walk alone," I said, "and no rain will come. This frog can also walk alone and there will be no rain. But they like to walk together with the frog under the dragon's jaw. He feeds off the dragon's saliva. In return, the frog scratches the dragon's chin." As I spoke, I looked at Westen. He was smiling. His head was nodding in approval. For a moment he was my little boy again with that hint of white teeth beyond his lips. Bright hazel eyes. Mr. Wang paused. I realized I'd missed the end of the story. He spoke again and I looked at the group. "When these two walk together," I continued, "storms come."

As we moved on, Westen seemed distracted, as if his head were in some other place. But perhaps some of this distance was something I was placing on him. Just then I saw him as a grown man, a tourist I did not know with his pale Northwest skin and dark brown hair just beginning to show gray. Yes, in truth, before this trip I could have passed him on the street and not recognized him as my son.

8

The tour is disappointed with the Shanghai waterfront;
a discussion leads the son to thoughts of his mother.

My father has quickly become the unofficial translator. Our guide's English is not very good. On our way out of Shanghai, I sit in the back of the bus, but my father sits up front at Wang's request. We drive by the waterfront of the Huangpu River, where everything is gray—the sky, the boats bleating at each other, the bank buildings that are strange European monuments to China's early brush with capitalism in the 1920s and '30s. The air smells metallic, like an alloy divested of some unnameable property.

"You want see?" Wang says, speaking overly loud into the microphone. His small body sways as the bus turns a corner. "You want see?" he asks again.

"See what?" the woman sitting next to me asks loudly. Her name is Sheri. She's maybe twenty-five and a chewing-gum smacker and she smells like bruised strawberries.

"This waters," Wang says, crouching a bit and pointing out the window. No one answers. All I can see are the backs of people's heads, black shiny Chinese hair, Chinese-American hair, the kind that gets lather, rinse, repeat, condition. But I can tell from Wang's expression that he's surprised. He says something to my father in Chinese. My father shakes his head, and then Wang checks his watch.

"Everyone look out right window," Wang says. "This waters a very important port in China. Many barges and ships do business here."

All of us are politely looking outside, but it isn't an interesting sight. There are coal barges moving slowly through an unappealing gray, and most of us turn quickly back to Wang. Sheri snaps her gum next to my ear. "He's really pushing *this waters*," she says, uncannily mimicking Wang, and I can't help but react with a chuckle.

"We could go back to Yu Yuan Garden," I say.

"Could you even stand that? Tables, chairs, walls, and ponds. That's all I remember."

"The rock lions," I say.

"I didn't see them until you pointed them out." She pops her gum again, loud as a firecracker.

"It's been a dreary start," I say.

"Except your dad is cool. If he wasn't translating I don't know what we'd do."

"Learn to speak Chinese maybe?" I look down on her lap at the slim red book on Chinese astrology.

"I gave up trying to speak it a long time ago," she says. "My mom and dad should've taught us. Do you know any?"

"When I was a little kid, my father used to talk to me in Chinese. But I don't remember any of it." I pause and look out the window, hoping to get away from the subject. Outside, the bus is moving through Shanghai's traffic at the base of skyscrapers. One of them is encircled by three-story bamboo scaffolding. The top platform is busy with painters. "Look at that," I say, pointing.

"They've still got their old ways. Primitive," Sheri says, with a hint of documentary in her voice. I try to figure out what part of her smells like strawberries. Her hair? Perfume? She's overripe, the crushed berry at the bottom of the plastic container I never find until I get home from the store. And I'm not sure, but

I sense a little sadness about her, something she's hiding. Birds of a feather.

"Old people come up to me all the time jabbering in Chinese because I look Chinese," she says, picking up the subject again.

"I don't have that worry."

"What does your mother look like?"

"She was blond," I say. "Very sharp-boned. But she died."

"Oh," Sheri says. It's the most sincere she's sounded. "Can I ask how they met?"

I tell her they met in college, which isn't true, but for some reason I like the sound of it. They really met on the beach. Fortunately, Sheri doesn't seem that interested and she starts telling me about her astrology book, which allows me to fade.

ONE MORNING WHEN I was seven my mother was taking me to school, but passed right by, passed the line of parents letting their kids out, passed the yellow school buses.

"Where are we going?" I asked.

"The beach, Love," Mom said. She pointed to the backseat, where there were two sack lunches and my bathing suit. Then she flashed open her robe to reveal that she already had her swimsuit on.

"How come?" I asked.

"I want to show you something. It's a surprise. Now hop over the seat and put on your trunks." She drove us to Santa Monica, near the pier. The morning sky was still thick and overcast, the beach a wide, smooth band pressed flat by high tide and the big tractors that raked debris from the sand. We sat on the hood of the car, the ocean breeze like feathers tickling our bodies. With the thin waves in front of us and traffic along the 101 behind us, it sounded as if we were between two coasts. Mom wore her floral one-piece with the ruffled straps. Her hair was twisted into a loose bun.

"This is where I met your father," she said. "By the pier. What do you think about that?"

I looked at her but didn't say anything. I never really considered that they hadn't always known each other.

She continued. "He was on a blanket next to me and some friends. We kept looking at him because we knew he was sleeping and it seemed like his back was getting redder and redder. Finally I woke him up and he kind of jumped."

"Was he burned?" I asked.

"Not too bad. We went out that night. We got along right away. We even talked about how we both wanted a little boy. So we were planning you from the very start. You were born out of instant love." This has always been a strange moment in my memory because she seemed to be saying these words as much for herself as for me.

Mom slid down and ran toward the water and I hopped off too, clomping as best I could through the loose sand. She was already in the water when I stopped and looked to both sides. We were the only people on the beach. The lifeguard tower was closed and unmanned. As far as I could see on either side, the sand was smooth and gray. Ahead of me were my mother's solitary footsteps, a trail of apostrophes leading to water's edge.

AS WE LEAVE Shanghai, Sheri pops in a fresh stick of gum— watermelon—and starts reading her book. After a while I can tell she's not reading because she stays on the same page. She's just staring at it, looking sad. "Something on your mind?" I ask.

She slowly tilts her head toward me. She has either swallowed her gum or stopped chewing it. "This trip," she says. "My family isn't talking about it, but it's for me."

"Is it your birthday?" I point to the Chinese astrology book.

"Something like that." She sits up straight and looks out the window. All the body language tells me not to pursue this.

"What's wrong?" I ask.

She looks at me, soft-eyed but without tears. "They organized this trip to help me through my daughter's birthday. She would have been a year old this week." Sheri pauses and then nods as if she feels she can trust me with the final part. "She was two months old when she died."

"I'm sorry" is all I can manage to say. I only know what it's like to lose a parent. Both, actually.

"The worst part right now is that we're all pretending like we don't know what tomorrow is. I guess that's the point of the trip. I've gone along with it, but suddenly I *want* to remember her on her birthday."

I offer a sympathetic smile, but I feel that Sheri doesn't need me to say anything more. I can tell she's heard all the comforting words there are. But I'm already thinking about what else I can do. I know there must be something.

JUST A COUPLE of miles outside the city and we're already driving through the canals that crisscross rice paddies and water chestnut fields. The road between Shanghai and Hangzhou is two slim lanes of opposing traffic. The shoulder is congested with small-engined vehicles pulling carts of straw and wood, and we have to steer carefully around these. Even from my seat in the back, I find myself gripping the armrest as we squeeze between the oncoming traffic on our left and the hodgepodge on our right. It becomes a strange, tense ballet and I admire the driver, who seems unaffected, slouch-shouldered. I look at my father sitting ahead of me and at Sheri at my side. Between them and the traffic, I feel like I'm at the end of some sort of stress-management training. Even the unpredictable can become routine, and suddenly, oddly, I understand bullfighting.

The son recalls the day his father gave him up;
he remembers the first words of his great-aunt.

Thin tree branches brush the bus roof, sounding like intermittent rain, and I watch my father nod in and out of sleep. The strobe of shadow and light across his face reminds me of that car ride the day he gave me up. When we pop over a bump, he wakes to find me watching him. "How long have I been sleeping?" he asks groggily.

"About twenty-five years by my count."

"What?"

"Nothing," I say. "I was just thinking about the last time I saw you."

"Yes, when I left you with your aunt." He pauses. "That was difficult."

"You told me it wasn't permanent. Did you believe that when you said it?"

"I did."

"Then what happened?"

My father begins to speak, but pauses, closes his eyes, and then looks directly at me. "To be honest, I came close many times. Yes, but that also brought back all the grief over your mother. I just couldn't."

I think an apology is coming, but nothing. My father simply

turns back toward the window and stares into darkness. This is something I did not want to know, that I was a reminder of my mother's death. Perhaps even now this is how he thinks of me. And I'm angry that his sadness was more important than mine. He lost one wife, but I lost two parents.

It was daytime, I remember, when he left me. We drove beneath an arch of white bougainvilleas as my father brought me to Great-Aunt Catherine and Uncle Cane's winter home in San Diego. The crescent lawn had been freshly cut. Stepping out of the car, I smelled the grass blades on the stone walkway. A peacock called out from behind the house, a sound I recognized from the times my mother took me to the zoo in the afternoons.

"This is just temporary," my father said, pulling my two bags out of the trunk of the car. He knelt down and reclipped my red tie with one hand while the other tucked my white shirt into my navy blue shorts. I kept my hands in my pockets, holding my mother's set of keys to our apartment. My father thought they were lost when he gave away her things.

I'd never been to my great-aunt's before. We stood for a moment in front of the redbrick house. The windows were arranged in a way that gave the building a face, and my aunt and uncle came out and greeted us from the center of its indifferent smile. I recognized them from my mother's funeral. I looked down into the tops of my new shoes, shined just for this day. I could almost see my face twice reflected, darkened by the black leather.

"They don't have any children. They'll spoil you to death," my father said in an unsure voice. He looked different to me. Two days earlier he had cut off most of his black hair in a way that reminded me of the other men in our Chinatown neighborhood. "You remember Westen," he said, introducing me to my aunt and uncle as they arrived at the car.

It was December and they were both suntanned. Aunt Catherine wore a wide straw hat, frayed and shot through with holes on the brim. She didn't use makeup to cover the freckles that layered the bridge of her nose and beneath her eyes. Uncle Cane had on all white. His cotton shirt hung over his large stomach. The long, coarse hair from the back of his hand tickled my skin as he tapped me on the back of my neck with his knuckles. These were my mother's relatives, nothing like my father's side. They were not Chinese.

My father turned to me. "You're going to be okay here," he said. "I promise I'll call." He held me by both shoulders and looked deep into my eyes, almost beyond me. "When I return," he said, his hands squeezing me tightly, "I will take you to China."

This promise floated in the air between us like a half-inflated balloon. He'd always talked about this trip when he put me to bed, telling me about the village where he grew up and how, at nine years old, he'd fled the Communists, his infant brother strapped on his back. Sometimes my mother broke us up because she said my father kept me up too late. He always reminded her of the nights we worked on our jigsaw puzzles. I felt for her keys in my pocket and found the one for the front door, rounded and worn, and the shorter one for the padlocked shed where we kept our bikes.

"I don't want to stay here," I finally said. My aunt and uncle looked at my father. We were all waiting for him to speak, but he said nothing. Behind him, the peacock stopped its walk across the lawn and cocked its head in a hard-eyed glare. "I have to go," my father said, kissing me on the side of the head.

"You don't have to." I held his arm.

He looked at me sternly, clenching his teeth and speaking in a monotone growl. "I cannot take care of you." Turning to Aunt Catherine and Uncle Cane, he changed his tone, saying good-bye and hugging them both. I felt weighted, as if I wasn't part of the moving world, as if I was staring into the dizzying center of a merry-go-round. The car door closed, sobering me. My father was really leaving.

The three of us watched him drive away, one arm waving to us out his window. I tried to catch his eyes in the rearview mirror. I thought I could hold him there with me if I just kept looking. But the car continued, rumbling over the cobbled drive and turning onto the road.

We stood quietly until Aunt Catherine whispered in my ear. "You're angry because you're being dumped off with people you don't know." Her voice had the soft cracking of age, and she smelled like tangerines. "We don't know you, either," she said, not unkindly. I looked at my uncle, whose entire posture had changed. He shrugged his shoulders and walked into the house with one of my bags. I didn't want to follow him, and I think my aunt sensed this.

"I'm going to show you the yard before we go in," Aunt Catherine said. We left my other suitcase on the drive. It was brown and scratched, an odd marker of where my father had left me. I was angry and promised myself never to utter a word to anyone again. My aunt touched my shoulder without speaking and guided me into the side yard, past ivy sweeping up through a tree fern and attached to the house like a tapestry. We walked by her herb garden, where she snapped off a sprig and held it out for me. "Sage," she said. It smelled sweet and dusty. She tucked the cutting into my pocket, and then bent down, pulling a large butter container from behind a clump of rosemary. A half-dozen snails floated around inside. "Beer," my aunt said. "Kills them. Your uncle could learn a lesson from that." She emptied the bowl on the ground and crunched the snails with the toe of her blue sneaker. "Just to be sure."

We walked around the corner of the house to the backyard. I felt Aunt Catherine watching my expression as I looked across the wide belt of grass deferring at the cliff to the Pacific and its soft blue sky. I'd no idea we were so close to the ocean. "Do you think you can live here?" she asked.

It was the first time anyone had asked my opinion on the subject. My father had simply told me where I was being taken. "I already have a home," I said. Then, remembering I wasn't going to speak anymore, I privately renewed this vow. Besides, I thought, this won't last long. My father will miss me. He will come back, maybe tonight. I knew he would be sorry, and in the morning I would wake up and find dates next to my bed. I looked at my aunt directly to make sure she understood my position.

"You do have a home." Aunt Catherine put her warm hand on the back of my neck, urging me forward. The calm breeze animated wisteria descending through the branches of a willow. Aunt Catherine guided me across the yard to a small table and white wicker chairs. I had never seen a lawn so large; it was like a park. As I calmed, I reminded myself I was angry. But I couldn't help wondering how my aunt and uncle took care of all that space.

We hadn't been sitting long when Uncle Cane walked out from the house, carrying a glass clinking with ice. His oversized black shoes slapped his heels at every step. He sat, resting his deeply freckled arms on the table. When he took a drink from his glass, I recognized the bitter-smelling mixture of tea and alcohol that my mother made for her relatives. "If we were at home," he said, "we'd be having hot chocolate."

"This *is* home," my aunt said.

Uncle Cane looked at me. "Your aunt still can't believe she married a country boy."

"I married a country old man."

Uncle Cane took another drink and winked at me. "When I met her, she kept that *Watchtower* in her hand all the time. She used to be quite a fanatic. Knocked on doors all goddamn day."

"I thought I was opening doors." Aunt Catherine's voice was

quiet and insistent. I'd never heard my parents speak to each other like this, and I wasn't sure if they were angry.

"She gave up all that crap when I built her this house." Uncle Cane swung his arm around, glass in hand, and pointed.

"Cane, faith is a conviction, not a denomination. I gave up nothing."

My uncle stared at his glass, which was now empty except for the pieces of ice. The three of us remained quiet for a few minutes. I felt the lump in my pocket, my mother's keys. She hung these next to the door when she came home from work. She had a rule that my father and I could not talk to her until the keys stopped rocking. Some days she gave them a sharp tap, creating just enough time to change out of her nurse's uniform. I was almost resigned to the fact she was gone, but I didn't understand why I had to lose my father too.

The sun was getting brighter, warming the grass around us. The rear of my aunt and uncle's house was nearly all windows reflecting the changing day over the Pacific. Uncle Cane leaned on the table in my direction. His eyes were dark and gray and shot with red streaks. "We're going to have to get you into school," he said. "One here, one in Washington."

"I haven't been since Mom died," I said quietly.

Uncle Cane leaned back in his chair. "You've got a little accent there." He laughed and stood up with his empty glass in one hand, the other roughing up my hair as he turned to leave. "Goddamn if you're not a regular little Hop Sing."

Aunt Catherine waited until my uncle walked away. "Don't mind him," she said.

But I wasn't offended. It was the first time anyone had ever said I had an accent. Uncle Cane was calling me Chinese and I welcomed it. Maybe this was the problem, I thought. My father had left me because I wasn't Chinese enough. Somehow I could prove I was. "Can we eat dim sum here?" I asked my aunt.

She gave a small sigh and shook her head. "I'm afraid your uncle wouldn't enjoy that. Besides, we'd need to drive to Los Angeles."

I understand now, that was the day I stopped living Chinese. There would be no bird's-nest soup or Chinese school on Saturdays. I felt as if I was being asked to become another person. I thought of my father's promise to take me to China when he returned. What if I did not remember how to be Chinese?

Aunt Catherine and I sat for a few minutes, watching the gray Pacific roll toward us. "When is he coming back for me?" I finally asked, looking at the imprint of the wicker on my legs, trying not to look at her. Because even then, though I couldn't have spoken it, I sensed my father had taken and given me something at the same time.

She continued to watch the ocean. "It may be a long while, Westen," she said. "And he'll need you when he does."

The son has not found his place in China;
the memory becomes a vision and a dream.

West Lake is hot and the air damp. Wang leads our group through the rows of sweet osmanthus. He holds a yellow flag that is supposed to be our beacon.

"I was here a long time ago," my father says to me, "when the osmanthus were in bloom. It was late September. You wouldn't believe how the air smelled."

I stop walking. "How often do you come to China?"

"Every five or six years, I guess. Now that things have changed there's money to be made." My father puts his hands on his waist and looks around as if he's surveying his own property.

"Did you ever bring Mom?" I ask, testing his reaction.

"We were talking about a trip before she died. The three of us."

He ends with a dead expression, as if this is not a topic he cares for. Wang waves his flag wildly. My father and I have fallen behind and we walk to catch up. The tour has stopped next to a rather unremarkable square pond. Other tourists begin tossing bits of bread into the water. Small ornamental carp bloom to the surface in massive groupings the shape of marigolds or a silent fireworks display. Each bit of food that hits the water causes a new rash of orange. A single large fish bullies its way along the edge and gulps at bread fragments.

"They're not so pretty if you look at just one," I say.

"Don't look at just one," my father replies. He turns to Wang and says something in Chinese.

"Goldfish," Wang says, "represents unity of beauty and ugly." He turns to the group. "Do you want to hear a fish story?" The response is surprisingly enthusiastic. Wang begins, speaking Chinese, and my father translates. I walk a few steps away and take a seat in the shade of a small tree, thinking of how Uncle Cane's first question would have been "How do you cook them?" Wang and my father begin the story.

"Two wise men met at the edge of a river and observed a number of fish. 'The fish are very happy swimming,' one of the wise men said.

"The other responded, 'You are not a fish. How can you know if they are happy?'

"'You are not me,' the first wise man said. 'How can you know if I don't know the fish are happy?'"

My father offers his hands forward to indicate the story is finished. Stepping next to me, Sheri pokes me in the side as the group patters a light applause.

Everyone begins to walk again toward the boat that will take us to the island at the center of the lake. We're on a long asphalt corridor bordered by grass and osmanthus, and Wang waves his flag, yelling to the group that we have to come back someday to see them in bloom.

My father asks me how I liked the story of the two wise men.

"I've heard it before," I say.

"Yes. Yes. It still makes you think."

We're walking behind Mr. and Mrs. Chow, the oldest couple on the tour, and I'm struck by how white the backs of their legs are. They're whiter than I am. My father is at my side, and I feel him looking at me for a response. It's at moments like this that I wish Uncle Cane were around. I wonder if he'd hear his echo, however dim, as I speak next. It is his voice passing through me, and not my father's as it might have been. "I have a problem with the idea of fish being happy," I tell my father.

"You don't think they can?"

"Well, sir," I say, pausing just enough to emphasize the formality, "not really."

"So when the people throw bread into the water, the goldfish aren't happy?"

"Every animal is equally happy, no matter what they do."

I feel my father sharpen his eyes. "You're saying a small fish swimming away from a larger fish trying to eat it is happy?"

"I guess. Both of them are being fish. They eat and are eaten. That's the natural course of their lives. They're fulfilling their purpose." I keep looking at the white legs in front of me, but I'm concentrating on the veins now, as blue and distinct as freeway lines on a map. Mr. and Mrs. Chow are made for each other down to their capillaries.

"And humans?" my father asks impatiently.

"Oh," I say, turning away from the legs and looking straight at him. "We're not happy. Ever." I do not like this bickering with my father, but I can't help it. For some reason, just hearing him talk makes me angry.

As we arrive at the narrow gangplank leading to our boat, he is shaking his head. I take a seat on the rear deck with most of our tour, my father sitting next to me, a model of my thesis on happiness.

The sun glares off the lake as we rumble away from the bank, the propellers churning the water as we pull out backward, separate from the dozen or so other boats just like ours waiting for their tours, waiting for people who've just fed the goldfish, heard the wise-men story, and walked through the rows of sweet osmanthus out of bloom, waiting for all the happy tourists.

"I'm hungry," I say, trying to change the subject.

"You should've eaten the *chong shi yu*," my father says.

"I don't like fish."

The night before when we'd arrived in Hangzhou, dinner was waiting for us. The main course was *chong shi yu,* a complete fish sliced into thick glazed wedges. The cantaloupe-ball eyes were a disturbing decoration, as if they'd served a zombie fish. I ate rice and a chilled raspberry-like fruit called *yang mei* and drank tea.

"If you don't like fish," my father says, "you're going to have a difficult time. You can't fill up on just fruit and rice."

"Then I guess we'll find out how long I can run on empty."

"Was it a mistake bringing you here?"

I think about this for a moment. "It was a mistake," I finally say, "to leave me."

My father shakes his head slowly.

"Don't expect this trip to be a panacea."

"No, no. But I am hoping for a kind of healing."

The wind from the moving boat whips hair across my father's face, mine too. "This seems impossible," I say. "What we're trying to do."

My father's expression grows intense, a flush of air pushing his hair entirely away from his face this time. I see all of him, the dark eyes that end in slight overlap, archipelagoes of age spots that emanate from the faint bridge of his nose. "Son," he says. "Westen, if I was a hundred, you in your eighties, and we knew I wouldn't make it to a hundred and one . . . would we be having this conversation?"

"Ask me in fifty years," I say.

My father nods quietly, his eyes looking away from me, but I sense not away from us.

"Wait," I say. "Are you sick or something?"

He pauses and looks at me as if searching for a hint of concern in my question. "No, no. It was just an illustration." He stands and pats me on the shoulder before he moves inside. "It's a bit windy. We'll do this again in fifty years."

Beyond the lake, the hills are green and featureless, not the China of my imagination. Nor can it be found where I'm standing, not in the distance, not on the afternoon ride back across the lake with everyone complaining of hunger, not in the stop to see the Camphor Buddha or in the teahouse. Not in the early dinner, the beggar's chicken, lotus-wrapped, or the watershield soup, tiny lilylike leaves harvested from West Lake, not in the grass carp that is starved for three days before it's cooked, not in the fried soybean-scum rolls, so crunchy with sound the locals call them "ringing bells." Not in the Dong Po pork, named after the poet, the dark sauce of ginger, onion, and sugar, nor in the ham cube seasoned with lotus seeds and osmanthus blossoms, nor in the Long Jing tea, which is best picked in March. Not in any of these things I've seen or tasted do I find the country I imagined. I do not know what China is, and I cannot feel it.

11

The father recalls his last days in China;
the father and son are awake in early morning.

That night in Hangzhou my sleep was in deficit, yes. Westen was asleep in the next bed—my son, yet we were strangers. If I were to wake him, I wondered, and say, "Next year I will not be alive," would he love me again? How would he respond? "I'm sorry," or "How can I help?" More likely he would say, "So you're leaving me again," and my heart would hurt because this was not only true, it was inevitable.

Lying in bed, I thought of my village when I was a small boy. Things seemed so much simpler then, though not for long. I saw the green rice fields surrounding our simple brick buildings. In my memory, each window was a dark rectangle in the morning light. Above every door, ceramic figures of dragons, roosters, horses, and pheasants. The smaller children were unattended in doorways. They played in the dirt. Old Da swept everywhere with her rice-grass broom. Ma used to say all Old Da managed to do was move the dust from one side to the other and back again. There was the pond where we drew our water. Sometimes we would sneak out to go swimming while our parents slept. Yes, yes, this was the business of my young life. *How would you be different if your parents disappeared? Would you hate them or did they do enough good for a lifetime?*

There I was, barefoot, the beneficiary of short pants and a brown shirt Ma had made from Papá's old clothes. Even so, mine were almost always in better shape than the other children's. I was carrying my tattered copy of *Hen hai*. I had read it many times just to get to the part where Dihau bites off a piece of her flesh to make a medicine for her mother.

I got very close to our home. Papá stepped out of the doorway and met me. "*Wo yizhi zai zhao ni,*" he said. But his version of looking for me was waiting for me at home. "Xin," he said. And he could communicate so many things by just using my name. This inflection meant he wanted me to follow him. I learned early not to speculate on what he might want. He often surprised me.

Yes, it was that one strange day when Papá did not leave the village for work. And I did not go to the rice fields. Papá led me to our local guard tower—there was at least one in every village. At night, men stood watch in each tower, looking out for bandits. In the spring when there was no harvest, the bandits might come and loot the village. Sometimes they kidnapped an elder for ransom. In the late summer or fall they came for the harvested rice. But in the daytime the towers were usually empty. Papá took me inside one, all the way up the slim stairwell. The top was a square room with low ceilings and two portals on each side. He led me even farther, up a ladder through a hatch in the ceiling. We sat down on the roof, facing east. The air was completely still. Not a single blade of grass moved in the fields. If not for the villagers working below, their straw hats moving, it would have looked like a painting. Yes, yes, our village lacked infrastructure to say the least.

Papá pointed beyond the fields to the border of our land. "Why is that mountain important?" he asked.

It was an easy question. "Our ancestors are buried there."

"Yes," Papá said. "Even my father, your *yeh yeh*, is buried there. But I will not be, and neither will you." He stood up and walked to the edge of the flat roof. I followed.

"Chan family is different from the rest of the villagers. You work in the fields sometimes because it is good for you. Not because you have to. This is our land. We own this and the business in town."

"I already know this," I said. It was clear something was on Papá's mind.

"I am not saying we are better. But at birth we were marked—landowners. That used to mean very little. Now things are changing. We are going to have to leave here soon." Papá was not emotional. I never saw him cry. No, never, and I cannot remember him touching anyone with more than a firm handshake.

This memory played back like a recording in my mind. I saw my awkwardly short haircut and Papá's wire-framed glasses that made his eyes look so large. "Why are you telling me this, Papá?" I asked.

He did not answer at first. The memory shifted and picked back up at the border of the rice fields, where Papá and I walked together. "This is all you know," he said. "I simply want to prepare you. There are people who will want to take our property. They might want to hurt us as well."

"Who would do this?"

"Men who want to run China."

"Foreigners?" I remembered my history lessons about the concessions. "The French? The British? Americans?"

"No," Papá offered soberly. "Chinese."

"Why would they hurt us?"

Papá looked down at me and put his hand on my shoulder. "I suppose there is some history they don't teach in school. China's greatest enemy has always been itself."

"What about the Japanese?"

Papá sat down on the dirt and I followed. Our rice fields stretched far on both sides of us. Yes, yes, this is how he told lessons. "It's because we fight among ourselves," Papá said, "that the Japanese attacked. Your *yeh yeh* used to tell how his brother was killed by the Imperial Government. Just before I was born, men would cut off their queues as a symbol of revolt against the Qing dynasty. One day men with scissors stopped my uncle at the city gate and cut off his queue. A barber working on the street reported him and my uncle was executed, even though he explained what happened. Your *yeh yeh* told me the saying was 'Keep your hair or lose your head.' "

"That's just one example," I said.

"Then there was the revolution and a new government and the warlords that fought each other and didn't care who got in the way."

I stopped Papá. "But Sun Yat-sen," I reminded him.

"Don't they teach you anything in school? Sun Yat-sen was a great man, but he let the Communists help him build his party. That's where they got their first taste of China. After he died, Chiang Kai-shek fooled them into helping the revolution and then he shut them out. Killed them. That's where they got their first taste of revenge." Papá paused. "You see. It is always Chinese against Chinese."

"What does that have to do with us?" I was beginning to get hot. Gnats flew around our faces.

"The Communists will not be shut out again. They will take everything." At that, Papá swiped aggressively at the flying insects near his eyes.

"Will they hurt us?"

"They can't if we leave." Then he turned away and spoke quietly to himself. *"Di er ci jihui."* A second chance.

•   •   •

THOSE WORDS WERE the only warning I had that we would flee the mainland. In my memory, my father's calm certainty was amplified. I thought of him often over the years, but I did not know why I remembered him just then in Hangzhou.

I was still awake in the middle of the night. In the small amount of light coming from outside, I saw that Westen was watching me from the other bed. "Can't sleep?" I asked.

"Weird dreams."

"I was thinking about your grandfather and me." I didn't elaborate.

"Let me ask you something," Westen said. "Do you dream in Chinese or English?" He sat up and leaned against the headboard. His cowlick bobbed to one side.

"English mostly . . . now."

"So my grandfather spoke English?"

"No. No. He didn't learn until we lived in Hong Kong."

I was surprised. "How about you?"

"Portuguese. Which is why I never understand my dreams."

I laughed. Westen smiled too. Yes, he did smile. I reached next to my bed and felt around for the pack of Hong Ta Shan cigarettes I'd bought earlier. I hadn't had them in years. At first I found my playing cards, which were far more important to me, but then I reached the pack. I lit a cigarette and inhaled. It was just as I remembered, a harsh, quick burn. I enjoyed the smoke merging with my lungs and the ticking sound of the tobacco being drawn down. It's unhealthy, yes, but then again, what does a dying man have to worry about? "Smoke?" I asked.

"Never."

"That's good. These are nasty things."

"I don't think you are supposed to do that in the room."

"Probably not," I said, but I did not snuff out the cigarette; it was already half finished. They burned so quickly. "So why are we both awake?"

"Why are we even here at all?"

"Because I promised you. Do you remember? You were seven and you asked me where I grew up. I promised to take you to China. You reminded me practically every day before your mother died. I even promised you the day I left you with your great-aunt."

"I remember," Westen said. "Do you know what Mom told me? She said sometimes people make promises they can't keep, and it would be a very long time before we went to China, if we went at all. And there was a Chinese woman in Blue Falls who told me you'd come back and bring me here."

Then I knew why that memory of Papá had come to me. He was passing along a lesson about strength and decisiveness. Sometimes you stand and fight, sometimes you are smart enough to simply leave, but you always do what you say you are going to. These were traits I could have used in New Orleans with Celia that night when we heard Elva Cartane sing, if I hadn't been so distracted.

"Since you mention your mother," I began, "let me tell you something about her before you were born." I had no idea how much I was going to tell, how much I could. As far as showing him the envelope in my luggage and getting it over with? Westen sat up straight and looked at me without speaking.

"We were in a bar in New Orleans once, when I was still so new to the U.S. She was in charge, which made her even more beautiful to me. If I could have frozen my life in place right then, I would have. There was this woman singing, Elva Cartrane, and when she took a break, Celia, I mean your mother, and I turned toward each other almost nose-to-nose. In that dim light her eyes looked almost lavender."

"That's awfully poetic for a late-night story," Westen interrupted.

"Yes, yes. I'll keep it simple," I said. "Your mother asked me playfully what I was thinking.

" 'Everything,' I told her. 'Have you ever thought about having children?'

"She placed her hand on my cheek. 'Not till now.' As if shaking off the moment, she took in a deep breath and turned back toward the stage as Elva prepared to sing again. 'It's too soon,' she said, 'and we're too young to be having this conversation.' She looked around the room and picked up her glass, raising it to a man sitting alone across the room. He nodded and lifted his glass in return. 'When I can't do that,' Celia said, 'it's time for kids.' "

Westen offered a curious expression. "So the point of this story is that my mother was a flirt?"

"The point is that she was fearless. Raising the glass to that man was an odd gesture, but she knew she wouldn't lose me. If we had left just then, I might have rescued the moment, preserved your mother's belief that I could be fun and spontaneous, youthful. But in less than a year she had you and neither of us would ever feel so young anymore."

Westen lay back on his bed and stared at the ceiling. "Much better," he said. "I was unwanted. Thanks for the bedtime story, *Dad*."

"That's not the point at all. Your mother wanted you for sure."

"Then what *is* the point?"

"Never mind," I said. "It's not coming out the way I hoped. That's enough for tonight." I was beginning to think I was the wrong man for this conversation.

What I could not tell Westen, what is hard to record, is this: In the middle of one of Elva's more upbeat songs there was a loud thud at the entrance. The entire bar turned to see what was happening. Three men stumbled in loudly. They cut themselves off when they saw the room staring at them. They were all wearing white T-shirts and jeans. Thick-bodied Caucasian men. They sat down at the table next to us. I looked at Celia and she rolled her eyes. The entire time Elva kept singing. When I looked at her on the stage, she was making eye contact with someone behind us.

"Looks like Chinky boy got himself a dolly," one of the men said. The dark-headed one. The other two were crewcut blonds.

Celia turned toward the three of them. "No," she said. "The dolly got herself a *man*. It should tell you something that I had to import him."

The three men laughed. "We lose," the dark-headed one said. He raised his hands in surrender. They moved their table closer to ours, squeezing me between them and Celia. But they were talking more softly now. Elva continued singing the entire time, no longer paying attention to them. They bought a round of drinks, and by the end of the night the five of us were drunk and hanging on each other like the best of friends. They mostly paid attention to Celia. They clustered around her. But I was not concerned. I was as happy as I'd ever been. I was part of the group. I was American.

Why did you stop here? Do you recall why your pen failed to tell the remainder of the story? No, it's as if you had to relive all your mistakes before you could record your worst, the one that led to losing your son.

"HELLO?" WESTEN ASKED, interrupting my thoughts. He was no longer smiling. We both understood this trip could not mean the same thing as when he'd been promised it as a child. No, China was not a memory to him as it was for me. I had taken that from him long before. There are no towers and rice fields. No fatherly lessons. Yes, in that way I failed him. What I had to give him now was pain and doubt, and though no father wants to do this, it was inevitable that it had to happen before our trip was finished. He must know his mother in a new way, and then, maybe, discover his father.

12

The father begins his explanation;
the son writes a letter to his great-aunt.

In our hotel room I lie in darkness wondering if this was all a mistake, a miscalculation. I close my eyes and red shapes appear, first round and disorganized, then elongated, darker, a shifting millennial red, the shape of a rabbit, dividing into two rabbits, the color shifting into white, the red now reduced to their eyes. And there are cages forming, lines of metal crosshatching around the rabbits, the vision pulling back until I recognize my home in Washington, the deep green surrounding the white house. But it's antiseptic, silent. Uncle Cane breaks the hazy frame of my sight, his always gray hair and his always plaid shirt, blue and white or red and black, the cages dissolving before him as he grabs one of the rabbits by the hind legs and hand-chops it behind the neck, leaving it suddenly limp. He hangs it from a board, both heels pushed over a nail. And there is the red again, gone from the eyes, pouring out the throat with a single cut, and then the slit down the abdomen, Uncle Cane aggressively scooping out the organs with his fingers, inspecting the gelatinous mass for worms, the intestines, the heart, all flung to the ground. Two slits at the ankles and he's pulling the skin, the white fur, over the torso, the pink underside of the hide separating from the bluish pink of the flesh, a thin, clear membrane tearing in between, all this pulled down over where the head once was.

How easily the pelt comes off, becomes a furry mound below the skinned body shining against the bloodstained wood.

I open my eyes and it is dark outside. I have no idea how much time has passed since I was looking at the ceiling and thinking of Uncle Cane, long dead, who didn't even like the taste of rabbit.

I ask my father again why he has decided to bring me to China. He tells me he is keeping a promise he made to me when I was young, tells half a story about my mother, but then falls silent. He lights a Red Tower Mountain cigarette and I lie back in my bed and stare at the ceiling. Outside, there is the sputter of an uncertain engine and here, our room already smells like cigarettes. Smoke sifts across me as my father sets his cigarette on the nightstand.

"Your mother's funeral was filled with Caucasian faces," he says, as if I should understand. "There were sympathy cards in English."

I get up and face him from the window, feeling light at my back, my shadow a rumpled clot across our beds. "What does any of that have to do with me?"

"No, no. That's my point. It had to do with *me*. I had to look at the bottom line. I tried so hard to be Caucasian, but without your mother around, it was obvious. When I first went to the United States I practiced speaking English every day so I could lose my accent, even lose the British influence. The entire time I was doing it I knew I was killing your *yeh yeh*. Every bit of Chinese I gave up was an insult to him. And then, with your mother gone, all I could think of was that I needed to go back to Hong Kong."

"You couldn't bring me?"

"No, no. I didn't know for how long I'd be there. I didn't

want to take you away from your mother's relatives." Sensing I don't understand, my father throws up his hands in frustration, but I am the one who has the right to be frustrated. I'm supposed to be satisfied with his solution to leave me with relatives I didn't know?

"What you're saying is that you wanted to run away," I tell him.

Standing now in his blue pajamas, he shakes his head, walking toward the bathroom and coming back quickly to retrieve the cigarettes and matches. He stops at the door and says, "It's a long trip, Westen. Have some patience."

When he leaves the room I sit down to write Great-Aunt Catherine a letter. In my backpack I find a pen and the rewrapped blue box, which I expose once again and set next to me on the desk, a boy's hope illuminated by the dull light of a hotel lamp.

"What's that?" my father asks from behind me.

I do not startle or reach for the box. "A surprise bon voyage gift from a friend."

"And you haven't opened it?"

"Not yet," I say.

"What's in it?"

"If I knew, it wouldn't be a surprise."

My father sighs. "Too many secrets," he says, returning to the bathroom, and I start my letter.

Dear Aunt Catherine,

I'm writing you early because I'm not sure how fast the mail will move. We're on our second city and we leave for Suzhou today. Gardens are very big here and from our itinerary, we'll get our fill. Gardens and temples. I hope they let us go off on our own so we can see some of the cities. We mostly see the Chinese people from the bus in between destinations. At some point I'd like to go to the market and stores and restaurants they go to, something more anthropological. Otherwise we're just taking a bus trip through a giant museum.

Yesterday we went to a place called West Lake, which is kind of like a well-manicured park, only it used to be private. Then they took us to Lingyin Temple to see the sixty-four-foot-high Camphor Buddha. Afterwards, we went to a teahouse, which was really just a sales pitch. We were told Mao fought off throat cancer with green tea. And then the tins came out and everyone in our tour crowded around to toss money at the women to get their tea. Smart country.

How are things at the house? I appreciate your staying there while I'm gone. I hope you don't feel too awkward. I have to admit, I felt a little guilty before you came because I'd made so many changes since you left. I figured you'd like what I've done to the wood floors, but knocking out the wall in your old bedroom seemed almost sacrilegious. And of course, putting the porch back on. I don't know why Uncle Cane thought a carport was better. He never used it.

As for my father and me, we're finding our ground slowly. We talked a bit this morning about why he wanted to take me to China, but it wasn't very complete. When I'm alone, I want to talk to him. But when I'm with him, I just want to argue.

Happy birthday, by the way. I'm guessing this will reach you in time, though I know you don't make a big deal of birthdays. Everyone in town still knows you, so go down to Madeleine's Diner and get some free food. There's a woman here on the tour named Sheri who has a little book on Chinese astrology and she read my sign to me and let me borrow it so I could look yours up. You were born in the year of the Tiger. "Tigers are unimpressed by power or material possessions. They are direct and expect those around them to be equally so. Still, Tigers tend to be acutely concerned with the opinions of others and can become depressed if they receive too much criticism or if they fail at something, which rarely happens. They rebound, however, very quickly from any adversity and are eager to move on." More precisely, you are a Water Tiger, the book says, which means that your "sign" is tempered by one of the five elements—Metal, Water, Wood, Fire, and Earth. "Water Tigers have unmatched intuition and insight and are very reasonable. They are more calm and deliberative than Tigers of the other four elements and would rather miss an opportunity than leap too soon."

That's it from China for now. I love you—Westen

P.S. I'm a Rabbit.

The son eats breakfast alone;
he remembers a childhood friend.

I address the letter to Aunt Catherine, but it's my address, my home in Blue Falls, Washington. I can't think of a person I'd like to share this trip with more than her, and it's not lost on me that there's something odd about a man my age writing to his great-aunt rather than a "special someone." I can't help but think about this, since everyone in town back home is interested in my singleness, my reluctance to even entertain the idea that I could spend my life with someone. Though sometimes—often—I think of two people I loved and who loved me back and I miss them. Well, three.

My father comes out of the bathroom and, as he leaves, tells me not to expect him for breakfast. I turn back to addressing the envelope. As upset as I've always been with him, I'm glad that if he had to leave me, he sent me to live with Aunt Catherine and Uncle Cane in Blue Falls. There isn't much in the town itself anymore, just Madeleine's Diner, the Steam 'n' Freeze, which has been falling apart since I was a boy, the building where the post office was, Joe Fellop's Bait and Tackle, and the little odds-and-ends store run by the McFaddens. Most everything else is just houses or closed-up businesses, and out from town a little bit is Lee's egg ranch, now closed, and a little farther, Jumper's Bridge.

But I caught the tail end of the time when things were still relatively good for Blue Falls. And now, for me, it's enough that we're right next to the Columbia, that we live where cool, wet days bring out the hard smell of the earth and hot days fill the air with pine. This is what I'm thinking about this morning, thousands of miles away in China, all through the "American style" breakfast, the buffet of pancakes, scrambled eggs, soft bacon, cold cereal, and orange juice, the exoticism of seeing this food here gathering my thoughts of home even closer.

Sometimes I feel like my life is a series of people leaving me. Patrick Glass was one of them; he owns the diner now. No one thought we'd see him again after his parents got divorced and his mother took him away. But a few years ago he arrived back in Blue Falls, a thicker, taller version of the boyhood friend I remembered, but still with the same loose, shiny blond hair and quick blue eyes. He started working at the diner and then Madeleine died and left it to him in her will.

I met Patrick shortly after my father left me in Blue Falls. I was tossing rocks into Pewter Lake when a bunch of older boys rushed me with homemade spears. Patrick was in the center, holding the largest spear, a bright-yellow broom-handle-and-butter-knife combination. Taking me prisoner, they brought me back to their fort for interrogation and checked my pockets. All I had was fifteen cents and a Bazooka Joe comic.

"What kind of kid are you?" Patrick said. He was obviously the leader.

"I don't know," I said.

"You the new kid that lives up at the Gray place?"

I was beginning to get more nervous. Patrick held his spear just a few inches away from me, and the two others, Mike and Gary, stood with theirs straight at their sides, almost at attention. "Yes," I said.

"I heard you was a Chink. You don't look it."

"Chinese," I said. "Half."

"Might as well be white. Guess your mom musta been on top." I didn't get it, but Mike and Gary busted up and Patrick acted like he'd just cracked the best joke in the world. "This is our lake," he said. "Get it? If you want to use it, you gotta ask permission." Patrick shook his spear to emphasize his point, and the butter knife came loose from the handle and fell into my lap. All of us started laughing. Gary and Mike were doubled over, and even Patrick didn't care that all his spear-wielding authority had collapsed.

"I could show you how to make better ones," I said. Uncle Cane already had taught me a lot in his workshop. The boys agreed to my proposal in an instant, so we spent the rest of that afternoon in Mike's garage making weapons, sawing into the ends of old garden-tool handles, looking for likely spearheads among the junk Mike's dad clearly never touched. We found an old spatula that we ground into a triangle, and from a ragged sheet of metal, Patrick tin-snipped a pair of blades he fit together to make dual points. It was the first significant amount of time I'd spent since I moved to Blue Falls not thinking about why my father had left me.

Patrick and I became best friends over the next few years. He was Blue Falls' version of a tough kid, a minor delinquent elevated by a lack of competition and the fact that he was trying to be two sons at once. Before I came to Blue Falls, his brother killed himself by jumping off the bridge outside of town, so Patrick acted like he had to live for himself and his brother too, as if that would keep him alive. I became his conscience. Once he showed up at school with a pocketful of candy I knew he couldn't afford. When I asked how he got it, he said, "If they're dumb enough to leave it out where I can steal it, that's their fault." I didn't say much then, but I didn't take any of the candy when he offered. A couple of days later Patrick walked up to my house, obviously upset. His bike had been stolen out of his front yard.

"I guess it's your fault," I said, "for being dumb enough to leave it out where someone could steal it." Patrick looked at me. His blue eyes could give a painfully hard stare. He sat on the porch, or what was left of it since Uncle Cane had begun remodeling.

"Where is it?" Patrick said.

"In the garage." He didn't ask me how I'd stolen his bike and he wasn't angry. Instead, he just nodded his acknowledgment.

But it's the night before Patrick left Blue Falls, the last time I saw him as a boy, that is most vivid in my memory. I was thirteen and he was a year older. We were floating out on the black water of Pewter Lake at midnight, each of us on our own log but locking arms to stay together, though with no current or wind it wasn't necessary. We had been lying back watching the star-splintered sky for so long it was like we were levitating in space, nothing beneath us and everything above us.

Pewter Lake was warm and soupy and full of all the infection teenage boys are immune to. The sounds of the annual rodeo and the bright moth-glow of the arena lights had ended.

Patrick and I left the rodeo early. We pooled the last of our money and bought a bottle of Coke and a bag of barbecue chips, both of which we valued for their flotation qualities. As usual, I had more to contribute than Patrick, but I didn't say anything. His parents never had money and, on top of the divorce, his dad had just been laid off.

After the store, we went the long way home, which would take us by the lake. Invariably we routed our walks home this way. We knew every reed and duck's nest along the shore. Our history and friendship revolved around this small body of water. In drier years the lake would shrink and the new shoreline yielded old golf balls, unmatched shoes, and one time an arrowhead.

It was ten o'clock when we got to the part of the lake where we kept our logs stashed. As we walked along the shore, crickets stopped their high-pitched chirping and occasionally one of us picked up a rock and tossed it into the water, breaking up the few reflected lights on its surface. The air smelled composted, thick and almost sweet. We stripped to our underwear and pushed out into the lake on our logs. In one hand we each held a stick to gondolier with. Patrick had the chips and I kept the bottle of Coke. We rode around the edge, past the small, rotting dock, rousting a few nervous ducks, and over the submerged ridge that became an island during drought years. Finally, Patrick and I pointed to the center and gave one final push with our sticks when they could barely reach the lake bottom. We gradually came to a stop, lit by a few bright windows in the distance and the open sky.

I opened the warm soda, took a swig, and handed it to Patrick. We both lay back and pulled ourselves close with our arms, the unopened potato-chip bag floating between us. We knew it was late, but neither of us was worried about getting home. His mother was packing their belongings for the move the next day, and his father was out playing a CB radio game called Turkey Hunt. Just before things got bad between Patrick's parents, we listened to the base radio in his garage. His dad was "Silver Eagle," and we heard him and the other CBers search out the "turkey" hiding within a five-mile radius. Patrick had a handle too. He was "Little Eagle," symbolized on his father's van as a flying egg beneath an enormous gray raptor.

Drifting easily in the April night in the middle of Pewter Lake, Patrick and I weren't saying much. We stared into the night sky, our arms between us, always in touch as if we were preventing even the slightest possibility of separating. "I wonder if she's riding with him tonight?" Patrick said, interrupting the silence. He sat up and took a drink from the Coke and handed it back to me.

"Maybe not," I said, finishing off the bottle. "It was probably just that one time." We both knew that was not true, that his dad, "Silver Eagle," was on the Turkey Hunt with "Midnight Lady." There are things you understand when you hear a voice without the contradictions of facial expressions. The last time we listened to the CB, Patrick's father and this woman had teamed up in his van for the hunt. The other CBers on the channel were breaking in and making jokes as "Midnight Lady" responded with giggly denials of impropriety.

Patrick lay back on his log, keeping the chip bag floating at his side. We reached out at the same time, again pulling closer together and grasping arms at the elbow. I held the empty bottle with my other hand, conscious of our five-cent deposit. After we stopped moving, the lake quickly settled into stillness again. In the black air not far from us, we heard something skimming the water. At the shore, the calls of frogs and nocturnal birds melded together. With a poke of his stick, Patrick sent the opaque bag of chips out into the black. It was a waste of money, but I didn't say anything.

We sat for a long while watching the sky, pointing out constellations of our own making, creating our own order. The stars and faint light from the shore threw a fine blue aura over Patrick's body, a line like a gas flame starting at his white underwear and angling up through one shadowed nipple. "Are you going to get married?" he asked.

"I don't think so."

"Me either," he said.

At that moment we were suspended, permanently weightless on the water. I allowed the Coke bottle to dip sideways into the lake. It filled quickly, weighing itself down in the water, wanting to slip away, a gravity and grace at my fingertips I wouldn't let go of.

We floated in the water for a long time, but eventually Patrick sat up, making us rock slightly. "You coming in?" he asked.

I shook my head. "Nah. I think I'll stay out here for a while." I didn't want to say good-bye.

"I'll call and stuff. Let you know about the chick situation in Tacoma."

"You better," I said, sitting up, but I didn't care about that at all. Patrick was smiling, and even in the dim light I saw that his eyes had welled up like mine.

Patrick didn't say anything else; he just nodded and pushed his stick off to the side, lying forward on his log so he could paddle with both arms. I watched him go in, gradually growing fainter until I could just make out the white dot of his underwear and finally nothing at all. Another person had left me. I lay back and set the full bottle of water on my stomach. A few hours later, when the sky began converting from gray to orange, I pushed for shore, keeping the warm glass close to me. Patrick's log was resting in its usual spot on the bank. I sat for a while watching the stars fade with the dawn, rolling the bottle full of water in my hand, planning how to cap it with plastic and wax so I could save it in my room.

14

The father feels his illness growing;
he leaves his son abruptly.

The pain got worse in Hangzhou. I could barely breathe in the shower. This was the dividend for being a bad father. Months earlier, friends had sent me to an old man in Chinatown. They told me he was not a doctor, but he was a healer who could help. I learned when I came to the U.S. to put such beliefs away, but no Western medicines had changed my condition. And after all, television in the United States was filled with men who packed arenas with believers seeking hands-on healing. The man I visited laid his palms on my shoulders and gripped them tightly. He had hardly any hair, and cataracts so dense his eyes were nearly white. He did not praise anything, or push me. His office was not filled with statues and burning incense. The room was sparse: a desk with a braille machine, cheaply paneled walls, and a window with a view of the next-door building.

"You are missing something, sir," the man told me in an almost British accent. "How long has it been since you visited home?"

"No, no. I live here," I said.

"Don't be dense. I mean China."

"A few years now."

"Go back, then, sir. Take your family with you."

I did not respond. What family could I bring?

The old man waited for a moment and put one hand back on my shoulder. "Do you have children?"

"A son," I replied.

"He must go too."

"How will that help my illness?" I asked.

"I didn't say it would, sir. But it will help something."

That was my healer, a blind man in a bare room telling me the thing I'd told myself for more than two decades and ignored. That was the initial reason I thought to contact Westen, because I could apologize and face up to the fact I'd left him, and because maybe it would help me live. A father survives through his son.

WESTEN WAS WRITING a letter when I came out of the bathroom. There was an odd box tied with a dingy red ribbon on the desk. He said it was a gift, but it looked much too old to have been received any time recently.

"Don't buy souvenirs if they tell you they're antique," I warned him. "They're all fakes."

He looked up from his letter, then at the box. "I told you it was a gift."

"That you aren't going to open?"

"Not yet," he said.

"You mean not in front of me." With that, I got dressed and went out. I did not tell him I was going to find an herbalist. Just another thing I would have to admit. *What man could find the words for that event you have not written? What could a father say to a son with so much resentment already?*

15

The tour stops for a lunch;
the son helps a tour member.

We are walking on gravestones broken into fragments. They form a narrow mosaic path along the edge of Slim West Lake, the smaller counterpart to its namesake. The Chinese characters are still legible, and one reads *1853*. There are very few blank stones, which seems strange to me, as if no one thought to at least place the inscriptions facedown.

"Look," I say, pointing to the ground, but Sheri ignores me, and my father is lagging behind us. I don't think he's feeling well. "What are these from?" I ask her.

"From gravestones," she says without looking down. Her voice is raspy and tired.

I remember that today would have been her daughter's birthday. Her relatives don't appear to be treating her any differently. They're all eating from a bag of fresh lychee fruit they bought outside the hotel before we left this morning.

When we reach the spot where Wang has stopped, he waves his yellow flag back and forth in tiny jolts as if keeping time. Bald Mr. Liu walks up and interrupts him just as he begins his tour-speak.

"Lookit here," Mr. Liu says. He peels a lychee in front of us, taking away the bumpy red skin very slowly, precisely. His son, Vincent, stands close to him and all I think is that he's not far away from losing his hair too. The whole group gathers around. "I learned this when I was a kid," Mr. Liu says. After he's done with the skin, he slips the plump little fruit out of its white membrane. He pinches the membrane together and blows into it, creating a small balloon. With a big grin, he slaps it into his hand and it makes a loud pop. Everyone applauds, but I am looking at Sheri, who seems more than merely unimpressed. It occurs to me the family isn't doing the right thing. She wants to talk about her daughter, but I'm not sure I am the right person for the job.

FOR LUNCH WE'RE eating almost cafeteria-style. We choose our own food and sit at long, benchlike tables. Sheri sits at one end, slightly separated, her shiny black hair secured safely behind her ears. She's fussing with her vegetables but not really eating, and suddenly I have an idea. I mound a perfect ball of rice on a plate and ask my father for a book of matches and stick one match, head up, at the top of the rice. I sit next to Sheri, sliding the plate in front of her.

"This is the best I could do," I say, striking a match and lighting the one on the rice. "Here's to a first birthday." Sheri looks at me, a bit startled, but I point at the dwindling flame and she blows it out.

"That is about the creepiest thing anyone has ever done for me," she says. Her eyes have already teared up and everyone is looking at us as she kisses me on the cheek. "But it's also the sweetest."

"What was her name?"

"Julia."

I raise my teacup to the table. "Happy birthday, Julia," I say. The group hesitates, unsure what to do, but I keep my arm raised and everyone complies in unison with a Happy Birthday salute. Sheri smiles, wiping tears from her eyes before they fall.

"You've got perfect timing," Sheri says to me. "I bet you'd make a good hubby."

It always comes back to this, so I offer the polite nod that I've programmed for this suggestion. Even though "get Westen married up" seems like a public mantra at this point, I still can't imagine doing that, saying I'll spend my life with one person when I doubt they'll spend theirs with me. My mother couldn't keep that promise. My father didn't.

I begin to eat my lunch, thinking about the first birthday I spent in Blue Falls, in the basement of Great-Aunt Catherine's church, my first time there, in fact. I cannot remember the Sunday school teacher's name, but I see her blue nylon dress with no sleeves and the belt with the green plastic buckle that matched her necklace. She smelled of baby powder and mouthwash. All of the children sat in rows facing her and she held up a coin bank in the shape of a small loaf of bread. "Today is a special day," she said. "We're going to make Father's Day plaques and we also have a very special birthday boy." She pointed, and the other children all looked at me as she continued. "Now is the time to pull out your pennies so we can take collection in Westen's name." She handed the small loaf-bank to the first boy, who plinked in his coins and passed it to the girl next to him, and this continued until I held the loaf in my own hands. It was light and vaguely brown on the top, as if it had been removed from the oven too early. I looked up at the smiling teacher.

"Go ahead," she said.

I shook the bank and looked at her. She continued to smile, but less so. "Thank you," I finally said, because I thought that's what she was waiting to hear.

"No, sweetie," she said, taking the loaf from me. "This

money isn't for you, it's for God. Don't you want to put something in?"

"Oh," I said. "I thought it was for my birthday. I don't have anything to put in." The class giggled.

"That's all right," she said. "I confused you. We let our special boys and girls take the collection loaf to Pastor during Big Church." She looked at the other students, who had started to talk among themselves about me. "Happy Birthday Prayer, everyone," she said.

They folded their hands, bowed, and immediately began together as if the teacher had pushed a Play button. "You are blessed all year long with Jesus' love and Angel song. But on your birthday we say this prayer to keep you safe from Satan's lair. May God bless you on your natal day, and give you love in his special way. And may he keep you from worry and harm and give you comfort through your parents' arms. Amen."

"Very good," the teacher said. "God answers the prayers of all deserving little boys and girls. Happy birthday, Westen." And then she started talking about Noah's ark, explaining how a wrathful God had flooded the Earth but thought first to save two of every animal type. She used a plastic model of the ark, with miniature animals standing on the deck, Noah the same size as the elephants.

When she finished her story, she passed out small pieces of unfinished wood and scraps of paper that said, "God Loves My Dad." The last few minutes of Sunday school were spent gluing these to the wood using the hardened rubber tips of mucilage bottles. Then we wrapped them in white tissue paper that we tied with blue strings. I held my Father's Day gift all during Big Church, even when I walked the loaf of money up the aisle and put it in front of the organ. Aunt Catherine never asked me about it, even on the way home in the car.

I had a plan for my plaque. As soon as we pulled into the

driveway, I got on my bike and rode down to the river, where I unwrapped the present and looked at it carefully. The paper was already curling up at the edges. The wind coming off the water was surprisingly warm and strong, and I swayed trying to keep my balance. The wood was unsanded and cut roughly at both ends. It felt light in my hands, buoyant. I knew the Columbia went to the Pacific and, vaguely, that the ocean went all the way to China and maybe Hong Kong. I tossed the piece of wood into the water and watched it float slowly into the current. The wind blew in my face and certain angles of refracted sun obscured the wood as it got farther away. I wasn't sure about the next part. I'd never prayed on my own, but I closed my eyes and put my hands together like I'd seen the other kids do. I prayed that my dad would find this plaque floating in the water and that he'd come back and get me. I prayed that Mrs. Cheung's box was for real.

So it has happened all these years later. He wrote me a letter and brought me to China. My father sits at the opposite end of the table. He really does look tired today, under the weather. I feel like I should sit next to him, but I stay where I am. And it isn't lost on me that I've just done this birthday thing for Sheri, someone I just met, and yet I can't even force myself to walk ten feet to have lunch next to my father.

16

The father and son walk through Zhenxing;
they attend to the father's business.

In Zhenxing the guide gives my father and me one hour to walk around the city. He lets us off the bus where streets converge in a circle, the flow of cars and bicycles a whirlpool of machines and people around a central, pagoda-like tower. "We've got some business there," my father says, pointing down one of the smaller streets. It's a dense corridor of outdoor vendors shrouded by a sycamore canopy.

"What can you possibly have to do there?"

"There is always business."

"You go alone," I say. "I think I'll just look at some of the shops."

My father places his hand on my shoulder and holds it there firmly. He looks me straight in the eyes, a band of black hair curving across his forehead. "Are you going to be this obstinate the entire trip?" he says. "If so, tell me now and I won't make an effort to show you anything." But before I can answer, he reaches into his belt satchel and pulls out a curious wad, returning his passport, tissues, and the worn envelope he had our first night. "Documentation," he'd told me. But now, seeing it again, I understand. It must be a check for me, compensation, but I do not mention it. When I get the offer, I will look at him and say no thank you.

The remaining item from the belt satchel is a deck of cards. "A proposal," he says. "We'll be fair about it. Whenever we do not agree, we'll cut for the highest card."

"What is this, Las Vegas?" I ask. But he holds the deck out to me and I'm willing to play his game. Seven of spades. He chooses the nine of hearts.

"That's settled, then," my father says, and he steps into the busy street. There is something so efficient and matter-of-fact about his plan that I feel I can't argue. We turn to the street, where bikes and cars move in a strange unity. And somehow even pedestrians manage to cross through all this.

"Come on," my father says. "And don't worry. *Qi che* are afraid of people."

"Key chey?"

"Cars." He nods and explains how we have to walk in a single rhythm and straight forward. "As long as the drivers can judge where you're headed and how fast, you're okay. Just don't hesitate."

We step into this broad street and begin to cross. I look only forward, focusing on a small red Chinese flag hanging opposite us. I count the gold stars to measure my walk, four small, one large, each a step. The flag hardly moves at all in this hot, breeze-less day. It's almost too noisy to think. Cars and bicycles surround my father and me as if we were wading through a river with no current, just the exhaust-heated air and waves of horns and tinny-sounding engines. I resist looking at the oncoming traffic. I continue counting the gold stars on the red flag, aware that somehow we're willing ourselves a pocket of space.

"Piece of cake," I say nervously when we reach the other side.

My father gently corrects me. "Piece of *gao*."

In a few minutes we're walking on a street beneath the broad branches of sycamores on either side. The heavy canopy darkens and cools, and the pace here seems calmer, though it's still packed with people. Vendors line the walkways, selling from carts and small canvas booths. The variety is slim. This street is about repetition. They sell spools of dull-colored thread, thin-looking cutlery, and all sorts of white-enameled cups and pans. I feel a tug at my elbow and a woman says something to me in Chinese. Her wide smile is accented by metal-framed front teeth. She points to her clothing booth of large button-down shirts pinned against the sides, flat and plain. Blue. Tan. It occurs to me she has my father's wardrobe tacked to her walls. "What is she saying?" I ask him.

As if he hasn't been paying attention, my father speaks to her and she repeats herself. "She says her clothes are American style and do you want any?"

I shake my head.

"Say *bu yao, xie xie*. No, thank you." He sounds it out: "Boo yow shey shey."

I try to mimic my father's intonation, but the woman doesn't react. He leans over and whispers to her. I notice that her earrings are stone settings without stones. She nods as my father speaks. It's odd that he's whispering because I wouldn't understand him anyway. The woman continues nodding and then walks inside her booth, coming back out with five-yuan and two-yuan bills, which she hands to my father. "*Xie xie,*" he says and we begin walking again.

"What was that all about?" I ask as we round a corner into a slim alley. My father takes out a pen and writes in Chinese on a pad of paper he pulls from his shirt pocket.

"Just a service. It's no big deal. Hardly worth it for a few yuan."

"What service?"

"Come on," he says, starting down the alley. "I'll show you."

There is barely enough space between the buildings for two people to walk side by side. The alley walls are white stucco, cracked and peeling where they aren't covered by the drying laundry hanging from nearly every window. The air here feels dense, smells like overdone meat. A man in white briefs stands in a large metal tub, pouring water over his dark brown skin. He scrubs himself without soap, every thin muscle shiny with wetness, his underwear pressed to his skin, thin as paper. "Doesn't he have any modesty?" I ask my father.

"Don't *you?*" he replies. "No one else is looking."

He has a point, so I turn away, look ahead to where a woman is chopping whole chickens on a large wood block. Next to her are two pans where she flings the parts without fear of a cat or dog coming by. There aren't any. The closest things are the children crowding doorways and pushing past us with canvas bundles slung over their shoulders. The smaller ones cling to the legs of their mothers, who are hanging out clothes or sweeping or chatting to other women. One little girl carefully watches my father and me from behind her mother's pants leg. Her eyes are wide and shiny. She has stubby pigtails and bangs straight across her forehead. I give her a wink and a small wave and she pops behind her mother.

This moment of chicken and children feels familiar. So many late springs come to mind. Uncle Cane and what he called Butcher Days, a week or so of chickens on the block, me the holder while he brought the hatchet down on their necks. Sometimes their headless bodies popped out of my grasp and flailed wildly across the yard, wings flapping in nerve-induced desperation.

"So," I ask my father, "are you going to tell me what we're doing here?"

"We're collecting curses," he says, patting me on the shoulder. "Be patient." A motorized cart plows through the alley, pressing us to the walls on opposite sides. My father splays his arms flat against the stucco. He's a two-armed, Chinese version of Leonardo's Vitruvian Man. He's art, his black hair and tea-colored skin against the sepia wall. When we step back into the street together, he looks happier than he has the entire trip.

When the street settles down, my father nods as if he wants to explain. As if he's actually eager to tell me. "Each time I visit China, and people here find out I am going to Hong Kong, they ask me to visit the Curse Ladies for them. Of course, I've always told them they are crazy to throw away their money. There are better investments. Now I think I've sounded like every conde-scending American I met when I first went to the States. This time around I wanted to correct that. Even up my accounts."

"But there's no such thing as magic or curses, so how does that help people?" Even as I say this, I think about the irony of Mrs. Cheung's blue box tucked away in my backpack.

My father offers an amused sigh and we begin walking again. "Yes. Yes. That may be true," he says, "but it doesn't mat-ter if there *is* such a thing as curses that work. It only matters that one *believes* there is." He stops himself and thinks for a mo-ment. "Like how you'll get well faster if you believe in the cure. So all these people are happier believing they are getting a little supernatural justice. Besides, it will be interesting once we get to Hong Kong. I've never actually met a Curse Lady." He pauses, seeing I'm unconvinced. "Do you know what a Field Tiger is?" he asks.

I shake my head.

"*Dì lao tu*. Field Tiger. They look like Jerusalem crickets. Large, unattractive bugs that eat the roots off plants." My father grins as if I'm supposed to understand.

"I don't get it," I tell him.

He holds the pad of paper and a pen and gestures with it like a professor. "If you want to kill a plant for sure, you have to get to its roots. That's the best way I can explain what we are doing right now." Just as my father finishes, a tall, slouch-shouldered old man walks up and greets him as if they are close friends. His clothes are thin and oily-looking and he smells like overcooked beans. My father nods at almost every word. The man's speech gurgles from his toothless mouth and I can tell my father is listening carefully because he begins writing on his pad of paper in Chinese. The two of them break out into eager conversation as the old man reaches into his pocket, producing a worn leather pouch. Both of his hands are heavy with tremor, but he manages to extract a small roll of yuan, which he gives to my father. They nod profusely at each other and the old man walks away, clearly happy.

"I don't suppose you're going to tell me what that was all about," I say.

My father slips the pad of paper back into his pocket and gives it a couple of pats. "That is between him and his Curse Lady."

17

The son recalls a trip to Mexico City;
he thinks of the man he met there.

The woman at the hotel shampoos my head gently, rinsing the lather with warm water. The sound track from *Grease* plays in the background. I keep thinking of how my father likes to play games, how answers here don't come easily. I consider the mosaic of gravestone fragments at Slim West Lake, how the dates and Chinese characters were still legible. I imagine a man with a blank stone in front of him, laboring with hammer and chisel, the hours spent on the summary of someone's life. Then it's broken. What sits above those graves now?

As the woman pats my hair dry with a towel, I notice she's barely as tall as I am sitting down. She has long French-tipped nails that point straight out from her fingers. No curve to them at all. I think my cut and shampoo are almost over, but she begins thumping on my head, using one hand to snap the fingers of the other onto my scalp. She does this all the way down the back of my neck and over my shoulders. I look in the mirror and from certain positions the woman is completely hidden. All I can see are her hands coming out of my back like I'm an Indian god.

The woman runs her nails through my scalp and I instantly close my eyes. This is how my mother used to put me to sleep, how Great-Aunt Catherine learned she could calm me. It's also how Gideon first touched me.

It was Mexico City after my second year at UCLA. That trip was supposed to be a kind of anniversary, two years with Margaret. But she came down with chicken pox. We decided I should go alone and we'd vacation somewhere together at Christmas.

I'd met Gideon by accident at Chapultepec Park. He was another American conspicuously alone. We ended up spending the week together, combining our itineraries. It was he who suggested the café in the Zona Rosa, my last full day before I had to go home. I think of us sitting there and procrastinating, the rain falling like I'd never seen, not even in Blue Falls, muting the sharp edges of the city. Gideon was so quiet. He wanted me to stay another few days with him. He told me he would pay for it. I wanted to say yes.

I hadn't called Margaret in days, and there I was sitting with someone fifteen years older than me, not wanting to leave him. It was the first time I'd felt like that for a man, for a particular man. The rain was bad. It sheeted off the awning above our table and it wasn't long before we could see our reflections in the cobblestones. The air smelled dense, tannic, like burning citrus. "It's too low here," Gideon said. As he spoke, he ran his smooth hand over his black rayon sleeve. I remember wondering what the rest of his skin was like.

I wondered, too, how I could ever explain this to Margaret. She was so beautiful, the first person I met in Los Angeles. I loved her. She was so completely Catholic, had even gotten me to attend mass with her. She had hinted about me getting baptized and about marriage classes. And sex came up once, a few months after we started dating. I was dropping her off at her sorority after the movies. "I want you to know," she said, "I really respect that you haven't pushed the sex thing. It's important to me." After that, she pecked me on the cheek and went inside.

So there was Gideon asking me to stay, the water edging into the café patio. He fingered a small silver crucifix around his neck. I looked for our waiter. The walls of the café were water-damaged, obscured by dozens of orange paper flowers. I heard the impatient breathing of the only other customers, a husband and wife, pink-skinned, chubby Americans. They sat at the back, under the near-leafless branches of a potted ficus. Their stomachs kept them pushed away from the table. But they were there together and I had gone to Mexico City alone, left Margaret behind. I looked at Gideon. "No waiter," I said.

He offered a sad expression. "They serve drinks here. So the food comes slow." The rain continued and the water at the base of our table crept higher. We moved inside, where we were slightly elevated. As we sat down, Gideon fixed on the small tan line on my finger where the engaged-to-be-engaged ring from Margaret had been. "What are we going to do?" he said. "We're both going to be in Los Angeles. We can't ignore that."

"It's a big city," I said.

He put both his hands on the table and leaned toward me. "Not anymore." He couldn't know how true I knew that was. Once I'd come face-to-face with my father in L.A. and he didn't even recognize me.

The floor of the café made a lightly fizzing sound as the rainwater advanced. We moved one more table back and I began to feel confined. I was leaving the following morning and the city was not letting go. I tried to remember my flight number as we looked out at the rain. "This could be Bogotá," he said, "or Portland or Belgium. We're the lovers sitting in the cafés waiting for the rain to clear."

"That's poetic, but we're not lovers." I said. "I just met you.

And I've never done anything like this." I was nervous and compelled at the same time. I didn't want to leave.

Gideon nodded without saying anything more. I thought I understood. Cities are defined through the eyes of couples. They are a confluence of perspective between two people. The trick is finding someone who shares your vision. I thought of Margaret at home, recovering, maybe venturing out to a coffeehouse, attempting to interpret the landscape alone. I wondered if she needed me, if I was the right one. If she was.

Seeking something, anything, to distract me, I looked toward the ceiling, which was stained with sprays of brown from previous seepage, a line of water following a crack just over where we sat. The tourists at the other table had obviously been to Chapultepec. They were talking about Carlotta, how sorry they felt that she'd gone mad, that Maximilian had put her in such a bad position. "She must have really loved him," the woman said.

A rusted-out Volkswagen bug pushed through the flooded alley in front of the café, sending small waves lapping against rolled-up throw rugs near our table. "They didn't put this in the brochure," I said.

Gideon's eyes brightened. "They always leave the best things out."

The rain ended, as if someone had shut off a valve. The waiter assured us our food was coming. Gideon looked at the flooded street. "This moment doesn't have to be the last one between us," he said. A flock of pigeons swooped close to the edge of the water, picking at the flotsam.

"You know, you never see just one pigeon," I said.

Gideon placed his hands on the table and changed the subject. "I've been wanting to ask, how do you spell your name?"

After I told him, Gideon gave me a curious look, then wrote it on his forearm with his finger. "Does it mean something?"

It was a question I asked myself frequently as a child, but wasn't able to ask my father. My aunt didn't have an answer. "I assume my parents made it up," I told Gideon. "Maybe something to do with my father leaving China and moving West."

"I'm named after a hotel Bible," Gideon said. "Honestly."

"I get the feeling you're honest about everything."

THAT NIGHT I felt uncomfortable about asking Gideon to my room, but I wanted our good-bye to be private, between us. So, instead, I took him upstairs to a storage area I'd blundered into when I first arrived. The muffled rhythm of the Ballet Folklórico at the National Theater reached us as we sat together on a stack of mattresses. I guessed at one time it must have been more than a storage room, since it had huge, semiglazed windows. They diffused the outside world, showing only feathery balls of green and red light pulsing with inconsistent current. "I'm going back tomorrow," I said quietly.

"I want to see you again," Gideon said. His skin was beautifully dark in this light, and his eyes were wide open and intent. He never looked away from me.

"I don't think it's right. I've got Margaret."

Gideon shook his head slowly. "Yes," he said. "She's a priority. But something happened here. It's possible this can't work out for lots of reasons, like I'm too old for you or maybe we shouldn't see each other, but let's leave that possibility open." He gave me his business card. On the back he'd written his home phone number. Across the street, the silhouettes of tree branches in the park created a fuzzed proscenium over a stilled fountain. The subtle Mexican music from the theater continued sifting into the space between Gideon and me, defining it.

I looked at the business card again. It was embossed in the

shape of a video cartridge. "Very L.A.," I said, and we both smiled.

Thinking of Gideon at that moment makes me feel good. I felt I'd discovered someone who understood me, someone who could protect me, too. But, happy as this memory is, it reminds me that years later Gideon didn't leave me, but sent me away.

18

*The father and son arrive at Confucius's temple;
the son recalls a trip to Disneyland.*

Poking me in the side with his elbow, my father rattles me to attention.

"You must know Confucius?" the guide asks. We give the disinterested nods and affirmative grunts we've gotten good at. "This man has made many famous sayings. Some are not so well known. 'If you can look into yourself and find no cause for dissatisfaction, how can you worry and how can you fear?'"

My father shakes his head. "I don't believe that is the entire thing," he says. The guide continues to rattle off more Confucian sayings, but I'm not listening. Instead, I'm watching my father's mood grow sullen. He puts his glasses on and looks out the window. The day is bright in Nanking, leaving no shadow on the gray, blockish storefronts. He shakes his head again.

"What's wrong?" I ask.

"This is the one city I never care to visit. It feels odd being a tourist."

"I don't understand."

My father looks at me as if he's considering his words. The guide is still speaking, and behind us, the group ignores him with their own conversations. "The Japanese," my father says, "tortured and killed a lot of people here during the war."

I look out the window at the people on bikes, at the pedestrians, and, when the bus stops in traffic, at a woman selling tea in tall, clear glasses. I am slightly taken aback to hear an emotion from my father that isn't related to us. It reminds me that this is *his* country. I am a tourist. "Everyone seems okay now," I say, inadequately.

"No, no. The Japanese came and raped the women and took the men out to the edge of the city and shot them. They killed hundreds of thousands of people."

"Were any of them our relatives?" I ask.

My father fixes his eyes on me, pinching his brow slightly. "They were Chinese," he says. "Does massacre require a family tree?"

I am cowed, my history courses surging forward, in which I learned of African slaves, Native Americans, European Jews. I am denied sharing this pain with my father. "I didn't know," I say.

"Of course not. Few do."

As we walk toward the Confucius temple, there is a visible change in the tone of the buildings. The storefronts are brightly painted in reds and yellows, with large, stylized Chinese characters advertising each store. Coca-Cola signs in Chinese and English hang everywhere, McDonald's and Kentucky Fried Chicken as well. Our group can't help but stop to take pictures with the larger-than-life statue of Colonel Sanders.

"It's like a carnival," my father says, as if he doesn't understand.

Inside the courtyard, a giant metal statue of Confucius stands before us. He holds one hand in the other as if preparing a welcoming gesture, and wears a broad smile on his bearded face. It is an almost cartoonish representation, as if he were ready to be covered with flowers and entered in a parade. Behind him is the temple, and as we step through, my father lets out a large sigh. Rows of rock vendors are lined up beneath long, dusty scrolls of Confucian sayings. Wang gathers our group. For some reason his hair is standing on end, as if he's been in a slapstick scare. "These rocks you appreciate are from Rain Flower Mountain," he says, but adds nothing about Confucius. The unpolished rocks soak in small, water-filled dishes, ovals striped with orange and white, maroon, blues of all shades. And egg-shaped stones veined in white. Some dangle on fishing line from above, lusterless but brilliant nonetheless. Somewhere in the marketplace beyond the walls, an unfamiliar rock-and-roll song is blaring.

"I was wrong," my father says. "This is not like a carnival at all. It's worse. It's Disneyland."

He's still shaking his head in disapproval, though I know he's not thinking what I am. I remember. The day before my mother's funeral, my father took me to Disneyland.

"This may be your last chance to go with me," he had said. He'd woken me early that morning. The house was full with the sweet smells of bacon and *lap-cheung*. I'd slept on the couch so Uncle Yi could have my bed. My father didn't sleep at all

When I walked into the kitchen, my father put his fingers to his lips and whispered. "Don't wake them. I haven't told anyone we're leaving." With a long fork, he set hot lengths of bacon and *lap-cheung* on a plate already piled with scrambled eggs. Bleary from sleep, I cleared a spot on the table. There were dozens of dishes, casseroles, cakes and breads, fried chicken—grieving food. The jigsaw puzzle my mother and I had been working on lay in its box on top of the refrigerator, set aside for all this food my father and I would never be able to eat.

I was just eight and still dazed after not even a week of my mother's death. Somnambulant. The relatives coming in and out of the house, the food piling up, all the sympathetic looks and head rubbings, people I'd never met, teary-eyed and assuring me things would be okay.

I stabbed at the sweet, gristly *lap-cheung,* my head resting on one hand. "Maybe we shouldn't go," I said.

My father shushed me. "I promised when you were old enough I'd take you."

"So I'm old enough now?"

My father sat down at the table, no eggs on his plate, just cold rice and sliced *lap-cheung.* He looked at me intently but said nothing. Behind him, outside our dirty kitchen window, the first of the hibiscus blooms blushed pink against the dusty pane. "Yes," my father finally said. "When a boy loses his mother, he is old enough to do anything."

He never looked more Chinese to me than right then, his eyes thin-slitted behind heavy black frames with thick glass, his brown skin and black hair shiny with oil.

Our group is now fully immersed in commerce, sorting through the Rain Flower Mountain stones to bring home to friends and relatives who outrank T-shirts but don't rise to the level of deserving embroidered silk. "I've got plenty of rocks at home," I tell my father. He leads me outside, where we sit facing the Confucius statue. It is a strange place, I think, China is. And then I think, No, it's not. Really it's me that's the stranger here. "How long did it take you to feel at home in the United States?" I ask.

"Your mother always made me feel like I fit in. Without her I never felt one hundred percent at home in the U.S."

"Because I'm just not feeling like China is my country."

"That makes two of us." My father sighs. "I'm not sure where I belong these days."

My mother's death was the catalyst for the separation with my father years ago. But it occurs to me it is also part of the context for this trip with him. The last time we spoke like this, admitted we were both lost, was that day before her funeral, when he took me to Disneyland. It was just an hour's drive from our house in Los Angeles, so we were there by nine o'clock, right when it opened, packed in behind a rope on Main Street with hundreds of other early birds, all the children strategizing about which ride to go on first before the lines got bad. I didn't really have any idea what I wanted to go on first. I looked down the thoroughfare and down the perfectly clean street bordered by a dream-replica of an early-twentieth-century main street: wood-slatted, bright paint even brighter on the ornate trim, penny arcade, sweet shops. A theater advertising *Steamboat Willie*.

I'd been here once before, when I was three, but my father said I wasn't satisfied with the kiddie attractions like Mr. Toad's Wild Ride and the Mad Hatter's Tea Party. He told me I kept pointing at the Matterhorn and got upset when he wouldn't take me. Disneyland had become a bit of lore in our family, something held over me when I wasn't good. When I'd ask if I could go again, sometimes they'd say, "When you're older," and sometimes "Have you been keeping your room clean?"

"Are you excited?" my father said, looking down at me.

"Yeah," I said.

"Good. What do you want to do first?"

It was as if we had an unspoken agreement that the reality awaiting us at home did not exist. I thought of all the possibilities at the park, the things I remembered and the things I'd heard my friends talk about. I stared at the white tip of the Matterhorn set off against the bright morning sky. That had to be first.

Suddenly the group started to push forward. Disneyland was open. I grabbed my father's hand and we started running toward the Matterhorn, not looking around, just plowing toward our first ride, kids screaming on either side of us, older kids without their parents passing us. I remember being upset that some of them were going to get to the Matterhorn first, worried as if there were a limited amount of seats.

That was how we spent the day, only stopping to buy tickets

for the rides, mostly "E" because the lower the letter, the tamer the attraction. We paused, too, for lunch, my father successfully reminding me that I might be hungry. We ate lukewarm hamburgers and fries at Tomorrowland Terrace. The sun directly overhead, hot and humming in my ears, made everything around us look washed out. The entire patio was filled, hundreds of people eating the same meal as ours, kids hurrying, taking huge bites and washing everything down with equally big gulps from soft drinks.

"Are you having a good time?" my father asked.

"Yeah," I said.

"See, I keep my promises." Then he started to cry, sob, putting his face in his hands. People at other tables looked at us. I wanted to cry too. I had always imagined going to Disneyland with both of my parents. But no tears came. I remember thinking one of us was enough. My father looked up from his hands, his glasses off, eyes already red and nose running. I handed him a napkin. "I'm sorry," he said. "This was supposed to be your special day. I just miss your mother."

"Me too," I said. The next day would be the funeral. That seemed to be the purpose of going to Disneyland, I understood later. It was a distraction to keep me happy, a gesture to relieve me from my own grieving. I'm thinking now it was a bad model, his lesson in how to subdue feelings.

We decided just to walk around Tomorrowland, where we found a ride I'd never heard of, Mission to Mars. There was no line. Outside, a mock digital clock gave the countdown to the next liftoff. We went inside and took our seats in what was made to look like the interior of a rocket ship. The lights darkened slightly. I looked at my father, who was crying controlled tears. I didn't know what to do. I wanted him to be happy. I wanted us both to be happy. A projection of our ship appeared in the center floor of our capsule while a narrator told us about the importance

of our voyage to the Red Planet. The countdown began and finally the engines roared. Across the way, a boy younger than I
sat between his parents, each holding one of his hands. I watched
my father, lights bright on his glasses, shielding his eyes like a
comic-strip mad scientist. I had no idea what we would do without my mother. The rockets fired. Our seats rocked. We were on
our mission to Mars.

1 9

The tour drives through Nanking at night;
the father tells the son about that night.

You lose something, even if you make a profit. I was coming to terms with this, yes. We drove through Nanking at night, Westen sitting next to me. One of the great stone gateways was lit in lime green. Large red lanterns dangled in the arch. In front was a square where couples waltzed and drank sodas. I listened carefully. The music was American: "Red River Valley." How could this be the same city Papá had told me about? I had even seen the photographs of the Japanese standing on that same gate. They had their arms raised in victory, guns in their hands. Below, their comrades were torturing the women and killing men. For so long the Japanese denied it even happened. That is why, as we passed the square where people waltzed, I felt I needed to tell Westen about his mother, that this time I couldn't fail to get it out. Our own history could not be covered up. Yes, even if I lost some respect by telling him, I thought there could be a net gain.

"There is probably a better time to tell you about this," I began. Westen didn't respond. I looked around the bus. Everyone was lost in conversation and he was lost in thought. I touched his arm and he looked at me. "I want to tell you something. It's about your mother."

"You keep bringing her up and then you don't say anything," he said.

"Yes, yes, I know. I'm sorry for that."

"I've been thinking about Mom all day."

"About what?"

"It began with Disneyland and the funeral. But all kinds of stuff."

"Well," I said, "I have something serious to discuss. Before you were born, your mother and I went on that trip to New Orleans I started to tell you about before. We got drunk and these men . . ." I paused. I did not know how to say it, but I came to the end with all calmness. "So these men took advantage of her. They tied me down." I didn't know how to continue with the most important part. Celia's face came to me with all its kindness, as if giving me permission. "They raped her," I said softly.

Westen's face was serious and his hands were visibly shaking, though he nodded quietly.

"There wasn't anything I could do to help her. No, the truth is . . . I don't even remember trying." It might have been the most painful sentence I'd ever spoken to Westen.

"What," he said, looking around and lowering his voice, "what are you telling me?"

"I didn't do anything to help her," I said. "I looked at my wrists and there weren't any rope burns. I hadn't even struggled." By then I was fully in tears.

"Jesus," he sighed, and his eyes were welling up too. "Who am I supposed to feel for? You or Mom? Why the hell did you drag me to China to tell me this?"

"Maybe if I had not gotten drunk. Maybe if I wasn't Chinese they wouldn't have bothered us."

"You're not listening." Westen grabbed one of my shoulders and looked directly into my eyes. "Why do I need to hear this? Is this the reason for the trip?"

"No, no," I said, "I promise. I would not bring you to China for this."

"The world is ugly," he said, halting, "with or without our consent." Then he reached into his bag and pulled out the blue box he'd had sitting on the hotel desk. He looked at it for a moment and pulled the ribbon, bits of old wax splitting open at the knot.

"What's that for?"

He placed his hand on the lid as if he were going to lift it off, but paused. "I'm not sure what it's for." Holding the box in his palm, staring at it, Westen did not speak. He looked at me and shook his head, retying the bow and returning it to his backpack. "It's not time," he said.

"Time for what?"

"No more."

"You asked me why I told you all this."

"Please," he said, "I can't handle anything else right now." He would not speak further. It was not easy, but I felt stronger telling Westen about his mother and me, that at least it was out. I wondered what the dividends might be. But I am relieved he couldn't yet hear the final thing, that his mother might have gotten pregnant that night. The bus pulled up to the hotel, and the group stood to exit. Westen and I stayed seated, dazed, even though we were in the front seats. Everyone was full of conversation, eager to get inside and eat at the hotel. I wanted to tell them this wasn't the real Nanking.

Yes, this is inserted here much later as you try to understand what happened. It could be a moral to tell a grandchild on a riverbank. Secrets, after all, are merely daily actions kept from those not worth trusting.

But why be so lofty? Your son will inherit this someday, remember. After that night in New Orleans when you were proud to be acting American, you woke up on the floor of the hotel room. No, *you couldn't recall how you got back. You saw Celia's foot hanging off the bed. As you moved to get up, you realized your arms were tied to the dresser legs. You called for Celia, but she didn't move. You said her name louder. She rolled over just far enough to see you. Her face was red and her hair was tangled and hanging in her face.*

"Did they touch you?" you asked. As you write this you are still not sure. Maybe she just saw the question in your face.

She nodded. "All of them." She wrapped a sheet around her body and untied you.

"We have to call the police."

"No," she said. She was shaking, almost ready to cry. "I just want to go home." You have always regretted agreeing to this.

A couple of weeks after that, you broke up. In another couple of months you were back together, planning a wedding, expecting a baby. Yes, yes, you had blood tests but you told her you did not want to hear if Westen was yours or not. The truth is, you did not want to hear that he wasn't. She knew that too. It never came up again. Not from her. Not from your doctor. But she knew and she sealed the truth in an envelope you never opened.

That is the story you planned to tell Westen in China. Harsh and implausible as it was, it was the only way you knew how to fill the hole you left in his life. You brought the old envelope with you, still sealed. You can forgive yourself for keeping it.

2 0

The son considers his mother's rape;
the tour visits a Beijing temple.

What am I supposed to say to my father this morning? Maybe I can't really talk to him because there are so many things I'm afraid to find out. We are already in Beijing. Last night wasn't easy. In our room, I lay awake, knowing he was awake too. I asked him if he'd gone to the police after my mother was raped.

"No. No," he said slowly. "Your mother did not want that. It was difficult."

"I imagine." These few words didn't seem enough. I wanted to yell at him. I never thought of my mother as a wounded person and I didn't want to think of her that way.

I was confused by what my father was telling me, loading this on with everything else we were trying to straighten out. I tried to unravel the purpose of his disclosure. He obviously went through something that night with my mother, lost some part of himself, and it struck me that maybe he had kept this inside all these years because he had no one in his life to confide in. I am it, I thought, if only because I am the last direct link to the woman he loved.

So I said nothing more. Our room remained silent, though neither of us got much sleep. Outside, Beijing rumbled in the night, as if we were poised above a volcano. At one point I got up and looked out the window. We'd arrived during a celebration week and the city was brilliant with colored lights strung along the avenues and on the rooftops.

I remember one of the last times someone tried to help me understand my mother. It was my second week in my new home, and Aunt Catherine and I were hanging out in the den. She and I were spending a great deal of time together because Uncle Cane was seldom around when I returned from school. Aunt Catherine sat on the edge of the avocado-colored loveseat and I was slouched in Uncle Cane's old brown chair, which sagged with his impression. The walls were darkly paneled and lined with shelves full of empty liquor bottles shaped like cars and trains and movie stars with screw-off heads.

"I have something to show you." Aunt Catherine pulled a small bundle of dull white satin from her pocket. She unrolled it on her lap, revealing a threaded needle and lace sewn across two edges. "I just found this in a drawer. I started it years ago," she said. "Look how it's yellowed." She slipped the needle into the material and began sewing. "I made your mother's wedding dress out of this material." She put her hand on my arm. It was warm and I was surprised how genderless it was, thick and knotted at the joints. "Your grandma passed on two years before your parents got married, so your mom asked me to help make her dress."

Aunt Catherine reached into her pocket again, producing a photo of my mother at her wedding. She held it out to me and I took it. My mother's hair was not the blond I knew, but a bright henna red, pinned back beneath a short veil dotted with pearls. She wore a knee-length dress bordered at the hem with the same lace Aunt Catherine showed me. In the photograph, dulled with age, my mother was waiting for the photo to be taken while my father stood in a white tuxedo, his hand on her elbow. But he was turned, talking to a table of Chinese, relatives or friends dressed in dark suits.

I wondered which image I would remember as my mother—the one in the photograph or the one I saw so often getting ready for work at the hospital, perhaps even the one at the viewing before the funeral. Her casket was draped with an ivy wreath laced with white gardenias and a spray of even whiter roses. She wore the jade-colored dress my father and I gave her for Mother's Day. The sharp green was an odd contrast to her face, which had given up its texture to a layer of powder. This is the image of her that comes to me first now, her soft face with pink lipstick on tightly closed lips, and eyelashes thickened like twigs with brown mascara.

Aunt Catherine continued sewing on the satin, the fragment left over from my mother's wedding. I ran my hand back and forth on the arm of Uncle Cane's chair, the friction heating my skin. I imagined this was the texture of the artificial turf covering the mound of dirt next to my mother's grave. As if those faded green rectangles were less conspicuous than fresh earth. As if the musty smell of wet soil could be covered up. I remembered how the guests divided themselves, Chinese on the right, Caucasians on the left. During the service, I watched for a pair of eyes that might meet mine. Afterwards, people filed by, shook my father's hand, patted him on the shoulder, but rarely looked at me.

I handed the photograph of my mother back to Aunt Catherine. My mother was dead, my father gone, and I was beginning to understand there wasn't much difference.

I FINALLY FELL asleep thinking about that afternoon with Aunt Catherine, about the two most important women in my life, about that time when I was young when everything derailed. And now I know that maybe it started even before I was born. But this morning as we tour yet another ancient site of gray stone, my father seems tired, as if last night wore him out. Wang calls him away from the wall to translate. The tour cheers him on as we arrive at an elevated marble platform, Wang waving the yellow flag as he begins to speak. Today he has a hand-shaped bruise on his right cheek, distinctly purple, and his words are half directed to the tour, half to my father. The day is humid and bright and all of us are squinting in the midmorning sun.

"This is Uyan Din Tan," my father says.

Sheri stands next to me. Today she smells like a melon medley, honeydew and cantaloupe, perhaps. "Your father is so great," she says.

"Yeah," I say.

My father continues to translate. "Couples come to this altar . . ." He pauses and speaks to Wang, shrugging. "Yes, altar. They come here to pray for twins."

Sheri pulls me back. She puts her arm around me. "I don't think I want to hear about fertility right now," she says between gum smacks.

"I understand."

"Have you ever wanted kids?"

"I have pigeons."

She pats me on the back like we are old friends. "For real?"

"I'm not sure I can handle children."

"Before Julia, I wanted three or four. Now I'd settle for just her. Maybe you don't appreciate what it feels like to be responsible for another life." I'm changing my mind. She smells like watermelon, I decide, and I find it strangely comforting.

"I guess not," I say as we continue to follow the group across the long plaza toward yet another temple. I want to tell her I *do* appreciate what it's like to take care of someone. To love someone. I want to tell her I've already been there, even at the end when it starts getting bad.

2 1

The son remembers a walk in the desert;
he recalls the beginning of the end.

The medication made Gideon nauseous and sometimes deliri-
ous. I remember the last time we stayed in the desert house. It
was ten o'clock when I awoke, and the sun hung low over the
still desert. I saw that Gideon was already on the stone patio
drinking coffee, ignoring the building heat. He was staring at a
pair of potted irises in the shade, which had opened overnight,
each stem allowing a blossom of dense purple and a slit of yellow
on the petal. One of the flowers looked as if it was already giving
in to the oncoming heat.

"It's so hot," I said.

"We're in the desert," Gideon huffed back.

"I wish you'd told me sooner," I said. "I would have left my
skis at home."

Gideon reached out to me. He had already gotten much thinner and his skin had taken on a bluish tint. He put his fragile-
looking arm around my waist. In front of us, the wall at the
perimeter was lined with clay pots, painted with hibiscus and
tropical fruits like faded tattoos. Some of them lay broken from
the day before, when Gideon had used them for target practice
with some of the stones he'd collected over the years. The pool,
too, sparkled with its bluish green refraction. Sometimes I would

spot it from miles away on one of our flora hiking trips, as if it were a chip of bleached jade.

"I took a walk this morning," Gideon said.

"Already? Where?"

"I had an episode," he began. "I don't remember all of it. I was thinking about going to the theater and how people pay to sit in the balcony, safe and away from the action. You know. It's so fucking sterile. No breath or nuance. So I was just thinking shit like that and I saw these amber shapes out on the desert, on the horizon I guess. It felt like an invitation, like there was a doorway or something out there I had to go through. I felt like I was being called out. So I just got up, slung my shoes over my shoulder, and started walking. I took the .22."

"The rifle? What did you need that for?" I sat down next to Gideon, already worried at the story he was telling.

"Hell, I'm not sure. I told you I wasn't thinking straight. Anyway, I got pretty far out before I looked back. The house looked so strange. It was this yellow stucco smear, like a dying flower or something. And then I thought of you and the tea stains on the sheets, the basil sprigs in the pillow slips."

"You shouldn't have been walking out there alone. It doesn't sound like you were all there."

"I already fucking told you that. I wasn't. I walked pretty far and after a while I guess I forgot why I was out there. I had a gun and my shoes off and I couldn't even see the house anymore. I got all the way out to Baker's Road."

"Jesus," I said. Baker's Road was a few miles from the house. I wouldn't have thought much about it before—we'd walked along its gravelly curves dozens of times—but thinking of Gideon alone all that way scared me. "Is that when you snapped out of it?"

"Kind of. I put on my shoes at least. And I realized I was sweating pretty bad. I just thought, *Fuck. What am I doing out here?* Then I saw this trail of dust whipping up in the distance. At first I thought maybe it was a whirlwind, but it was a car, a white station wagon. So I kind of plopped down under a grove of tree chollas and waited in the shade. Thought I could get a ride or something. The station wagon gets pretty close, so I stand up, like an idiot still holding the gun. Imagine this." Gideon stood up, the .22 held at his side in one hand.

I shook my head.

"I know, I know. It sounds like the beginning of a crappy made-for-TV movie. Hell, it sounds like one of the shows I've produced.

"So, anyway, this fucking car rushes by me. Just keeps going. Like I should have even expected someone to stop. It heads off over that little hill with all the saguaro. I kind of knew I should go home, but I also thought maybe I should try to get a ride. I started walking up the road and I started thinking of you because there's all this desert star and purple owl clover and I remembered our first walk out here with our native plants book."

"Okay. Okay," I said, getting impatient. "What happened?"

"I don't know. I went over the ridge and I saw this woman get out of the car. I think she was releasing rattlesnakes. The next thing I know I was back here."

"I didn't hear a car pull up."

"You wouldn't wake up if I spontaneously combusted in bed right next to you." Gideon smiled, trying to take the edge off the moment. But I couldn't join him.

"You know," he said, "it's all going to be up and down from here. I'm thinking about finally calling my mother." Gideon had avoided speaking to his family since he started getting sick. Since there was no longer time between symptoms. He'd seen his mother nine months earlier at a family reunion. She'd guessed what was wrong. "I'm sure she's wondering about me."

"I always thought it was weird that you two hadn't spoken anyway."

Gideon smiled, and even though he was thinner and his skin no longer the smooth light brown of when I first met him, I could still see what had made him so handsome. "You're one to talk," he said. "How many decades has it been since you've spoken to your father?"

"Not decades," I said, caught a little off guard. "And besides, *he* doesn't speak to *me*."

"Whatever. The fucking point is you're a big boy now. You could find him if you wanted to."

"Exactly." I gave Gideon a look that told him I didn't want to talk about my father anymore and he understood. He'd always been good about not pushing me about certain things.

THAT NIGHT WE took a blanket into the desert where we'd made a clear spot for Gideon's painting and meditation. The ground felt warm against our backs as we looked up at the stars. Gideon liked to say he could hear music coming out of the sky. On any given night, Bach or Chopin or someone from the next century experimenting with silver notes on a black canvas.

"What are they playing tonight?" I asked.

"Baroque." He held my hand, the grasp hot and firm.

"Again?"

"Yes," he laughed.

I scooted in close to him, curved my body into his. When we first lived together, after Margaret, I could lie like this for hours, feeling his hand run through my hair, the thickness of him a place of safety. But that night, lying together on the blanket, I stayed close to him because I didn't want him to think things had changed. He was so much older than me, frail with disease, and I was still looking to him as a safe harbor. Even after all the weight loss, I wanted him to know I still needed to be close to him, that he had something to offer. And that was true. "I could stay here all night," I said.

Gideon squeezed my arm. "I wanted to say I'm sorry about wandering off today. I don't want to worry you."

"What are we going to do?"

"Well, kiddo," he said, scratching my head softly, "I think I'm going to put the Beverly house and this one up for sale. I'll move into Silver Lake."

"That's awfully small for the two of us and all our things."

"I know. We have to talk about that. You need to make some decisions for yourself now."

The air was cool. I stared at our yellow patio light in the distance, as still and bright as a brass doorknob in the darkness.

"I've been thinking," Gideon said. "I love you so much. But you're pretty fucked up. You know that, right? I mean, you're with an HIV-positive guy fifteen years older than you." He paused. "Hell, it's AIDS now. We've never had sex, and you don't speak to your father. And we both know your aunt could find him in a second."

"You're right," I said quietly. "I am messed up." Gideon didn't say anything more. We lay there together on the desert floor, everything still and cool, the ceiling of stars seeming close enough to touch. I knew he was right about me, except about not allowing sex between us. That was partly him not wanting to risk getting me sick. For him, I could have. But I wasn't worried about myself. Just then, I was only concerned with how long we had together. As it turned out, not long at all.

22

The acrobatics begin;
the son wonders about his talents.

The seats at the Beijing Acrobats' Theater are covered with worn yellow fabric and the walls are undecorated. George, a retired dentist and uncle brought along by his relatives on the tour, sits near my father and me. "I understand this is quite a show," he says. "They say if you come to Beijing you shouldn't miss it."

"Here we are," I say, smiling and nodding, trying to be as eager as he is.

"Makes you proud to be Chinese. 'Course, I wouldn't trade living in the good ol' U.S. for anything."

"George," I ask, "how many generations of your family have lived in America?"

"My family? I think we built the goddamned railroads." He slaps his knee, pleased with himself.

I turn to my father and whisper, "They're about as Chinese as Wonder Bread." As I say this, I think of how everyone I know has forgotten I'm half Chinese, as if that part of me is no longer relevant. At least George gets to look the part. If my mother had made this trip with us, I wonder if I would feel less conspicuous, especially if I didn't know about that night in New Orleans. Would her sharp Caucasian features make me look and feel more Chinese, if only by comparison?

. . .

THE ACROBATS ARE difficult to watch. They amount to painted-up children contorting their bodies, girls in white tights balancing on one arm, smaller girls in pink tights and beaded tutus balancing vases on sticks and rolling around like seals. And this is just the opening act. The crowd loves it. I look at my father. He's watching, but with very little expression.

A boy leaps onto the stage, two streaks of rouge giving him cheekbones. He's a boy from the waist up, but his legs are as thick as any man's, straining under silvery white spandex. Four other boys enter. All five have on red tops. They hold their hands out wide. This, and the way their costumes cling to their bodies, makes them seem like underdressed matadors. For five minutes they leap onto each other's shoulders, slide through open legs. Clasped together like a tank tread, three of them roll across the floor. All of this set to high-pitched Chinese music, all strings and percussion.

I have a dim memory of doing somersaults on a blue mat. I remember other children flopping around beside me and parents looking on. It's not a solid vision, though, nothing I've ever thought of before. I lean to my father and whisper, "Was I ever in gymnastics?" He does not reply, so I poke his knee and ask again.

He thinks for a moment, his eyes searching his memory skyward. "Tumbling. When you were three. But not very long." He looks at me. "I'd forgotten about that. We put you in all kinds of crazy programs."

The music heightens, the set changes, and two girls come out and lie on padded supports. They reach behind themselves with their feet and each lifts up a ceramic pot as tall and fat as an extra-large pumpkin. They hold these high above their bodies, white tights leading to red slippers leading to seemingly precarious pots that begin to spin as the ankles and feet below them go into motion. But always the legs themselves remain almost perfectly still. It's interesting, but I've seen it all on television. In a while they'll start tossing the pots to each other, catching them with their feet and throwing them back immediately. "What other programs?" I ask.

My father shakes his head. "All kinds. Violin, piano, art, chess."

"How come I don't remember any of that?" I notice they've gotten to the tossing part on stage.

"You were young. I'm surprised you remember tumbling."

"Why all the classes if I was so young?"

My father pushes his glasses up on his nose. He's half looking at the stage, half at me. The girls are rapidly tossing their pots back and forth to each other. The audience is applauding loudly. "We were seeing if you had any talent."

I think I know the answer to my next question, since I don't play an instrument, or paint or play chess. "And?" The girls with the ceramic pots run offstage to large applause and the curtains close, a white spotlight appearing on the dark fabric. Stagehands bring out a platform with a Y-shaped steel brace pointing up from the center. A girl of about eleven appears and leaps onto the platform. "And?" I say again.

"Your motor skills were average and you didn't have any concentration." The girl grabs the steel brace and lifts her entire body with one arm, no strain, just pure focus. Nothing about her obeys gravity. Her outfit, a satiny combination of white and light blue spandex, shows every tightened muscle.

"So then what?"

My father looks at me sternly. "Maybe you had other aptitudes. Can we talk about this later?"

Both of us look back at the girl. She's doing a handstand, then curving her body backward, as if her hips can dislocate, as if she can float her bones inside her skin. Every move is smooth and precise, slow. She's hovering like an angel. But it occurs to me I've never seen a Chinese angel. They're always blond and fair-skinned. It's always a white God and his white entourage.

I look again down our row, my father already ambiguously engaged, George entranced, eating it all up. What's it like, I ask myself, when everything tastes as wonderful and exotic as you've always imagined it? What's it like to be someone who knows his aptitudes? The girl continues her balanced contortions, each precise pose seeming inevitable. I wonder when it will not be so easy, how many performances from tonight until her body betrays her and she is no longer useful. Eventually the world reminds you not to take it for granted. I learned that lesson as I watched my father drive away from me, and again when Gideon told me it was time to end our life together, both of them, I understand now, confronting some mistakes, making new ones.

23

The father and son talk over beers;
the son watches a Chinese opera.

T hat was kind of grotesque," I say to my father.

He shakes his head and raises his hand to the waiter. After the acrobats, we've decided to have a beer in the atrium of our hotel. "No. No. I think it was a profitable experience for both of us. How often do you get to attend such a show? Every time I see those children, I can't believe it."

"The operative word is *children*. They're like trained seals." Our waiter brings us two lagers. My father is silent. We both look around the atrium, the huge expanse capped by a skylight that is the entire roof. We're surrounded by rooms with windows looking down on us. Chinese music blares from two speakers set on a small stage covered in red carpet, an unattended grand piano sitting like a beached whale in the back.

My father clears his throat. He pours the contents of his bottle into a glass. There's a precision to it. He starts low, and as the bottle empties, he raises his hand higher. He takes a drink. "When the United States sends forty-year-old gymnasts to the Olympics," he says, "we can have this argument. And I'm not so sure that beauty pageants for five-year-olds are the healthiest thing."

I lift my bottle to my father. "Touché."

The music from the stage cuts off for a moment and switches to something grander and high-pitched. The canned voice of a Chinese woman makes an announcement.

"She says the show will begin in five minutes," my father informs me, laughing.

"What kind of show? Why are you so amused?"

"I'm going to bed," my father says, looking at his half-finished beer. "You'll have to find out for yourself."

"Wait," I say. "What were my other aptitudes?"

My father is halfway out of his seat, but sits back down. He folds his hands on the table and looks at me. "You were sensitive." The sour smell of beer rides his breath.

I wait for him to continue, but he says nothing more. "That's it?"

"We thought it was significant. You were always curious about other people's emotions. If someone was laughing or crying you would walk up to them and watch until you were laughing too, or pat them like we did for you when you cried. It was very sweet."

I take another drink and consider myself as a sensitive child. "Aren't all children that way?"

"No. No. You were like a emotional barometer. It was a special quality. I guess that's why I fail to understand you now. You are not the same at all."

I finish my lager and order another. I don't ask my father if he wants one too. I don't know what to say. I want to show him I haven't changed. I haven't. But I also know he hasn't seen any evidence of it. It's not something you can point to and say, "Look at me. I'm being sensitive like when I was a kid."

The recorded female announcer speaks again as my father stands and says goodnight. I'm a little annoyed that he isn't staying.

The music begins, Chinese opera style. A woman appears onstage in a flowing robe and headdress with two long pheasant tail feathers trailing, quivering, behind her. Only it's not a woman, it's a young girl, maybe twelve, lip-synching to the high, nasal voice of a much older woman. Now I know why my father was so amused. The girl moves around the stage with precise choreography to what sounds like a lament. A man appears, a boy really, and the music gets more dramatic. Both the girl and the boy wear nearly the same makeup, white foundation with pink around the eyes. A second boy appears. They all draw tassel-covered swords. They move in front of the grand piano as if it weren't there at all.

I make up my own story. The warrior princess is in love with the first boy, but the second boy is her betrothed suitor. A battle ensues, not just among these three, but among their families. In the end, the two jealous men accidentally run their swords through their princess, and then each commits suicide. The warrior princess lies between them, a pile of shiny pink fabric. In her palm she holds a square of white satin, which unfurls as death overcomes her.

I might not be an emotional barometer anymore, but I feel the irony in this moment. The woman needlessly dead at the hands of her two suitors. And even though this is an actress, a child playing a woman, it doesn't escape me that I'm affected because I'm reminded of my own mother. I could have told the warrior princess to avoid love and saved her the trouble.

24

The father recalls a tender moment with his child;
he agrees to the son's drunken request.

At times, yes, the pain was intense. The herbs I purchased early on failed to work. It might have been smarter to tell Westen I was very ill, but also I did not want guilt to be a reason for us to get along. Of course we did not. That was very difficult for me to get used to. We were closer when he was a boy, yes.

The evening of the Beijing acrobats, he seemed very curious about his childhood. And defensive. I was not feeling well. I did not have the patience to argue. I went to my room and lay down. My insides felt as if each individual organ was in a vise. I took some tea and tried to sleep. Of course, Westen was on my mind. Yes, he was. I knew he was downstairs watching scenes from a Chinese opera performed by an all-child cast. When he was a boy, we put him in expensive classes and set up private instruction to see if he had any special talents. It did not pay off, no. He did not do well at anything. Except every instructor mentioned that Westen was very curious about the other children. He always wanted to help them. Sometimes before the instructor realized help was needed.

"He is not good at anything," I said to his mother while we were waiting for a seat at dim sum one day.

"His talent is empathy," she said.

At the time I did not understand this. Papá would not have accepted an answer like that. Each of us had to specialize. I was the child who was good with numbers. My mother told me he placed an abacus in my bed when I was two. When I was eleven, I was checking his business receipts at the end of each day. My sister was a perfect seamstress and my brother excelled at math, piano, Ping-Pong, and chess. No, Westen's empathy hardly impressed me.

"Don't underestimate your son," Celia said. "Someday you'll find out how important empathy is, and how difficult it is to maintain."

Yes, she was correct. A month later Papá fell very ill in Hong Kong. I made flight reservations but they were not until the next day. When I picked Westen up from preschool, I tried to act like everything was fine. I said hello to his teachers and put him in the front seat of the car. When I got in on my side, the first thing he said was "What's wrong, Daddy?"

I looked at my son. He wore a Superman T-shirt and blue Toughskins that were dark at the knees. A good clothing investment for a boy. He stared directly at me, insisting on an answer. I started crying. "Your *yeh yeh* is in the hospital," I managed.

Westen slid close to me and put his small hand on my shoulder. He patted me the way his mother and I did when he hurt himself. "I know why you're sad," he said in his new English. "Because daddies are important."

I found myself half smiling and half crying. I cleared my eyes the best I could and started the car. "Thank you," I said. Westen nodded sweetly and scooted back to the passenger's side. We were on our way home.

Yes, that was why the China trip was important. In a strange way, I wanted to hear him say I was valuable to him. I do not know how long I lay in my bed thinking. When I heard the show finish downstairs I got up and looked out the window into the atrium. The stage was empty. Almost everyone was leaving. Westen sat at the table where I'd left him. He looked small, like my little boy. It was so easy to talk to him back then. I understood things were not the same at all now. I took the letter from his mother out of my luggage, wondering whether if I showed it to him, his aptitude would reappear. No, more likely it would make things worse. It was best, I thought, to put the envelope back into my luggage and leave it there. My aptitude, I understood, was knowing when someone needed a product and making them feel so even if they did not. What I didn't understand was how to sell myself to my own son.

Still, it was clear that if there was ever to be a time for Celia's letter, it was probably not this trip. What he was trying to recover was not the potential loss I could offer. For the first time in a long while I felt like a parent, protecting my son from the harsh world. *Yet you might have destroyed it, finally. You knew it was inevitable that he should have it.*

After a while, Westen came into the room. He turned on the light and leaned against the wall. He'd obviously had a few more beers after I left. "I'm sorry I'm such an asshole," he said.

I did not know how to reply. "It's awkward for both of us," I finally said.

Westen fell onto his bed face-first. He turned his head and looked at me with one eye. "But you've been so good about all this China stuff." His words were heavy. Run together with no spaces between. "I mean, this must have cost a bunch of money and all I do is come and complain and tell you what a bad father you are."

"It's not much." I could see that it wouldn't be that long before he was asleep. *And you wanted him to sleep rather than talk.*

"No, really. I was thinking about Mom and you and me, and me being sensitive. You're right that I haven't been like that to you, but I *am* like that." Westen closed his eyes.

I thought I should get him ready for bed, perhaps watch him fall asleep like I used to. It was at these times, when he was a boy, that I convinced myself how much he looked like me. But, seeing him as a man, I thought he looked more like his mother. Not Chinese at all. Maybe a mix of something else. His hair was dark, but not black like mine. His jawline and cheekbones had taken on angles, and his skin was not as olive as when he was a child. If I am his father, I thought, he has not kept much of me. *You thought more, much more than just this.* I turned out the light and let him be.

"You know," he started again, a little motor gassed by lager, surprising me, "part of the problem is that I'm here and you're here and I'm not sure what we're doing here. I don't really care about all these temples and gardens or any of these cities you never lived in. What about where you lived? Do we still have any family? Why don't we go there?"

I stared into the darkness. Westen was drunk. I doubted he would recall any of this. "It's just a village. We have a few cousins."

"I want to meet them and go."

"It's not on the tour." That was accurate. It was also accurate that I did not want to visit my village. Every time I had gone back there it was hard, yes. So many people who remembered my family.

"Screw the tour. Let's just go."

I usually never liked to see anyone drunk. On Westen it was a nice change. I even forgot about my pain. "I will see what I can do," I said. I doubted he would remember. It was a cost-free promise. *You know now that no promise kept or unkept is free.*

"Thanks, Dad," he said. Dad? I could not sleep the remainder of the night.

25

The son arrives at the Great Wall;
a man guesses he is half Chinese.

A hangover translates in any country. I wake up to my father opening the curtains to the bright morning. He's already dressed, wearing a bright blue short-sleeved shirt I haven't seen before. "Good morning," he says. "How do you feel?" He sounds unusually happy.

"Headache."

He sits on the edge of his bed to put on his shoes and I notice he winces as he bends over. "Yes. Yes," he says. "How many did you have last night?"

I sit up and run my hands over my face. "I guess around seven or eight. I stopped counting. I'm a lightweight."

My father really does not look well at all. He starts making coffee in the room's four-cup. His movements are tentative and his skin looks clammy, a hand shaking slightly as he pours water into the machine. "Are you all right?" I ask.

"Yes. Yes." When he turns to me I know he is lying. His eyes are dark and glassy.

"No, really. What's wrong?" I stand up next to him, my own hangover working my head. I put my hand on his arm. He's sweating when there's no reason to. "You're sick. I'll get a doctor."

"No. No," he says. "I appreciate that. It's just a touch of diarrhea. Common." He sits on the bed and dabs his head with the sheet. "But you're right. I'm not feeling well. I don't think I'll go with you today to the Great Wall."

I understand it's not serious, but I'm still worried. "I'll stay too, then," I say.

"No. No. I've seen the Wall before. You haven't. Go get my money's worth." My father seems to brighten, walking back to the coffeemaker. "I'll be fine. But I like the fact that you're concerned."

I like that fact too, I think to myself. "Listen," I say, "did you mention something last night about us not finishing the tour? Something about going to your village instead?"

My father turns away from the coffeemaker, obviously surprised. He takes off his glasses and inspects them away from his face. "No. No. *You* brought that up. I just said it was possible."

"Right," I say. "Well, I think it's a good idea."

"Maybe," my father says. He thinks, walking around the room. That and the smell of coffee are nauseating me. I close my eyes.

"I will not go to the Great Wall with you today," he says. "Maybe I can get us a flight from Beijing to Guangzhou."

I keep my eyes closed but it's not dark. There are swirls of red and green light. "I can stay here too," I say.

"No. The Wall is worth seeing. Trust me."

A FEW HOURS later my head is starting to clear, at least enough to bring along Mrs. Cheung's blue box. If the Great Wall isn't the right place and time to open it, I can't think of what is. Maybe my father's absence is a sign that this is in fact the opportunity. On the bus trip we've gotten an entire history of the Wall, but it's what's happened recently that interests me. I think the

Chinese have got it right. In the mid-1980s they refurbished this part of the Wall for tourists. It's not ancient, not all of it. But as we approach on the new highway, it is still a surprising sight, the Great Wall running along the Badaling Mountains like exposed vertebrae. On this day the mountains are dimmed by a wet haze, they look indistinct as shadows in fog, but somehow the wall itself stands out.

Our bus parks at what must be an entrance. There are T-shirt shops all around, and vendors run to us as we step off. They hold up all kinds of shirts that say I CLIMBED THE GREAT WALL or have crudely colored renderings of the Wall with Chinese writing beneath. *"Bu yao, xie xie,"* I say, and I stop walking, not because I've never said this phrase, but because I didn't *think* before saying it this time. The vendors crowd around me, but I am not paying attention. I look up at the Wall, past the restaurant and flimsy T-shirt stands. It's tall, not impressive like a skyscraper or even a football stadium, but there's something about it. I try to think of a time when we couldn't imagine aircraft that would take anyone thirty thousand feet above the earth, when we didn't have artillery that could blast a hole through this stone as if it were foam. I think of a man like me a thousand years ago, even a hundred years, staring up at the stacks of dark-gray stone, knowing there was no passage through, that he was kept in as much as any man on the other side was kept out. There are two sides to every wall, and the trick, I suppose, is doing your best to imagine the side you can't see.

When our group reaches the top, forty feet up, we have a choice to turn left or right. It's a choice of a very steep climb and immediate gratification, or a longer, more gradual hike to a higher point. Unlike most of the group, I take the latter and head right. Before me is a multicolored ribbon of people on a broad gray background. Flags snap in the wind. I think of soldiers who patrolled these walls and wonder if they would ever consider us invaders, all these people in shorts and sneakers trampling the smooth stone. In some places along the wall, Chinese characters have been carved into the rock. It makes me think of tombstones and permanence and, for some reason, of having children. They are the mark we carve in time and that time itself wears away.

I'm faster than the rest of my group. Eventually it's just me, some eager Chinese children, and a waddling but sure-footed old man whom I imagine to be their grandfather. He's wearing jogging shorts and a white T-shirt that says AMERICA'S FINEST CITY. All of us arrive at the same turret standing on the top, overlooking the mountains. The day has cleared and the countryside is gray-green, shrub-covered, not a tree in sight. The old Chinese man taps me on the shoulder and holds out a cigar. "Thank you," I say. "But I've never smoked one."

"First time for everything." His voice is surprisingly American. Even with the T-shirt, I expected him to at least have an accent. I take the cigar and he shows me how to smoke it. He warns me not to inhale, to start with small puffs until I get used to it. He puts his to his lips, making sucking noises as he takes in the smoke, one hand on the cigar, one hand patting down his comb-over.

I'm tentative at first, like he warned me. The cigar feels heavy in my hand, but I'm surprised by the smell, something like heated apple skins. I take my first few puffs carefully, feeling the smoke roll around in my mouth like a living thing.

"Good," the man says. "You aren't even gagging. A natural. By the way, I'm Hank Fong." He lets go of his cigar and extends his hand. It's thick and dry and surprisingly sturdy. "You on one of these goddamned tours too?"

"Yep, but it's our last day," I say. The children have left the turret and Hank yells at them to stay close. "Where are you from?" I ask.

"San Diego. Born and raised. Bricklayer. Retired. Now all I

do is haul my grandchildren around for their mother." He laughs again, a skittering sound like a rock skipped across a smooth pond. "You ever been to California?"

I take my longest draw yet from the cigar. I think Hank is right. I may be a natural. Maybe I've found my aptitude. "Lived on and off in San Diego. And I went to school at UCLA."

"No shit. My daughter went there. She's a doctor now. You don't know how many goddamned bricks I had to lay to pay for that."

We're quiet for a few moments, both of us leaning over the side. There is no guide to explain what we're seeing. It's all just perfectly reconstructed, smooth gray stone for as far as we can see. Below us, the ribbon of people continues in both directions, but they're silent from our perch here. It's just me and the sound of Hank puffing away.

"I tell ya," he says, slapping the rock, "those bastards sure went to a lot of trouble. Just getting the materials into these mountains had to be a bitch."

"My guide says they rebuilt this in the eighties."

Hank slaps the stone again. "Yeah, I seen the pictures of where it's falling apart. Have a photographer friend who went all the way out into the goddamned Gobi Desert to take pictures of the tail end where it's just mounds of clay." He faces me with the cigar clenched in his teeth, hands perched on his waist like an emperor. He looks me up and down. "So, you half Chinese or what?"

"Excuse me?" I say, even though I know exactly what he said. No stranger has ever guessed this. Most of the times when I was with my parents, people would question whose child I was. Once, when I was seven, we were eating at a restaurant when the waitress asked my mother if I was her nephew.

"You look like *something* half," Hank says. "Now, with my grandchildren you can't even tell. But maybe that's because their mother is dark-skinned and dark-haired."

"Well, Hank," I say, "I am half Chinese, and you're the first to notice." I take a drag off the cigar. "My father is Chinese."

"No shit," he says and leans against the stone, propping his elbows on the ledge behind him, cigar held tight between his fingers. "Usually it's the mother. Military and all. Well, all I got to say is you lucked out, boy. Best of both worlds."

"What do you mean?"

Hank stands back up and calls his grandchildren again to get ready to go. I look ahead to where they are playing, nothing for miles but the rugged undulation of the mountains and wall. "What I mean," Hank says, "is that you got to be Chinese and look white."

I turn to him. Pale smoke rolls out of his mouth. His teeth are a waxy yellow. "And what exactly did that get me?"

"None of that prejudice shit. No Chinaman crap. I've had to put up with it for years. It ain't what maybe the blacks got, but still."

Hank's grandchildren are all around us, running back and forth. I can see it in them now, the not-quite-Chinese nose, the not-quite-Chinese eyes. But still, they're what I wanted to be when I was young, they look more like my father than I do. I think of those kids who teased me because I looked Caucasian in a classroom of Chinese faces. For the first time it occurs to me that maybe they were just giving it back, that maybe somewhere, someone had mocked them with eyes pulled back at the corners with their fingers or offered some butchered imitation of Chinese, *Me order flied lice.*

After I say good-bye to Hank and his grandchildren, he hands me another cigar for my father. The sun paints us with a sifted yellow light as we shake hands. I'll have to leave soon too. Our tour guide will be nervous, needing to keep us on track so we can get to the next garden or souvenir shop right on time. But I'm not ready to leave just yet.

It's just me and Mrs. Cheung's blue box. I reach into my backpack and pull it out and separate it from the tissue. It strikes me that it doesn't at all resemble the gift I was given the day Mrs. Cheung handed it to me, no more butterfly bow with a red wax body. Now it is held together by the hasty knot, tied after my aborted attempt to open it in Nanking. As I untie it I realize I'm surprisingly nervous. It really cannot be much, I understand, but at the same time, once it's open, it's done. I will have closed a chapter of my childhood and I'm not so certain I want to. Still, with the view across these mountains from this high point on the wall I cannot imagine another, better time on this trip. Taking a deep breath, I lift off the top of the box. There is no bright light, no guiding voice. Just a small note sitting above white cloth protecting the contents. The note says, "You still unhappy, boy? You *sure* this the right time?"

So there is a kind of voice, Mrs. Cheung's. I have an immediate answer to her first question, which is largely *yes*. And to the second, I could lift back the white cloth and find out, but I suppose the mere fact that I could only know for sure after the act means it is not time. Instead, I close the box and retie the bow, attempting a reproduction of Mrs. Cheung's butterfly. After a couple of attempts I have to satisfy myself with what I can maybe claim as a wounded moth. I will tuck it away in my luggage, I decide, and wait for my father's village, where surely I'll feel like I'm standing on more authentic ground. For now, I'll linger for just a while longer and finish the cigar Hank gave me. He and his grandchildren continue to descend below, become smaller on the Wall, and meld into the bright crowd of tourists. I will follow shortly along their same path as so many thousands do each day, only I will be alone and without anyone to watch my progress.

26

The son and father announce their departure;
the son recalls a fishing trip with his uncle.

For our last large meal with the tour, we all have Peking duck, small slices of crunchy-skinned roast duck in hoisin sauce, sprinkled with scallions and served over thin, round bread. "It's much better in Los Angeles," my father whispers to me. But everyone else is digging in. Sheri's wad of red gum is perched at the edge of her plate like a patient pet. She's looking much happier than when the trip first started. Her father tells everyone how authentic the food is and, without segue, asks the table to guess what the oldest living tree in the world is. "The giant redwood," he says, without giving anyone a chance. The collar of his over-starched white shirt stands high, almost touching his cheeks and satisfied smile.

"That's not right," I say. My father taps my leg with his foot to get me to stop. "I believe it's the bristlecone pine." The table looks at me blankly. "Check the *Guinness Book*."

Just then George, our awkward cohort, stands up and breaks into the moment. He makes a wide gesture with both hands, which are disturbingly clean looking. He's wearing a light-blue button-up shirt with short sleeves, as if he could step right back into a dental office. "I have some bad news for the group," he says. "Xin and Westen are leaving the tour after Xi'an."

There's a collective sigh of disappointment, which surprises me, and then I notice that everyone is looking at my father. They're sorry *he's* leaving the tour. Someone yells, "Speech," and there's eager affirmation of the request, so my father stands. "Yes. Yes," he says. "I want to take my son to my village." Everyone nods and murmurs their approval, without ever looking at me. Behind us is the clacking din of the restaurant and a woman who sounds as if she's haggling over the price of a silk wall hanging. "It's very strange," my father continues. "My family ran away from this country so many years ago. And now the only thing on my mind is bringing my family back." He pauses and I see in his eyes that he's sad and sincere, but then there's a sudden smile and he picks up his teacup. "So, here is to the next couple of days in Xi'an with good friends." Everyone raises their cup and I follow suit, but when I tip mine back, I find that it's empty. I fake a gulp, though I know no one is watching me. I'm stuck on the word *family*. As if that's something you can take off and put on like a winter coat, something you put away for a few seasons until it's useful again.

Great-Aunt Catherine and Uncle Cane were the ones who got me to school and fed me and ran me to the hospital when the Buckles' German shepherd bit me. They saw me deliver my valedictorian speech and sent me off to college as if I were their own child.

It was Uncle Cane who was tired of seeing me mope around the house. "Your dad ain't coming back anytime soon," he said to me one day. "Let's go fishing."

We left early the next morning, driving miles out of town to a spot high on the Blue River where it's a sharp gash in the black rock. As we walked through the woods, Uncle Cane said nothing, most of our gear dangling from his shoulders. All I carried was our lunch and a thin rod he and Aunt Catherine had given me the night before. I watched Uncle Cane's thick hands for signals on direction and speed. His large back, covered by red flannel, led me. It amazed me how easily he maneuvered through the tendrils of undergrowth. We were so silent. I began to feel like I was in on a secret. After a few minutes I began to pretend we were convicts escaping from prison.

We came to the river, a narrow rush of water inset between high, charcoal-colored cliffs. "This is as good a place as any," Uncle Cane said. "Jump." He gestured toward the cliff and looked at me. I stood completely still. He pulled a length of rope out of a satchel he carried at his side. "Guess we'll have to do it the sissy way."

"I'll jump," I said, "if you go first." I looked again at the cliff. I knew there was no way either of us could possibly make it that far down.

"We got us a little smart-ass." Uncle Cane gave my head a friendly shove.

The riverbed was solid rock, swept clean by high water except among the crevices and fallen branches that created snags for woody debris. The river was not wide, but it was a dizzying rush of white, and I had to keep from looking at it as Uncle Cane led me along. He showed me the berry vines growing out of the cliff, and I plucked the only ripe berry I could find, something like a blackberry. It was small and bristly in my mouth, bitter, nothing like I expected.

"Here we are," Uncle Cane finally said softly. We had come to a pool where the river seemed to stop, its surface reflecting the morning like a dish of mercury. Three branches reached from the water, straight as lost arrows. Uncle Cane checked me for silence. Birds clattered in the branches as he arranged our gear and sat down. He looked frustrated at even this amount of noise. His blue eyes widened as he turned to me, and I knew this was someplace special to him.

"The water'll tell you everything," he whispered as I sat down. I felt his arm around me positioning my viewpoint. I stared into this flat, quiet place that divided the river. All I saw was a perfect reflection of the cliff and the pine trees at its edge.

"What am I supposed to be looking for?" I asked.

Uncle Cane grunted, realizing I did not understand. "Hell. It's not as still as it looks," he said. "What would you see if this were empty?" He pointed to the branches sticking out of the water. "Start there."

I looked again. I followed the branches to where they met the bright surface. I saw nothing. I repeated this several times until I wasn't thinking about it anymore, and suddenly I saw *below* the surface. The branches merged under the water and led toward a dim log surrounded by slow-moving ovals. Trout. "I see them," I whispered, excited.

"Hot damn." Uncle Cane slapped his thigh, and then, catching the loudness of his voice, said quietly, "That calls for a drink." He pulled out his thermos and poured himself some whiskey. "You're too young for this." He winked. "Wait till you're fifteen or sixteen." He handed me a smaller thermos of hot chocolate, holding his plastic cup up in a toast before he swigged back the contents. After a thick, satisfied exhale, he opened the tackle box and began preparing our lines with small hooks. A thread of sunlight ran across his face, outlining his red, roundish features. "Fishing's all about good eyes," he said. "A guy ain't for shit if he can't see past his arm." He handed me a tangled mass of gray, chainlike metal. "You're in charge of this," he said. "It's a trout stringer."

"Are you going to show me how to use it?" I had never been fishing before.

"You'll figure it out." He handed me my pole. "Besides, it's about goddamn time someone treated you like a man."

That is the problem, I think now, watching my father eat and talk with such ease to the other people at our table. He came for me after twenty-five years looking for a boy, and I showed up hoping to be a boy. It's clear that before we can be a father and son again, we have to treat each other like men first.

27

The tour arrives in Xi'an;
the son is taken to real China.

Outside Xi'an, our bus passes fields that are dry and empty, striped black and yellow as if charred. In the distance, a nuclear power plant with four looming stacks puffs away. Wang taps the microphone to get our attention. "Some very important thing," he says. "Xi'an was once the capital of China. It was a very great city. Very important on the Silk Road. Tonight you see a big show at your hotel about this history."

"It's strange," I tell my father, who sits next to me. "We come all this way and they don't let us see the real China. It's all gardens and temples and everything else is explained by a show."

My father looks serious. "It's stranger that we travel this far and we don't show each other our real selves." He takes his glasses off and begins cleaning them with a small cloth. "Yes. Yes. That's true," he says, agreeing for me. "Tell me, Westen, what do you think the *real* China is?"

It's a good question and I nod because I'm not quite sure what my answer is. My father waits for my answer and starts going through his Curse Lady notepad, flipping pages, counting in his head. "I'll tell you something real about me," I finally say. "I keep waiting for the moment when I feel Chinese again."

"Why are you just waiting?" my father asks without looking up from his pad.

"What else am I supposed to do?"

Now he looks at me. "Yes, it's a problem. You were a Chinese boy, and now what?" He pauses and takes a long, controlled breath that looks somewhere between contemplation and pain. "Back at the hotel I have something to show you."

"What is it?"

He gestures with his hand for me to be patient but does not speak. Instead he returns to his pad of requests for the Curse Ladies.

The bus slows. A jackass-pulled wooden cart overloaded with straw is halfway in the road. Here the fields give way to squares of deep-green ponds of lotus for harvesting. Each block looks like a playing card, a game waiting for a child to turn them over one by one to find a match.

"I know there's more to China," I say after a long while, "than fresh red paint."

My father closes his notepad. "Yes. Yes," he says. "There's always more than the veneer. But that rule applies to everything. You cannot pick and choose if you're going to start seeing the world that way."

AT FIRST WE go in with everyone else at the factory where they demonstrate the method by which the Terra-Cotta Warriors were made. Of course, there is a generous supply of miniature warriors available for sale, grayish brown Chinese soldiers, sullen-faced, standing ten rows deep and all nicely dusted for an ancient effect. "They look like an army of dressed-up rats," Sheri whispers to me. The walls are lined with decorative tiles of the Chinese zodiac and landscapes and Chinese characters, all for sale. At the side are two worktables where the factory guide tells us these tiles are painted by the "artisans." I look out the window at the side of the main factory with its smokestack billowing a black streak into the air, and I wonder how many artisans, sitting at how many tables, are at work right now making tiles and miniature warriors.

My father looks at me and rolls his eyes. We step back out of the group and he removes the deck of cards from his pocket.

I take the top third and he selects a middle card.

"What are we deciding?" I ask.

"You were right. So either we're going to stay here or see your 'real China.'"

"There you have it," he says darkly as we flip our cards. "Queen of hearts beats jack of diamonds."

"You sound like a spy movie," I say, heading toward the door.

Behind the factory we walk down a thin lane lined with vegetable vendors for as far as I can see. I reach to take out my camera, but my father puts his hand down to stop me. "It's not polite to take the real China home," he says.

It's noisy here—everyone seems engaged in an argument. Each two or four or five feet is a new vendor, selling plums, corn on the cob, Chinese cucumber, chives, dried shrimp heaped in piles, red meat on a chopping block blackened from years of use, eel and dressed chicken, even *live* chickens with white feathers and black skin—"The bones too," my father says—red chilies and entire carts of ground pepper in bright orange mounds, bags of beans (green, red, black) and spinach, bok choy, cauliflower, brown potatoes, green peppers, bunches of yard-long beans tied together, thin eggplant, and eggs—white and blue and flats of brown. Behind each stand is a tired Chinese face with a smile of worn teeth. Some of the women hold lethargic babies in one arm while they use the other to deal with customers. The air smells sweet and dusty and I feel a lot of eyes on us, on me.

"Is this what you wanted to see?" my father says.

"I suppose," I say. "If this is what you think real China is."

My father stops and looks at me as people pass around us on either side. "It is," he says. "Just like Appalachia is the real United States."

He is a smart man, my father. I look up into the overcast with its odd slip of blue sky like a tear in gray flannel, like a peephole. He leaves me standing and I watch him round the corner toward the bus. I'm jostled on all sides by people of the market, people of real China. This image of him walking away startles me, reminds me so much of the day I stood in Great-Aunt Catherine's driveway and watched him get into his car and drive away. The feeling comes back and I understand why it has always been easiest to simply say my father abandoned me as a child.

28

The tour discovers a theft;
the father recalls a story about Tao.

We returned in the evening. The air was still hot, and I was weary. I had one more task ahead of me, however. Westen wanted to know if he was Chinese. Yes, I could answer his question with the simple opening of his mother's envelope. *Yes, you must have been tired if you thought being Chinese was hereditary.*

In the hotel lobby our guide gathered us around him as the manager whispered urgently in his ear. "This manager must speak with you," the guide said. We were told in Mandarin that our floor had experienced a burglary and we should check our luggage when we returned to our rooms. Because the translation was behind, I was already looking at Westen when he understood the news. His mouth opened slightly and he shook his head. "Is this the real China?" he asked.

The thefts were consistent in all the rooms. They used a key and took only the smallest luggage. Few lost much of value, since our cameras, money, and passports were with us. Mostly, all of us were upset, physically disquieted to think that strangers had such easy access. In our room the loss was even higher. Yes, both Westen and I had luggage taken, though he suffered more. When the thieves opened mine, the profit for their efforts would be vapor rub, cotton swabs, bandages, cough syrup, and aspirin, yes, almost a medicine cabinet. Though I had no prescriptions. Those proved useless months earlier.

Westen sat on his bed with his head in his hands. "I don't believe this," he said.

"What did they take?" I asked, sitting on the bed across from him.

"Nothing," he said. "Not nothing, but nothing to you."

He wasn't being clear and I wasn't sure I should press. Then he looked up at me with red eyes. "What did you lose?" I asked again.

"I guess it doesn't matter now. That blue box is gone."

"The bon-voyage gift?" I could tell by his reaction that was not what it really was.

"It was more than that. I guess it doesn't matter if I tell you now." The story was brief. Yes, the box was more than a going-away gift. Westen told me about a Chinese family in Blue Falls, about a woman who gave him that box with the prediction I would someday return for him and maybe he would know happiness again. It seemed a risk to promise a child such a thing. What could she have put in there that would have helped? Yet he kept it all those years. My heart hurt knowing this, that he held out hope for so long. Even to the end he kept his secret as instructed, waiting for the right time to open it. No, I knew right then I hadn't been a terrible father after I gave Westen up. I hadn't been a father at all.

"I'm sorry," I said when he'd finished. "What do you think it was?"

"I almost found out on the Great Wall, but decided to wait until we got to your village." He sat up straight and cleared his eyes. "They get anything important of yours?"

I couldn't do it, risk adding to this sadness he'd carried

around all his life. I could not show him his mother's envelope safely tucked away in my large suitcase. I lied. "Yes," I said. "On the bus I told you I had something to show you. It's gone."

"What's gone?"

"I had a note from your mother. It was like your blue box, to be opened at the right time."

"And you don't know what it said."

I shook my head slowly and Westen plopped back on his bed in disbelief, running his hands through his hair, pulling it. I told him I was tired and he said he didn't think he could sleep. He wanted to keep checking about finding our bags. In the meantime I would rest and he would go ahead to see the T'ang dynasty dancer in the hotel's playhouse.

I HAD BEEN out of balance for a long time, yes. By the time Westen left the room I felt dizzy and out of control. I did not know what was the right thing to do. Whenever I felt this way I recalled a story my father had told me more than once. Stories are what I tell myself when it feels as if my own life is being written by another hand. *Yet now you are correcting your own record. You are the final editor of your life.*

Papá's story was told this way: Not long ago a grandson and his *yeh yeh* sat together eating an afternoon meal on the bank of Cháng Jiang. They watched cars being ferried across the great muddy river and barges going both up and downstream for as far as they could see. And on each side, cities had been built up almost to the water's edge. The grandfather shook his head.

"What's wrong?" the grandson said.

"Just look at how they treat the river, Xiao. They don't remember."

Xiao looked out at the river traffic, at how the ferries seemed to time their crossing just perfectly so that they squeezed between the oncoming ships and barges. It all seemed slow and controlled, despite the choppy, fast-running Yangtze. He looked across the river at the city that sloped down to the water's edge, where the ferries began and ended their crossings. There was a long line of automobile traffic waiting for a turn to cross the river. Xiao wondered how so many people could have business on this side of the river that they couldn't do on their own side.

"I don't see what's wrong," Xiao finally said.

"Let me ask you this: Who is the master, the river or the people?"

This seemed an easy question to Xiao, and he answered quickly. "The people."

"That, Xiao, is the problem." The grandfather said nothing more despite Xiao's pleading, and the two finished their meal in silence.

The next morning the grandfather woke Xiao up quite early. "What is it, Yeh Yeh?" Xiao said, rubbing his eyes.

"Get dressed," the grandfather said. "We've got a very long trip today."

"But I have school."

"*Aiya!*" The grandfather stood up straight. "You'll be lucky if you ever learn as much at school as what I will teach you today."

By midmorning the grandfather and his grandson arrived just outside an unusually small village bordered by rice fields and a slim, gray-yellow river. "There aren't many rivers left like this in China," the grandfather said. "See, so few boats and not even a footbridge. If the river is high, no one crosses. When it is low, the boats rest on the sandbars."

"This is what you wanted to show me?" Xiao asked, a little disappointed.

"I wanted you to see what isn't here," the grandfather said. "They subordinate their activity to the whims of the river."

"I guess that's why they aren't very prosperous," Xiao said. "Look at their village."

The grandfather shook his head and began walking toward the river. It was hot, and Xiao noticed how much he was sweating. He looked out into the nearest rice field, where a line of women in wide straw hats were sticking rice plants into the mud. They must be even hotter than we are, Xiao thought.

When the two came to the river, they found a grassy spot and sat, each laying his unopened bundle of food at his side. The grandfather looked at Xiao. "I could easily tell you what is on my mind, but it's better if you come to understand it on your own. What do you think is the guiding principle of our universe?" In his heart, the grandfather knew this was a big question for a ten-year-old boy. But he hoped that maybe the bloodline would pass along information to his grandson that he was sure his son had not. The night before, as he thought about taking Xiao away for the day, he imagined Xiao sitting in front of him, a little Confucian, a little Taoist, explaining the interplay of yin and yang. So here they were, the question offered, and the grandfather waited for Xiao's response.

Xiao thought for a moment. "I know the answer to this, Yeh Yeh. The struggle between good and evil is the guiding principle, and Jesus helps us battle evil."

The grandfather sighed. "I am sure your mother would be proud of that answer. I'm thinking of something older than Jesus."

Xiao frowned.

After he thought for a moment, the grandfather spoke again. "There are two forces always at work in the world, a masculine force and a feminine force. This north bank of the river, in the bright sunlight, on this warm, dry sand, this represents the masculine force." The grandfather pointed. "Over there is the feminine force, the south bank, shaded, wet, and with soft earth. There is never a river with only one bank. Just the same, these two forces are always at work."

Xiao looked at his grandfather slightly openmouthed, a question forming slowly like a droplet of water on a leaf tip. "One never overpowers the other?"

"Good question," the grandfather said. "Sometimes, when there is disharmony, it means that one is prevailing over the other. But it is always temporary, and when they are in harmony, there can only be good." After this, the grandfather instructed Xiao to gather some small pieces of wood so they could have a fire to warm their food. As they lit the small pile of sticks, the grandfather spoke again. "And watch how the wood can turn from yin, the feminine, to yang, the masculine."

"And back again when the fire is out?" Xiao said.

"Yes," the grandfather said, smiling. "It is not enough, however, to just observe this balance. You have to find a way to achieve this harmony in your own life."

"How do you do that?"

"That is Tao," the grandfather said.

"What is?"

"Two opposites producing order. They can do that because Tao is the force of integrations, the supreme force."

Xiao sat watching the fire, waving his tin of rice and vegetables over the flame. He looked up to ask a question, but then returned to the fire.

"It's too big to explain, Xiao. You might think of Tao as a path or the right way, and everything that is good acts in accordance with its way."

Again Xiao looked to his grandfather. "Jesus died for our sins," he finally said. "And then he became one with God."

The grandfather nodded calmly, trying to conceal his

sadness. "All the gods observe Tao," he said. "Even yours." With that, the two ate their meals silently on the north bank of the river, in the sterling sunlight, beyond them the rice fields and the north face of a hill, still half in shadow.

This story Papá told you was a kind of forecast, yes. You mixed East and West, risked balance. Westen is proof, Celia's envelope. You thought you were strong enough to right the scales. Yes, you were weighing feathers against lead.

29

The son sits through a show while the father sleeps;
he listens to an impressed American couple.

The Terra-Cotta Warriors had better be spectacular tomorrow because our rooms have been broken into and the T'ang dynasty dancers are not much of a distraction tonight. The first act is a travesty. It's like the performers know hardly anyone is watching. Their movements are loose and unbalanced. But maybe it's me. I am sick over losing Mrs. Cheung's box. Even now there is someone rifling through all our luggage, coming to mine and finding that box. He will tear off the ribbon, rip off the lid. I imagine him disregarding Mrs. Cheung's note, flicking it aside to peel back the white cloth. And this is the difficult part because I cannot imagine what it is he uncovers, and I wonder if when he does, some truth is revealed to him that should have been mine. Maybe losing the box is a sign in itself. The actual gift I am to hold on to from this trip is the worst kind, my father's news about one terrible night in New Orleans—a weak man and a damaged mother: Here, son, I wrapped it myself.

For the second act of the show, Sheri sits next to me and we talk briefly about having our things stolen. She lost a jade souvenir necklace, some costume jewelry and makeup, but otherwise she made out fine. Tonight she wears a black dress with pearls, as if we were going to the opera. She's not even chewing gum.

Onstage, papier-mâché horses rise on either side, framing a twilight blue background. A large silk cloth billows in the center as warrior-like figures, silhouettes, tromp to the foreground. It looks as if everyone in the cast has been enlisted. They are costumed in black tights, with all body shapes represented. The music is loud and percussive, full of gongs and drums.

Sheri looks at me and rolls her eyes. "My elementary school put on better shows than this," she whispers.

I'm comforted that she doesn't like the show either. "I played Snoopy in sixth grade."

"Tortoise," she says. "Fourth grade. A whole fairy-tale retrospective."

WHEN THE SHOW is over, it doesn't seem as if anyone in the audience knows whether they should clap. It feels too conspicuous with so few people. But the dancers come out and we offer meager applause that ends quickly. The cast reacts as if it were a standing ovation. Then the houselights immediately pop on.

"What a show," a blond woman says to the man with her. "How can they afford to do this every night?" Sheri and I are walking right behind them.

"And all that history," the man says. "These Chinese are ingenious."

"Yes," the woman says, holding the man's hand. "I wonder whatever happened."

Sheri elbows me and clears her throat. "We all moved to California and opened restaurants," she says loud enough for the couple to hear. "Do you know where your dog is right now?" The couple pauses, but keeps walking without acknowledging her.

Sheri grabs my arm and holds me back until the few remaining audience members leave and we're alone in the small lobby of the theater. Her grasp is warm and moist and I recognize for the first time how beautiful she is. "I just want you to know," she says, "I'm really lucky you were on this trip and I'm sorry you're leaving."

I blush because I do not know what to do with this compliment. "You were fun," I say.

She kisses me on the cheek. "And you're a sweetheart. You'll make someone a good hubby. And you'll be a good dad."

When she says this, I think of Margaret and Gideon and my father, how far down that road I was and how much the idea of having my own children scares me. I'm not sure I have that much love to give, and if I do, how to give it. Sheri looks straight at me, wanting a response. "I barely make a good me," I say.

30

A tour member hands out pennies and balloons;
the father and son discuss the value of the trip.

Y ou really surprised me last night," I tell Sheri. We are at the Small Wild Goose Pagoda. The day is bright and hazy and there is a smell of burning rubber. Sheri is back to her usual self, chewing a large pink wad of gum and wearing a too-tight cotton shirt the color of an underripe avocado. We walk near the back of our group. Behind us, I hear the busy chatter of schoolchildren. There's a small boy at my waist in a crisp white shirt and blue shorts. His shiny black bangs run evenly across his brow. "Hello," I say.

"Hello," he barks back with a smile that's missing two front teeth.

"Well, well," I hear from behind me. It's George, with his hands in his pocket and a broadly pleased expression. "Look at all the kiddies." He takes a handful of balloons out of his pocket and distributes them to the children. They crowd in and begin to yell. When he's out of balloons, George pulls out pennies and gives them away one by one. It's ugly and condescending. Two female teachers, both with sweaters wrapped over their shoulders, yell and push forward. They're obviously upset. Positioning themselves between George and the children, one of them gives a stern lecture to her students.

My father stands by my side and whispers to me. "She's telling them they're acting like beggar monkeys and they should have more respect for themselves." Then my father walks up to George and explains to him what's happening.

The children line up, and one by one they walk by George to return the pennies and balloons. "I didn't mean any harm," he says. My father pats him on the shoulder and speaks to the teachers. They offer a few sharp bows and forced smiles as they gather up the children. As our tour moves into the pagoda grounds, I stay behind with my father and he introduces me to the teachers. They both look surprised and I figure they've just gotten the news I'm his son. One of them puts on a pair of thin, black-framed glasses and looks at me closely.

"They're teachers," my father says. "First grade."

I shake their hands. "Nice to meet you. You have very polite students."

After my father relays my message, the women giggle as if I've said something kind but ridiculous. The children stand quietly, waiting for instruction, and all of us begin to walk. Each has a lunch sack or pail, and as soon as we get inside the grounds they fan out with a single word from their teacher, taking spots under trees and on benches and random patches of grass where sunlight seeps in. My father says good-bye to the women and we look around for the tour. They are already entering the pagoda, which is tall, brownish gray, and unremarkable. I'm reminded of stacked pancakes.

One of the teachers walks up to us and speaks to my father. He nods a few times as if he's concerned. Then he takes out his pad and writes down her information, letting her look to see if it's correct. The pad is amazingly full. I don't know when he writes in it, but each time I see it the number of words seems to double. This isn't even the same pad he started with. The woman thanks him and leaves.

"Are you ever going to tell me what curses they ask for?" I say, pointing to his pocket where the pad is already safely tucked away.

"You are standing in the middle of China on my dime in one of its oldest cities, and the only thing you're interested in is what I have in my pocket?" He pulls out the deck of cards. "High card wins."

These cards have somehow become the way we communicate, as if we both agree that chance and destiny are more reliable than ourselves. I take the deck from him. "This time you cut." I shuffle the cards a few times and hold them out. He lifts a third of the deck and turns over the four of clubs. I take the next card. Three of diamonds.

"The gods smile upon you," I say, trying to sound a tone of levity. The problem with this outcome, however, is that it means the gods are not smiling on me.

31

The son and father see the warrior compound;
the son focuses on what has yet to be excavated.

No news about our luggage. The Terra-Cotta Warriors are our last stop before going it on our own. My father seems like a different person as we approach. He's anxious-looking, like a boy waiting for an elephant ride. "I have waited a long time for this," he says.

Inside, the building is dim and cool, bigger than a football field, with halogen lights and steel beams running everywhere, as if we were in the rib cage of an enormous animal. And in the center is the excavation pit, where hundreds of the life-sized warriors stand guard in perfect rows too wide and deep to count, waiting in dirt trenches ten feet below topsoil, excavated and restored, all empty-handed, their swords and crossbows looted in another millennium. And all of their armor perfectly replicated in clay down to the last rivet, with bunned hair, groomed mustaches. And terra-cotta horses too, dressed for battle. It's a remarkable sight, not only for what is in front of us, but for what once stood here: ten thousand new clay warriors protecting an emperor in the afterlife. One man harnessed all this human effort for his resting place, had the unapologetic ego to have human-sized figures cast and hand-painted, each head individually designed after a real warrior.

"Do you believe it?" Wang says. "They are in such good condition. This is very much hard work from skilled archaeologists."

The longer I look, the more uneasy I am. Every sound is swallowed by the air and stilled. And the warriors stand ready for battle, unarmed, as if at any moment legions may sweep down and overtake us. I look at my father. He is peering over the railing, shaking his head, pleased.

"Impressive," he says, waving me over. "What an achievement. Makes you proud to be Chinese, doesn't it?"

I don't answer until he looks at me. "I hadn't thought of it that way. This is *our* accomplishment?"

"It's what we're capable of."

"You know something," I tell my father, "I've always heard about the Terra-Cotta Warriors. But in school we only learned about Stonehenge. Our teacher told us it was possible some distant ancestor of ours assembled those giant stones."

"Ancestors of *yours*," my father says to clarify that he is not included in the statement.

"Exactly," I say. "Here we are, looking at a field of an emperor's giant dolls, and I can't imagine being connected to this in any way."

"At last," he says in a kind but mocking tone, "we have something in common. We've never had ancestors even close to Xi'an."

"That's not what I was getting at," I say.

"No," my father says casually, "but it should have been."

I appreciate the assumption, but I don't believe it, that I am included. But how can I be? I live as if History consists of just two eras, the one before my father left me and the one after. Perhaps I expected this trip to be the beginning of a third, though more and more it feels like one knuckle-dragging age. I have no tools and no hope of them.

Wang moves us farther down the pit and we get a better idea

of why the lines of warriors end where they do. The excavation is not complete here. These figures represent how the others were discovered, upturned, broken, and coated and trapped in dried clay. There are limbs sticking out everywhere from the light brown earth, a few heads like an orgy frozen in place. But to me it looks like a mass grave. It looks like devastation.

32

The son and father visit a zoo;
the father becomes ill.

Before we left, the hotel was not optimistic about retrieving our luggage. Their one clue was a housekeeper who stopped coming to work and who had not shown up at her home. When my father left instructions on where to contact us, the hotel manager nodded grimly and told him that when such thefts happen, stolen items are rarely found.

Now we are on our own, away from the tour, our first stop thankfully not a garden or temple. Still, the giant pandas are a disappointment. They're lumped in the corner, faceless as black-and-white beanbags. They sit curled up and motionless behind thick steel bars. I consider this a sign of intelligence. All the animals here are caged like this, but most of them pace their obsolete enclosures, sticking to the perimeters in a constant motion. At least the pandas have caught on.

I'm not sure why my father brought me here today, why the Guangzhou Zoo had to be on our itinerary at all. I ask him this as we walk along the cages where they keep the big cats.

"We have to fill time somehow," he says. "Your relatives aren't home."

"You didn't tell them we were coming?"

He stops to look at a black leopard. It halts in the center of the bars and stares back at us, panting, vague spots shining through its dark coat. My father takes a handkerchief out of his pocket and wipes the back of his neck and forehead. "Of course I told them," he says. "But they can't just drop everything for us. They work."

I notice he is sweating profusely again. The air is humid, warm, but not this bad. Something is definitely wrong with him. "Are you okay?" I ask.

"Yes, yes. Fine. Fine," he says, waving off my concern. "Let's walk a bit more." He continues mopping himself and I watch him out of the corner of my eye as we move toward the tiger area. There are dozens of people congregated here, and the air is punctuated by excited Chinese voices. From behind, the sun reflects from their hair like the white centers of shiny black flowers. I can barely make out the cat beyond them.

"Let's skip the tiger," my father says, smiling and dabbing at his forehead. "They're probably auctioning off its testicles."

His face is pale. I can tell he needs to sit down, but all the benches are occupied. "Standing room only," I say. A sour breeze rolls over the pond in front of us. I'm not sure where we should go and I turn in a complete circle, slightly frantic.

"Jesus of Buddha," my father says. "I'm not dying. Let's just sit."

3 3

The father rests;
he recalls the death of his brother.

My son asked if I needed a doctor. *You were finished with Western doctors by then.*

"I always need a doctor." I laughed. "I'm an old Chinese man."

"They probably have someone right here," he said. He is humorless.

I tried again. "You want me to see the zoo doctor? You've seen how they take care of the animals. I'm fine, anyway." I just wanted to make it to Hong Kong. There was some treatment there I wanted to try. *He knew that you were ill. Why didn't you tell him then? Why didn't you tell him everything?*

"We've been doing a lot of walking," I told him. "I guess it caught up with me all at once. Let's just sit there for a second." I pointed at a bench under a banyan tree. I sat down. He told me he was going to find some water.

I've had these episodes before. The doctors tell me it is normal. The previous ones seemed more serious. I felt hot inside, yes. The Chinese medicines had not worked, but I'd heard of a doctor in Hong Kong who might help me. Maybe it was the trip that brought it back on so fast. Perhaps it was Westen. I knew I only had to stay outwardly well for a few more days, a week at the most. They would give me something in Hong Kong. I was worried. *A mistake. It was serious enough to tell him.* This was like looking at a balance sheet at the end of the month when all the checks and bills are about to come in.

"I appreciate the attention," I told Westen when he brought back the water, "but I'm really okay."

He looked worried. When his mother and I were first married, I worked three jobs. She had the same sharp, inspecting eyes and taut jaw. Our first arguments were over my health. "You don't have to slave like a Communist," she told me once. "It's not good for you."

I replied too fast. "One lazy American in our family is enough." There were plenty of days I thought we might have divorced had our son not been born.

Westen sat next to me. "Maybe we should call it a day," he said. "This is a lousy zoo anyway."

There really was no reason to stay. But I liked the attention Westen gave me. I felt like his father again. "No, no. Go take a look at that," I told him. "I prefer to sit here for a while by myself." I read the Mandarin for him. "It says 'Dog Breed Exhibit.'"

"I should stay here with you," he said.

"No, no. I'll be okay. Just go. I would like a moment of quiet." I took out a map of the zoo to fan myself with, while my son went to get in line. With his cowlicked hair and thin body, Westen reminded me of myself at his age. He looked back at me and waved as if I were sending him off to school for the first time.

Yes, it *was* an awful zoo. But then, it could be an awful country too. Like so many times before, my thoughts went to the night we fled the Communists. Our family was considered bourgeois because Papá owned our land and was a grain merchant. He woke us up in the middle of the night. He was dressed as a peasant, pants rolled to his knees and a dirty, oversized cotton shirt.

He told us to put on as many clothes as we could, but explained nothing. Ma strapped my baby brother, Yee, to my back in a kind of pouch. She and Papá both carried large bundles wrapped in blankets and slung over one shoulder. Outside, the village was dark. We all held hands as Papá led us across the rice field. The water and mud went almost up to my knees with Yee's extra weight on my back. I remember the sucking sound each time we pulled our feet out of the water. Papá asked us to be quieter.

I wondered why we weren't using the paths between the rice fields, but as we got to the edge of one, I saw a tiny flare of fire and the speck of orange that would be a cigarette. Later, Papá told me they had posted guards on our property, that he had seen them in the twilight. That was why we had to leave so suddenly. We were lucky there was no moon.

When we were almost at the end of our property, I could barely make out a water buffalo and a wooden cart full of straw. I wondered how Papá had arranged this. Ma and I and my older brother crawled into the back under the straw. We scooted close together. Yee started to cry and I felt my mother's arms reach around me. I could tell she was touching my brother's head. Until that moment, he had remained remarkably silent.

The cart started to move and we wobbled a bit from side to side for a long time. The straw scratched at my face with each movement. Ma warned me not to make a sound no matter what. At several points the cart stopped and I heard Papá talking to other men. The final time this happened, the man sounded like an official. He wanted to know what Papá was doing out so early. "Trying to make a living," Papá said.

"Maybe you have contraband," the man said.

"Only if the Communists have outlawed farming too," my father said, affecting a strong but respectful tone.

"So you won't mind if I shoot into your straw?" the official said.

"Not at all," my father said. "If you want to waste a bullet."

I imagined a gun pointed right at us, and I waited for some sort of explosion. Instead, I heard the official poking into the straw around us. We could see nothing. Ma found my lips with her finger to ensure my silence. What I think was the barrel of a rifle slid past my ear. My brother started to squirm and I was afraid he would cry at any moment. "You can pass," the official finally said.

The cart moved on. Less than a minute later there was a loud gunshot and I felt a thud on my shoulder and then a stinging sensation. Somehow I remembered not to yell. The pain was not bad, but I thought I had a serious wound. I felt hot blood soaking into my layers of clothes. Then a horrible thought occurred to me. "Check Yee," I whispered to Ma. Her hand moved around my body and she let out a small gasp. I knew my brother was dead.

34

*The father and son visit the dog exhibit;
the father proposes a conversation.*

And now, a marginal zoo at the edge of a dirty city.

I'm not interested in the dog exhibit, but it's a good chance for both my father and me to get a moment alone. As I pay the extra yuan to get inside, I look back at him. He sits under a banyan, fanning himself with a zoo map. His posture is a bit slumped. I'm struck by the vision of him, not unlike Gideon during some of his hot flashes. My father looks almost ghostly in his khaki pants and his green striped cotton shirt with its dark triangles of perspiration. It's a camouflage, as if this man sitting on the green bench will recede into the background and never be seen again. The cup of water I brought him rests on the ground between his legs and he picks it up, waving at me to go inside, offering a posture of comfort I don't believe.

At the entrance I see a man with two beautifully groomed white dogs. They sit as still as stuffed toys, not even panting. I ask what breed they are, and the man tells me in English I can take three pictures for ten yuan. "No," I repeat slowly, "what kind are they?"

"Three picture. Ten." He holds up his calloused fingers to show me the figure.

I don't reply even though I've relearned how to say "no thank you" in Mandarin. I enter and stop at the first row of outdoor cages. The long-haired breeds are first: shih tzu, English sheepdog, poodle. Each breed has a hand-painted sign with red letters in both Chinese and English. At the second cage, I think about turning around. The sheepdog lies flat on wet, mildewed concrete. Like the other dogs, his fur is damp and matted, nothing like the two out front. These are definitely not three-picture-ten quality.

I watch a large poodle race back and forth inside his small cage. He looks as if he's been wrapped in a black tangle of frayed yarn as he stops and pees on the corner of his concrete doghouse, the urine running down the wall and across the cage to the edge, where it troughs out the back. Each new cage I approach is nearly the same, the dog racing around, then pressing its nose into the wire mesh, sniffing at me nervously.

"They look like prisoners," my father says, surprising me from behind.

"I thought you were going to rest."

"I felt better." He has stopped sweating and the color has returned to his face. He wrinkles his nose. "It smells like a wet rug in here. Let's move on."

We quickly pass by dalmatians, German shepherds, dachshunds, rottweilers, Akitas, Chihuahuas, and boxers until we come to a sign that stops me: MONGREL. Inside are three medium-sized dogs jumping around, all of them speckled with dark, short hair. I wonder if they were an accident, if a caretaker turned for a moment and one of the German shepherds mounted a boxer, or perhaps it was the other way around. Is the difference between a breed and a mongrel a human's controlled whim?

"Look at this," my father says. In the last cage is an orangish brown dog with a rectangular muzzle and a scarred face. He lies near the front of the cage. His sign simply says PETER. I look back at the mongrels and then again at Peter, four dogs with no certified lineage. Peter doesn't move. My father taps his cage and the dog lifts a brow but drops it quickly, uninterested. Walking back to the other cage, I wonder if there is something I've missed, some other sign, but I find nothing. I turn to my father, hoping that maybe he is wondering the same thing I am.

"I want to talk," my father says. The words are heavy and unexpected. He keeps his eyes on Peter's cage as if something interesting is there. "I should have started this trip by talking to you about everything that's happened. I have given you parts, but I don't want your history to become a jigsaw puzzle."

"I'm good at those, if you remember."

"I do."

"Mom and I were working on one when she died."

"A boy flying a kite, I know. It did get finished."

"No. You pushed it into the box when we got all that food."

"I made many hasty decisions after your mother died." My father offers me an expression of disappointment. "After I drove you to Catherine's, before I went back to Hong Kong, our apartment was so quiet, but your mother seemed present everywhere, her clothes, her magazines. The kitchen was the only neutral place. Your puzzle was on top of the refrigerator. I brought it down. So much of it was intact, Westen. The boy was complete. How could I not make an attempt?"

"You finished it?"

"In a day. But no, *we* finished it. I just patched together what the two of you had already accomplished."

"I would have liked to have seen that," I say.

"I have a photograph somewhere, but it was so long ago. I wish I could have shown you."

"You could have."

"That is water under the bridge. I know you have many questions. I haven't pleasant answers," he says. "Be prepared for that. And if you don't mind, I'd rather we didn't begin this in a kennel."

He's wrong about that. My questions are few, perhaps boil down to even one. *Are you sorry you left me?* Everything else I can think of pales beside that. And the answer can't simply be regret. I need to hear about loss and damage, that he has struggled with his separation as much as I have.

We follow the exit signs, which first lead us through a small building stocked with pet supplies and three puppies in individual cages. One is a shar-pei with small, bloodshot eyes, and stitches behind the right ear. Apparently they are for sale. A woman in a blue smock dozes in the corner at a desk. We continue through the building, which opens into a small grotto with a half-circle of cracked, orange fiberglass amphitheater chairs. Behind it, past a tall fence, an African elephant stands, pinkish red from the clay ground. It slowly curls hay into its mouth. In the center of the grotto is an oval of worn artificial turf and at the side, a red wagon tied to a dozing Saint Bernard. I wonder if we have just missed a show. I look around for a trainer, but there is no one. We walk up to the dog and I pet it beneath the harness. Its fur is thick and hot. "Where is its water?" I wonder out loud.

"You had a dog," my father says, unhitching the tether that leads from the Saint Bernard to the wagon.

"I don't remember that." I was never allowed to have pets because of my asthma. Once my mother brought home a small rosy boa that one of her coworkers had found curled up in her garage. I'd only had it for three days when I left it in its coffee can on the windowsill, baking it to death.

"Maybe you were too young to remember it." My father leads the dog back toward the shade of the building and I follow. "It was an Australian shepherd," he continues. "But it made you too sick." He stops at the door. "Go and get that woman."

I walk inside and with a purposeful cough wake the woman. "The dog," I say, "I think it needs water." I point outside to where my father is kneeling and petting the Saint Bernard.

"Picture?" she asks. "You want picture?"

I wave for her to follow me, and we go outside, where my father speaks in Chinese to her. He nods as she replies and counts on her fingers. Finally she repeats his words three times. I guess she is saying, "We don't have time."

"She says," my father begins, looking at me, "that the dog is fine. One of the other dogs just had fourteen puppies and they haven't had time to put him away." The woman looks at me for some sort of response.

"*Shui,*" I manage, water. She nods and bows slightly.

"Very good," my father says.

The woman runs inside and brings out a large silver bowl of water. Immediately the Saint Bernard begins lapping at it. Looking at me suspiciously, the woman speaks again.

"She wants to know if you want to buy me a puppy," my father says.

I look at him. "But we couldn't get one out of the country."

"I told her I was your tour guide. She thinks I live here. I must be keeping my accent in check." My father looks at the woman and tells her we don't want a puppy. She frowns slightly and goes back inside.

"Why didn't you tell her you're my father?"

"It was easier."

I walk down a few steps to the orange fiberglass seats and sit down. My father sits as well, leaving a seat between us. Behind us the Saint Bernard is still drinking, making the sounds I imagine come from someone drowning. "I don't get it," I say. "You tell me you want to talk and a minute later you do something like this."

Pulling out his handkerchief, my father dabs at the back of his neck and stares straight ahead. "You are my son."

"That," I tell him, "is biology. What else?"

He shakes his head, holding back tears that I am surprised have come almost instantly. "I am your father. I should be. I want to be."

I look beyond this empty grotto, with its torn synthetic grass. On the other side of the fence, the reddish elephant continues to swing straw into its mouth. Behind us I hear a clamor of barking from the exhibit dogs. I wonder if Peter is one of them, if he even bothers to stand anymore. How much easier is it to sag flatly onto the wet cement and stay there? Why bother standing, actually, if the only thing that makes it out of the cage is the bark? I look at my father, who is tight-lipped and silent and holding back. I'm not sure which way one more question will push him. And it dawns on me that what I have to say is simple: *I have always wanted you to act like a father*. But what I actually say is "Did you have this much trouble talking to your father?"

He considers this, looks into the corner of his mind. "After I met your mother it became more difficult."

"He didn't like her?"

"No, no. It wasn't about *like*. She wasn't Chinese."

"Then he wouldn't have liked me."

My father considers me sternly, so quickly clear-eyed. "Will you stop that? Every time we talk about you being Chinese you put up a roadblock. It sounds more like you are rejecting the idea than it's rejecting you."

"I hadn't thought of it that way."

"Yes. And maybe that is a way to reject me."

Is that it? I ask myself. Has this trip not been about rediscovering my father? Is it about retribution, turning the tables? Somewhere in the back of my mind, am I imagining watching *him* in a rearview mirror as he stands alone next to a piece of luggage? I do not want this to be true because if it is, I will have failed Gideon and Aunt Catherine—my mother too. And now I am plunged into the proposition, the fear, that all these years have been about spite, a kind of pilot light inside me, a low flame in wait.

3 5

The father and son visit relatives in the city;
the son's paternity is questioned.

It has been an afternoon of near silence. My father weary and clearly ill, and me afraid to say anything, which is just as well because the city is so loud we can see the lightning but can't hear the thunder. It begins to rain and we move as best we can down an alley past empty wooden produce stands. The wet air tastes like chewed aluminum. My father stops at a tall apartment building and we step into the alcove, where a man sits in front of a cardboard box of DVDs. They have the names of American movies on the front, *First Blood, Jurassic Park, Mission Impossible,* and one without a title, just a picture of a man with a briefcase running away from a fiery explosion. "Didn't that just come out?" I say to my father.

Breathing hard, he wipes the rain off his glasses with his shirt and looks at the picture. "Yes. Yes. That's that lawyer movie," he says, pointing to a hand-painted sign written in Chinese. "And you can rent it for . . . ninety-nine cents."

"I'll keep that in mind," I say, following him up the stairs. Our relatives live on the seventh floor. The stairwell is surprisingly hot. "Smells like fish," I say.

"When you live next to the water, you smell like fish. When

you live inland you smell like rice." My father pauses for a breath, though we've only gone up two flights. This is not right.

"Are you sure you're okay?"

"Fine. Fine. I just need something to eat. That zoo fare was not exactly nourishing."

We arrive at the door and my father knocks. A Chinese voice calls from inside and my father responds. The door opens, a crack at first, and I find myself looking for a face at my own level. My search quickly takes me a foot lower to the hazy brown eyes of an old woman who smiles with gold-filled teeth and slowly welcomes us in. The small room is full of people. I count nine, including a little boy watching television and already in his pajamas, Smurf bottoms and a pink Hello Kitty top. The old woman motions us to sit, and my father and I take the two places that have obviously been saved for us. The introductions begin, all in Chinese.

The room is small and neat, with gray marble floors and mahogany-stained Chinese-style furniture, low and ornate. These people are not rich, but they take care of what they have.

The old woman opens a red tin of cookies and passes them around. Everyone seems reluctant to take one except my father, who takes three and acts like it's the biggest, most pleasant surprise he's ever had. He hands the tin to me. "Do the same," he says. I take a few cookies and bite into one with an exclamation of pleasure, nodding the biggest thank-you I can, and the room is suddenly happy, as if they've succeeded at something.

"This is your grandmother's youngest sister, Pingmei. You call her Yi Po," my father begins as the cookies go around a second time. He's talking about the old woman. She's wearing a Mao-style gray outfit that's stiff on her thin frame. Her pale gray hair is gathered in the back, as short as a lamb's tail. "And next to her, her first daughter, then her other daughter and her husband, her first son and his wife, her second son and his girlfriend and I'm not quite sure who the boy belongs to. I'm supposed to know."

As my father speaks, the others watch us eagerly, as if we are the most exciting thing that's happened to them. I realize they don't speak any English. I give them each a wave so they know they've been introduced. They nod in return and begin talking to me in Chinese.

"They say you are very handsome," my father translates. "They say your mother was very beautiful."

I manage a polite expression. "That sounds like an insult to you."

My father listens to more questions and comments, but they are directed at me. He translates randomly: "When will you marry?" "Love is gradual." It is a bit overwhelming, but I get a sense my father is acting as a kind of buffer, since his translations are so pared down.

The little boy is sitting on the ground, staring at the television. It's the lawyer movie we saw downstairs, the exact scene from the picture. Only the perspective is odd, almost angled, and the sound is terrible, muffled. Then I understand why. A silhouette scoots past the screen, and it's not part of the movie. Someone bringing popcorn and a drink back from the concession stand.

"That's a bootleg," I tell my father.

He shrugs and returns to his conversation, standing quickly, as do the rest. "We're going to dinner," he says. "You'll like this. Real China." He gestures quotation marks around the last two words.

THE RESTAURANT IS outside the larger city. It's surprisingly big and new-looking, squared off with fluorescent lighting and large picture windows. We are escorted to our table, but no one sits down. Our waitress, a tall, thin woman with a single braid framing each side of her face, walks ahead and leads us outside to an area with dozens of buckets, tanks, and containers of various sizes, each with a different kind of living creature—large, moss-green scallops with shells thin as fingernails, scorpions, sea snails, smaller scallops and clams, stringy pink sea worms.

"What do you feel like eating?" my father asks. The waitress stands next to him, pencil poised over her pad.

"I haven't decided," I say. "Or have you forgotten how I feel about seafood?" My father speaks to the woman in Chinese and she begins writing. He points to a bucket of the mussels, and a man selects a dozen or so and sends them away with a young boy. "Where's that going?" I ask.

"To the kitchen," my father says, smiling. "If you don't want fish, feel like snake?" We're standing next to a glass tank full of snakes in inch-deep water. A young couple has just ordered one, and the attendant reaches in and grabs the reptile behind the head, separating it from the body with a quick slice from his knife. Just as quickly he runs the knife down the length of the body and guts the snake, finally peeling the skin off in one fast, even motion. He sets the fresh pink carcass on a tray and sends it off.

"I'll pass on reptile tonight," I say, noticing how all this live food smells familiar, like cotton candy.

"Do you see anything you want?"

The wall of fish tanks is a mosaic of bored-looking captives inside each one. "It wouldn't be China without a whole fish on the table," I say. "But not for me." My father calls to our waitress and he points to a specific fish.

"I don't suppose they have any hamburger swimming around here," I say.

"No, no, but how about some *long sut*," my father says. "It's just like hamburger."

I'm suspicious. "Show me," I say, and my father leads me to a large blue vat that from a distance looks like it's filled with crude oil. The attendant reaches in with his net and scoops out dozens of black water beetles. He dumps them in a silver bowl and off they go to the kitchen.

"How much should we order?" my father says slyly.

"Those make the scorpion look good. I'll pass."

We walk inside, where most of our relatives have already returned. As soon as we sit, everything we ordered outside starts arriving on our table: first the large mussels, which smell like rain on asphalt; steaming clams on a bed of lettuce; the whole fish we ordered, pale and startled-looking; and some things I don't ask about, slim strips of silvery meat I imagine is eel in brown sauce, a plate of white stringiness that could be noodles or sea worms and smells like corn, and a heaping bowl of steamed rice, which seems amazingly friendly. Yi Po signals to me to begin and I look at the table, all eyes on me. I turn to my father, who seems worried. These are the relatives he knows, and I will not embarrass him. I think I know what I have to do. "Give me one of everything," I tell him, and I begin with the dish that looks like eel.

As soon as I start serving myself, the table comes alive, the lazy Susan in constant motion. Each time the fish passes me, it has lost a little more of itself, looking less like dinner and more Jurassic with every turn. One of the wives stares eagerly over my shoulder at one more entrée coming to our table. The waitress sets down a large oval plate of blackness, dozens of upturned beetles as big as my thumbnail in a shiny, clear sauce. The woman who was so eager for these to arrive quickly spins the dish to her side and spoons out five or six of the insects. They go around the table slowly, but no one else is taking any.

"*Tun yun mei sek,*" my father says. "Countryside bug. This is not city food."

The woman is now only half engaged in eating her chosen dish. In fact, she looks a little embarrassed. Her husband has a slight scowl on his face, and I imagine the scenario. He married a girl from the country, and just when he thought he'd trained out all her country habits, she pulls this in front of company. The plate arrives in front of me. I look at the woman once more. She is soft-looking, very tight-eyed with a rounded chin. Her fingers, holding one of the beetles, are as thin as straws. I grab the spoon and put three on my plate. "Ask her how I do this," I tell my father. He doesn't look happy.

As he talks to her, the woman beams. I carefully follow my father's translation, removing the black outer shell that protects the wing, then taking off the wing, always holding the head, avoiding the needlelike point protecting the thorax, and then finding the tiniest piece of meat to pluck out like a seed. I pop it in my mouth and swallow without chewing. "You're right," I say to my father. "Just like hamburger." My father repeats this to the table in Chinese, and everyone laughs. "Was that a good thing," I say to him almost under my breath, "or a bad thing?"

"You're very generous," he says. "You made seven people feel awkward to spare the feelings of one."

I look at him because I'm not sure how that was meant, but he's already into a mouthful of fish and he shakes his head as if he's done. "It's not polite," he says. "They'll think we're talking about them." He takes a pot of tea and pours into my cup, then into my cousin's on his left, and then into his own. He checks the other cups with a question in his voice and puts the tea on the lazy Susan, where it makes its rounds and everyone fills up.

Yi Po catches my eye. She is neither smiling nor frowning. Just inspecting. Her face is mottled with dark spots and freckles and she has almost no eyebrows. Her front teeth protrude slightly beyond her bottom lip. She looks at my father and asks him a question. He shakes his head.

"What did she say?" I ask.

"Nothing. Nothing important."

"No, what did she say?"

My father swallows his food and looks to the ceiling briefly. "She wanted to know if maybe you were adopted."

"Why would she think something like that?"

"Because," my father sighs, "she says you don't look a thing like me."

36

She is Yi Po to Westen and Pingmei to me. By either name, she had always been blunt. *Perhaps had you been as forthright, your son would have understood you.* Ma told me once that when they were young girls, Pingmei said to her that she would never be married because men did not like moles. She said the one on my mother's cheek made her impossible to love. As it happened, Ma slipped down a ladder and scraped it off so cleanly it did not grow back or leave much of a scar. After that, the women from Papá's village took a new interest in her. Pingmei never got as many offers of marriage as Ma.

I never called this woman Aunt. She told me not to. She married a man in the same village as Papá's, so I saw a great deal of her when I was young. But she was not friendly. Even to her own children she was not motherly. Ma frequently attended to their scrapes and bruises from horseplay, because Pingmei would simply look at the blood and say it was their fault.

She once told me I had the ugliest hair of any boy in the village. She asked me if I wanted her to shave it off. But I told her I preferred not. *"Wo bu yuanyi,"* I said and she became very angry. Not for what I said, but with my tone. She told Ma that I had been disrespectful to her. That night when I went to bed, Ma sat by my side and ran her fingers through my hair. Her hands were rough from work, but I did not mind. "Your auntie is a difficult woman," she said. "But you must respect your elders. If you do not, for our family this is a loss of face." *Díu lian* were her exact words.

No, it did not surprise me that she would say Westen and I did not look alike. She had a vaultful of brashness. But to ask if he was adopted did surprise me, as if she did not know I married a Caucasian woman. Westen was clearly not pleased. I suppose he shouldn't have been. The ride back from the restaurant was quiet, at least between us. Our relatives, though, were full of questions for me. Why had it been so many years since my last visit? Why had I lost so much weight? How come I'd waited so long to bring my son to China? Peppered between these were queries about my finances.

The next day Pingmei was going to take us to the village. She instructed me on the respect I should have for my roots. She told me to make sure I had plenty of money to give. *"Mun gan zap zok,"* she said. "It is an unwritten law."

Westen was looking out the window of the car. "What's she saying now?" he said. "That I'm actually your daughter?"

"Don't sulk," I said. "She's just an old lady."

"Being adopted would explain a lot of things."

"You are not adopted."

"Actually, I kind of was. By Great-Aunt Catherine and Uncle Cane."

IN OUR HOTEL ROOM, Westen remained quiet. He lay in bed wearing a white T-shirt and boxers. It was the same slender body I had at his age. I did not think I could afford to allow him to remain upset at this stage of the trip, so I took a calculated risk. "I can prove you are not adopted," I said.

He looked at me but still said nothing.

I walked to my suitcase. Each brass lock snapped open surprisingly loud. Inside the slim pocket next to where I kept my
new cache of bandages, ointments, and some leftover cassia bark
for abdominal pain, I also kept his mother's letter. The paper of
the envelope was duller and more wrinkled than when I first held
it, but it remained closed. Celia's signature over the sealed flap
was faded but perfectly intact. "This is the envelope I told you
was stolen with our luggage."

"Why would you lie about that?"

"It's a letter from your mother. She wrote it because at one
time we were not sure if I was your father." He sat up. "It has to
do with what happened in New Orleans. We had blood tests. I
told her I didn't care to know. She kept it for me if I ever thought
it mattered enough to know for sure." Yes, finally it was out. I
was both relieved and afraid of what might come next.

As I expected, Westen appeared stunned. "And you've never
opened it?" he asked. I handed him the letter and he turned it
over in his hands. He ran a finger over his mother's signature,
tracing the lines as if he was writing it himself.

"No, no, no, no. I have always been too afraid to open it.
There have been many times I was tempted. You can open it if
you want. I just wanted to show you that at the very least you are
not adopted."

He stared at the envelope and at my name written in thin
blue letters. "Why haven't you mentioned this before?"

"Because I think you are my son," I said. I sat down next to
him on the bed. "It's why I was so emotional at the zoo."

"No doubts?"

"There are always doubts, Westen. But they don't last. I
know it's not scientific."

He handed the letter back to me and began crying. I didn't
know what to do. If it was anger I would have understood, but I

didn't know how to interpret his reaction. I wanted to reach out and hold him, and it hurt to think I didn't know him well enough for this. Instead, I slid closer and put my hand on his shoulder. When he was a boy, I rarely saw him cry. Not because he didn't cry, but because he didn't like to cry in front of us. One night I walked past his bedroom door and heard him sobbing. I stopped and asked what was wrong. He told me that his friend had gotten in a fight at school and that he was afraid his parents would punish him even though it was not his fault.

So there was my adult son, crying. "I understand it's hard," I said, pausing to take a long look at him. In seconds we could go from being father and son to what? I had to ask the next question, though I hoped Westen's answer would be no. "Should we open it?"

He sat up and cleared his eyes with the back of his hands. His face was red and wet. "I really don't think I can handle it," he said, stuttering an inhalation. "Not right now." He leaned back on the headboard. "I don't want to know I've wasted the last twenty-five years being angry with someone who's not even my father."

"Yes, yes. I know. But if we open it," I said, "you might be able to forgive the one who is."

He looked at me for a long time. Neither of us said anything. Even though he was half Chinese, I couldn't understand how people did not see our common features. If I just looked at his mouth, his lips, and the teeth behind them, I could say he was my son. And where did he get the color of his skin? Even the shape of his nose, though more pronounced like his mother's, came from me. I was sure of it. Or I wanted to be sure of it.

"Really," Westen said calmly, "why haven't you opened this?" He tapped the letter sitting next to him.

"Because I do not need proof that you are my son," I said. But with little conviction.

"I don't believe that," he said. "I think it's because you feel the same way I do. Only you don't want to find out that you've felt guilty all this time for nothing."

"Okay," I said. "It scares me."

He reached toward the nightstand. I thought he was going to turn off the light. Instead, he grabbed my deck of cards. "You're open and I'm sealed," he said, shuffling the deck. "High card wins." I watched his hands, young versions of my own. Quick, with clear nails. Smooth veins running into the knuckles. He held the deck out. I picked up all but the last three cards. Ace of diamonds. So that was it. We would open the letter and know after all these years. For me it was an old question, but for Westen it was brand-new. For so long I'd been able to resist opening the envelope because I simply resolved that Westen was my son. But I had other reasons, I can admit to myself now. If I lost him, if he was not my son, it would also mean that night in New Orleans I had let Celia down even more than I already understood.

I certainly had the high card, so I reached for the letter as Westen turned over the next card. Ace of hearts. Incredible. He nervously shuffled again. This time I selected high in the deck. Ten of clubs. Westen nodded in a way I could not interpret. Was that the card to beat or the card to get under? He turned over the next one. Ace of Hearts again.

"What are the odds of that?" I said.

He handed me the letter. We both stared at it as if it were a stack of counterfeit bills we wondered if we should spend. "Put it away," he said after a long silence. "Whatever the two of us have to figure out won't change because of that letter."

I returned the envelope to my suitcase. I knew we would need it later.

3 7

The son writes a letter to his great-aunt;
he recalls a choice between a man and a woman.

I am shaken, hollowed out. The very person I should naturally
talk to is the one man I most want to avoid. It occurs to me that
nowhere is more than halfway around the world from where I am
at any given moment. And it's a small planet, small enough that I
can, in a way, bring close to me the one person I can count on.

Dear Aunt Catherine,
  Some startling news. One of three things is true. I
am adopted and my father is lying to me, I am my
mother's son but not my father's, or I am their son and I
am Chinese. I doubt you know the story and I apologize
for being cryptic, but I prefer to tell you in person. One
thing is for sure: up to now I hadn't thought visiting my
father's village could be so important to me. Now I
think I have to go, to prove something to myself and my
father.
  I should be telling you, perhaps, about the water
lilies and carp we see in every pond, or about the brass
funeral coach complete with horses buried with the
Terra-Cotta Warriors, as if the emperor's soul could be
carried off, as if this and the warriors themselves had

some sort of agency. The cynic in me says these things are simply alloy and clay, but the optimist wonders if maybe there's a piece to the archaeological puzzle we've missed, a pulse or a current that can no longer be measured. Or maybe it's just the Western ear, the scientific notions that render everything implausible without a control group. But think about the implications. These things which may have had life, may still have. And think about the possibilities of man to create and for art to transport. When I think of it that way, I can believe in intuition and I can let the rest of this trip proceed with a little more promise. I hope this is realistic.

Which is nothing really about China, I suppose, but it's what I'm thinking about, and of course you're the only one I can talk to about all this. We're going to see a bit of Guangzhou tomorrow, run some errands with Yi Po, and then go to my father's village. I'm continuing to ask myself what I want from all this, because when we began I just wanted to show my father how angry I was.

Hope you're doing well. I've got a T-shirt from the Great Wall for you. Though, now that I think about it, I've never seen you wear a T-shirt.

Love, Westen

Even after all this time I'm struck by the ease with which I confide in my great-aunt. Writing to her made me recall how dishonest I'd been with Margaret. We'd been going out a long time and it'd been a year since the last time we talked about marriage. "Is this going to happen?" she asked me. All I could say was wait. Later she told me that's when she knew.

But the night we actually broke up, I had invited her over to dinner, the two of us along with Gideon and his friend Mark.

Gideon had just told me he was HIV-positive and symptomatic, and somehow that made us closer, though I guess technically we were still just friends, and landlord and tenant.

Margaret brought a bottle of blackberry Manischewitz, which was a private joke between us because the only time we'd gotten drunk together was at a Jewish wedding reception. Gideon gave Margaret a big hug, bigger than the one I gave her. I remember the entire house smelled of Greek olives and garlic. It was a good dinner. The four of us knew one another well and I'd gotten used to Margaret and Gideon being in the same place at the same time—and with Mark there, we were all squared off.

We talked about the usual things, Gideon's next bad TV-movie project, Mark's boyfriend of the week. But Margaret did something she'd never done before. She brought up the possibility of our wedding.

"What do you think, Gideon?" she said looking right at him. "June?"

Gideon was halfway into a wedge of toasted sourdough dabbed in jalapeño olive oil. He seemed to hang there in mid-bite before setting the bread down and looking to me for help. Finally Mark spoke up. "Sure, sweetie," he said. "Summer weddings are for good girls." Mark was a nice guy, a corn-fed blond from Iowa who'd gotten Los Angeles down pretty fast.

Gideon recovered and, sweet as he was, I never knew him to back down. "You two kids are about as good as it gets," he said, making quotation marks around the word *good* with his fingers. "You still haven't, um, you know . . . have you?" He didn't say it, but we both knew what he meant.

"We're waiting," Margaret said, glaring at me for telling Gideon about our intimate life, or the lack of it.

That was about the saddest thing I'd ever heard. Gideon

looked straight at me and said, "How long are you going to wait?" I could tell he clearly wasn't talking about Margaret and me.

Mark stood up and grabbed his plate. "If this evening is going to devolve into a conversation about abstinence and heterosexual sex, then I just don't have anything to contribute." I got up with my plate and Margaret's and went into the kitchen after Mark. The two of us cleared the rest of the table while Gideon and Margaret sat quietly, Gideon refilling his wineglass and Margaret playing with the lemon slice in her water.

"What are you going to do about that mess?" Mark said to me in the kitchen. I didn't respond.

Gideon walked into the kitchen just then and came over to kiss me on the cheek. "Thanks for clearing the table," he said. I returned the gesture, just pecked him on the cheek, but Margaret had come in on cue. In a few seconds she was out the door and at her car, fumbling for her keys. I followed and caught up with her, grabbing her arms.

"I wondered," she stammered, clearly shaken. "I wondered what was wrong and I thought maybe this was it. But I just couldn't believe it."

"It is and it isn't," I said.

"Just tell me, Westen. Are you having sex with him? He's sick, you know."

I couldn't help but sound incredulous. "Not once. I've never even kissed him."

"Because if you are, I can pray for you but I can't save you. It's one thing to be tolerant." She pulled away from me and leaned against her car, arms crossed.

"You think I'm going to hell? It's not like that. I just rent a room. We're close friends."

Margaret got in her car and closed the door, unrolling her window. She gave me a long, sad look but there were no tears, just her wide-set brown eyes firmly locked on mine. "You never want to be the bad guy," she said. Then she sighed. "Gideon has three houses. He doesn't need to rent out a room. Seriously, Westen, if I told you to choose, to stay here or move out tomorrow for me, what would you decide?"

I could barely look at her. "I'd have to stay," I said.

"Yes, you would," she said touching me on the hand. "I'm really sad for you, but I'll pray." Then she drove off. That's how clean it was, except for a message on my answering machine the next day and a box of things I'd left at her apartment. I had nothing to return to her.

The son admits to a failed engagement;
he walks through a fish market.

We're up early, hungover, it seems, from our conversation about my mother's envelope, and neither of us seems to want the hair of the dog that bit us. Thankfully, the walk from our hotel to Yi Po's apartment is short. Guangzhou is tall and even more shiny and metallic the farther away I look. But it's dark and crowded where we are, and the buildings have orange stains running from cracks and corners, as if the walls were bleeding, showing rusty stigmata.

We walk up the alley to Yi Po's, the same place we came through last night that seemed so black and empty. The light is gray-blue, the street clogged with people selling dried mushrooms, lychee, string, chopped meat, and fresh greens.

"Your *yi po* doesn't have to go far to do her shopping," my father says. He walks directly behind me because there's not enough room for us to walk side by side.

"Maybe we should bring them something," I say loudly, turning around.

My father raises his eyebrows. "What did you have in mind?"

"Lychee?"

"Look," he says, pointing to a vendor not far from us. She's sitting behind two piles of lychee, a bumpy fruit the size of a Ping-Pong ball, with its unmistakable pinkish red color. "Now look up the street." All along this narrow row, between the crowded shoppers, I catch glimpses of lychee, flashes of color that let me know this fruit is for sale everywhere. "It's in season," my father says. "And it grows near here. That would be like going to Colombia and bringing your host a pound of coffee."

"Or a bag of coke," I say.

He doesn't yet get the joke. "The drug," I say. "Not the drink."

"Yes. Yes," he says.

We begin moving again and just before we get to Yi Po's building, a man sitting against a wall with a straw basket catches my eye. His beard is pepper-colored and patchy. He stares directly into the basket of small fruit he's selling.

"How about some of those?" I say as we get closer.

When my father walks to the basket, the old man does not look up. *"Wong pei,"* my father says. "I haven't seen this in a while."

The bunched fruit is small and yellow with brown speckles, almost like golden hummingbird eggs on long green stems. My father speaks to the man, who never looks at us but replies in a soft voice. He appears to be in his sixties. Plucking two pieces of the fruit from their stems, my father hands me one. I watch him peel back the skin on his, which is thin as a plum's, its meat greenish white and slick.

"Too much trouble," I say, popping the fruit into my mouth. It's sour, like biting down on a lemon with a pinch of sugar, and my eyes water a bit. But the most surprising thing is that it's nearly all pit. I spit it out into my hand and it's green as a lime, a shudder running through me from the tang.

"See?" my father says. "That's a good sign. Most Chinese don't like sweet."

"So Yi Po will want these?"

"I happen to know she does," he says. "She cannot taste very well, so she appreciates anything that's strong."

My father speaks again to the old man, and he lifts up a handheld scale made of wood, twine, and lead weights. We put some fruit in the wire-mesh basket and the old man runs his finger along the top of the scale. He's blind. He says something to my father, who takes out a few yuan and places them in the man's dark palm. Grasping the money, the man offers a semi-toothless smile and wags his finger in my father's direction. He takes one of the bills he has just received and gives it back to my father along with a piece of string.

"Tie the stems together," my father says, handing me the string and fruit. The old man talks to my father, making broad gestures with his dark, thick-knuckled hand. My father takes out his pad and writes in Chinese, occasionally affirming that he's listening.

We part and walk toward Yi Po's. "More curses?" I say. "Or should I even bother asking?"

"When the Communists came to his village, they mistook him for the son of a landowner and smashed him across the back of the head. That's why he can't see."

"And what were you writing down?"

"Just that and some names," my father says, waving me forward.

Yi Po calls to us and approaches, plows through the crowd with the eagerness of a neglected child. She's wearing an orange button-up blouse and a black vest with a raised floral pattern. When she reaches us, she says something to my father in a disapproving tone and then turns to me and speaks. I listen and nod, although I'm at a loss for what she's saying. But my father laughs and so do I, though I have no idea why.

"She says that you shouldn't be on this trip with an old man like me. You should come to China on a honeymoon. She wants to know where your girlfriend is."

I know I must look a bit startled. "I don't have one," I say, and my father shrugs as he translates. Examining me from head to foot, Yi Po looks incredulous, speaking the whole time.

"She's saying that you look fine. Maybe a little skinny. And that she knows a matchmaker in Hong Kong if you want her name."

I manage a response, though not eagerly. "The truth is," I say, pausing so my father can follow. "I had a fiancée but it didn't exactly work out."

It takes a moment for my father to process this. He looks over the top of his glasses to check if he heard correctly. "Your aunt didn't mention a fiancée."

"I'm sure there are many things she didn't mention," I say, gesturing with my hand for the translation to continue.

Yi Po straightens up and nods her head as if I've said something she understands. We remain in the middle of streaming pedestrians pushing my father and me closer together while Yi Po manages to stand her ground.

Scooting his glasses up, my father offers Yi Po's reply. "She says that your girlfriend came from a bad family."

I'm not sure why, but I feel that I owe Margaret more than this. "It wasn't that," I say, overcompensating for my lack of Chinese with dual hand gestures. "I made her jealous."

My father starts to translate, but stops before the first word comes out. "Are you sure you want to say that? Yi Po is a busybody."

I look at Yi Po and nod affirmatively. "Sure," I say, watching for her expression. When my father is done, she closes one eye slightly and gives a slow nod, methodically grinding out a few words.

"She says if you had another woman, you are more of a Chinese man than you look."

I want to say that it wasn't two women, that it wasn't like that at all. That I'm not like that. But then I realized there's no difference. There were two people and I chose one over the other. So I just nod and say I'm not proud of it, and my father offers a final translation. Yi Po shakes me by one shoulder.

"She's telling you not to concentrate too much on the past. Focus on the one you chose."

"I wish I could," I say, but then I tell my father not to translate. I don't feel like explaining. It's not because of Yi Po, but because I don't know how to tell my father about Gideon or what happened. Instead, I end the conversation by handing Yi Po the *wong pei* we bought for her.

She thanks us and walks us down the street into a covered market where they're selling whole fish. I welcome this distraction. It's dim here, each vendor's wares illuminated by one or two small bulbs. At the first stall, a live fish lies on the cutting board, only it's not whole. Half of it is filleted away and most of the tail is missing. All the internal organs remain in the center, intact, even the air bladder, as white and luminous as a pearl. The fish's heart beats slowly and the gills continue to flap, sucking air into a body that's no longer there. Surprisingly, even the remaining portion of the tail flaps a bit.

Other tables have whole fish and shrimp and crabs in low, shallow buckets. At the perimeter of the market, vendors sell whole barbecued duck behind greasy Plexiglas. Each duck is reddish brown, like a scale model of a vanquished dragon. One bird is purchased just as we pass, and is chopped up as the customer yells out her specifications. Suddenly the air is filled with the sweet odor of duck meat.

The lights, the *clop-clop* of fish beheadings, customers dickering, it all has the effect of a mammoth pinball machine in a dark arcade. Maybe, I think, that has been this entire trip, the two of us launched into the game, banging into rubber bumpers, truths half realized before we're shot off into another direction. My father's invitation, *bing,* my mother's rape, *bing,* her letter, *bing bang,* my fiancée, *bing.* And each time it seems we are about to roll out of the game right down the center, we are flipped back in.

Bing. "Your *mamá* would shop for us at a place like this," my father says. Yi Po is already at the other side of the market, uninterested. But my father and I linger. I notice that the concrete is stained nearly black from years of foot traffic and fish guts.

"Uncle Cane and I used to go fishing all the time," I say. "I can fillet anything from trout to halibut, and I thought I was pretty good until I saw this." I point to a table where the fish is being carved up alive in front of a woman watching intently as if at any moment she could reject it.

"You two spent a lot of time together."

"I was his little project. Someone to make a man out of."

"He did a good job," my father offers quietly, quickly turning away as if it's not something he wants to repeat.

Yi Po leads us into a small side street lined on both sides by fish tanks and buckets gurgling air. It's a street of bubble-eyed goldfish dumbly lumbering about in the water: ornamental carp, tetra, moonfish with their transparent backs the colors of gasoline on water, bettas, black and orange mollies, freshwater shrimp, caged turtles, flute fish and knife fish, which look exactly like the scalloped half of a lasagna noodle.

"When I was a boy," my father says, "I wanted a business like this."

"Selling goldfish?"

"It seemed exciting, yes. And they didn't even have so much variety then."

"How much time did you spend in Guangzhou?"

My father nods to himself a few times as if counting. "Your *yeh yeh* had a great deal of business here. He kept a bed with some relatives and we stayed here with him a few months at a time, depending on school."

"Was it difficult to go back and forth like that?"

"It was important to be near him," my father says. We look at each other because this is my cue, only I am so wrung out I don't have it in me to say the obvious thing.

We walk around a corner and into the sun. It's startlingly bright, and my father and I raise our hands to shield our eyes. But Yi Po continues forward. "What are we doing?" I ask.

"Your cousin Ding is working and we're picking her up so she can go to the village with us." As my father says this, Yi Po leads us around another corner, suddenly busy again with people. Not far from us, a few women sit facing each other, and as we get closer, I see that one set is doing something to the faces of the other set. We arrive in front of the woman I presume to be my cousin. She is attending a female customer whose hair is pushed back off her face with an elastic band. Ding has a thread gripped in her teeth, the two ends held by her hands. She scissors this across the woman's face, concentrating on the air where the thread intersects.

"Pulling out hair," my father says, anticipating my question. "*Lai meen mo.* When they put their makeup on, it helps it stay smooth."

My cousin finishes and offers the woman a mirror. She inspects her face closely and runs her fingers over her cheeks and across her forehead. She removes the elastic band and fixes her hair. She's surprisingly professional-looking, in a dark suitlike dress. I realize that I've developed an expectation of what Chinese women should be, and this isn't it. It strikes me how American this scene seems, like an ATM, a walk-up facial, *dozens of locations to serve you.*

Yi Po is approached by a woman who looks to be her senior, hair thin and gray, lopped off in a straight cut just above the shoulders. She could be seventy or one hundred. Yi Po turns to us and introduces my father first. He greets the woman enthusiastically, as if he knows her, and I wonder if this is something I should be doing as well.

The woman steps close to me. Her vision is obviously bad. She says something in Chinese and my father responds. The woman takes my hand in hers and squeezes a bit, moving up my arm as if she's considering a purchase. Her hands feel dry and rough against my skin and she smells like camphor and root beer. She stops her inspection at my elbow, offering an affirmative-sounding murmur. We walk away without saying good-bye.

"What was that all about?" I ask my father. Yi Po is in front of us, clearing a way through the crowd. For an old woman, for anyone at all, she has a willfulness about her that I respect.

"That woman was one hundred three years old," my father says. "Our family has known her a long time. She used to help deliver babies in our village. She delivered me."

"So why was she feeling my arm?"

"She wasn't feeling your arm. It was your bones she was interested in."

39

The father considers the importance of this trip;
he recalls an early moment with his wife.

I always imagined I would be proud to show my son where I came from, yes. *Did it matter, really? Did it make a difference?* Once we got to Guangzhou, I began to worry even more. I wondered how he would experience China off the tour. Home never seems primitive when you are growing up. But even I was startled by some of the things I had forgotten. I had become used to fish fillets on Styrofoam trays. Seeing a fish carved up live reminded me that "fresh" has a very different meaning in China. I did not say anything to Westen, but everything seemed so dirty as well. This was something I rarely noticed before. China was wealthier than ever and still the economic situation was terrible. Was I so Westernized? It was not so long ago that I was one of them. Much happier as well.

One time I stayed with Papá in the city, just he and I. I had not seen him for some years. He took me out to a big dinner with his city friends and a few relatives. We had a whole suckling pig brought to our table. Its skin was oily brown and it had large red cherries for eyes. Seeing it on our table made me feel rich. For each plate the waitress cut a square of pigskin along with onion and a small piece of bread. Then we were given a piece of the white pork. I remember the soup ladled out of the cooked winter melon. And the orange crab, too, and deep-fried custard balls. Papá said we were very prosperous. He wanted to share our good fortune.

I thought Papá was very sophisticated then. He seemed so tall and handsome. He could afford glasses that didn't make his eyes look as if they were bulging out of their sockets. And when he was in the city, he wore a dark gray suit with a white shirt and a thin black tie. It seemed to me then that he was a very important person. Everywhere we went, he greeted people who knew him and wanted his advice. He introduced me as if I were his proudest achievement. Everyone remarked what a fine boy I was.

The differences on the trip with Westen could not have been more clear. With my own father, I was validated as a worthy heir. Westen seemed to be a cause for questions. Yes, I felt as though people were seeing in his features the thing I feared. When we were passing through the fish market, we met an old woman who used to live in our village. She had helped deliver me. When I told her who Westen was, she said he smelled like steamed rice. Which was her way of saying he did not seem Chinese to her. She could not see him, so she grabbed his arm. "Not Chinese bones," she said. "Not Chinese."

I did not tell Westen this. One more doubt. *But if you had told the truth then, it might have changed the outcome.* One more piece of backward China. Although I was relieved that Westen didn't seem to find China exotic overall. In fact, he seemed bored much of the time. When we were driving to the village, I asked him about this. The road was new concrete and the locals took advantage of it. For miles the sides were lined with rectangles of drying rice. Water buffalo stood here and there, grazing and tethered by the nose.

"Does it seem impossible to you that I came from this?" I asked.

"No," he said. "It seems impossible that *I* came from this."

I understood then what I was doing. I was untangling a mess that I had started when I met his mother. She was a beautiful American woman willing to talk to me. I did everything I could to show her I could be American too. At the time, my English was still poor and I made many mistakes, like mixing my pronouns. "She was a very good president," I said about Kennedy on our first date. Celia laughed so hard I thought they would throw us out of the restaurant. That was something I learned quickly, the American laugh. It is full and unashamed.

Yes, I changed the way I dressed too. No more of the boys-school look that I had carried over from Hong Kong. White shirt and black slacks. I bought jeans and colored cotton shirts with no pockets for pens. The denim felt itchy and stiff, and sometimes I reached for a pen where there wasn't one. I stopped listening to any music that sounded remotely Chinese. Instead, I got used to Petula Clark because she was Celia's favorite. I studied the music on Ed Sullivan as if I were reading a textbook. I figured each song I remembered was an investment. *Even then you tried too hard in the wrong ways.*

Once, Celia and I parked under some eucalyptus trees in Balboa Park and left the radio on. I wanted to show her I fit into American culture. "That's the Brytones," I said. They were local, singing their only minor hit, "Johnny Backdoor." It was about a wealthy girl in love with a boy who delivers groceries to the back of the house. Of course, the love is forbidden. The finest part of the song is when Johnny Backdoor is struck by lightning as he crosses the girl's lawn. He's carrying a ladder because he's on his way to elope with her. Just at this moment they sing with a dramatic pause—*Struck down—but not out of my heart*. It's not a classic, but Celia seemed impressed I knew what it was.

"Do they have this kind of music where you're from?" she said. She looked so beautiful. She wore a red and green dress with a white collar and no sleeves.

"Yes," I said, and she looked surprised. "Not the music. The stories are the same." I explained how you could change Johnny Backdoor and the wealthy girl to a peasant boy and a princess. It would be like a Chinese song, except the princess would fall on a sword.

"You're pretty okay," she said.

After that night, I got even more serious. I bought Coca-Cola in the long green bottles. I forced myself to watch *Gunsmoke* and *Bonanza,* with the embarrassing Hop Sing, and even *Gilligan's Island*. I learned to be for the Vietnam War when I spoke to people Papá's age, against it with people my age. It was not long before I felt that I deserved my own car. I bought a Valiant from one of Celia's friends for a few hundred dollars. It was white with blue accents and a peeling dashboard.

You were everything but blond. I did everything I could to forget rice fields and Hong Kong and Communism. I was going to construct myself as an American. The last part of all that effort was Celia. When I felt I had remade myself, I asked her to marry me.

Yes, that was the beginning. I was even more certain the trip with Westen was the end. My course had seemed so certain in those early years with Celia, so promising. Then, those decades adrift, the navigation random. No, even then I could not promise Westen we would arrive in safe harbor.

40

The son sees the father's childhood land;
he considers his own labors.

I am slightly disappointed. My father rented a white van, which my cousin drives, and the road to the village is brand-new concrete. There are rice fields on either side, people raking the yellow grains into rectangles as wide and long as king-sized beds. But it doesn't feel as rural as I expected. My father and Yi Po talk almost the entire way, as if negotiating, and it appears that she is coming out on top.

"What are you two talking about?" I finally ask when it seems like there's a break.

Shaking his head, my father throws up his hands. "She says the village needs money for a new bridge. They're expecting me to bring them enough to cover the costs."

"An entire bridge?" I say.

"I'm the only one who keeps in contact."

"But how can you afford that?" My father does not respond. He looks out the window, the sunlight curving over his face like a quarter moon. "How much do they want?"

"I'm not sure," he says, reaching under his seat and pulling out a plastic bag. He opens it and shows me the contents, dozens of yuan-filled *lai cee* envelopes, red and slick-looking as fish hearts. "Let's hope this is enough."

. . .

AS WE DRIVE, I realize the actual road to the village is hard dirt that winds through the center of a wide valley, rice fields spread out like a yellow lake dotted with dark, harvested sections, each small village an island. We drive through the first of these, a mesh of whitewashed brick homes. Yi Po waves as if she's a grand marshal in a parade, and the few people we pass wave back, seeming to know her. The van comes to an unexpected stop and we all look out the front window. A family has dug a trench across the road for some kind of pipe extending from a house, and we can't pass. Yi Po says one word with an outstretched hand that clearly means "stay in the van."

We watch Yi Po walk to the trench and talk to the family. Her gestures are fast and direct. The man does most of the listening. He's tall and thin, with skin that looks even darker under his dirty white T-shirt. Yi Po points at the piles of dirt and gravel and at two shovels. The man she is talking to seems to grow smaller as time goes by. In quick order, he and a boy are shoveling the piled dirt to the side and the woman is dropping planks over the trench. In minutes they've made the road accessible. Offering a broad smile, Yi Po opens her arms as if blessing them. She waves the van forward and waits until we pass over the trench before she gets in. The family waves limply at us and we are on our way.

"Does she always get what she wants?" I ask.

My father does not respond, but speaks in Chinese to Yi Po. She looks back at me and shakes her head, saying something with scratchy amusement.

"She says she *only* gets what she wants."

The van rocks from side to side and lurches as we proceed over the uneven road, past the end of the village and into the midst of the fields. Broad straw hats move in the greenish yellow fields like heavy flowers, the bodies beneath them thick stems. Here, no one stops to wave as we pass. In the distance is another small grouping of white buildings. "There is the village," my father says, sitting up. And then he squints through his glasses. "And if you look at that mountain beyond, that is where our ancestors are buried."

Yi Po is watching us talk, and she speaks to my father. I can tell he's translating our conversation because she simply nods as if she approves. Then she adds something.

"She says she would like to see how long you would last in the rice fields."

"Tell her I'd do okay," I say.

Chuckling at the news, Yi Po launches into something intricate, my father stopping her now and then, repeating words as if to get the pronunciations. I open the side wing window and the humid air lurches in, solid and hot. The van is immediately filled with a smell I can't pinpoint, something tinged like a mix of red clay and lemon. My father translates. "Yi Po says that when she was your age a vacation was a half-day off. She says that no American can possibly know what hard work is like."

I have not had a hard life. But it has not been easy. When I think of myself and work, I think of my hands. I see them impossibly stained after changing the oil in Uncle Cane's truck, and dry and cracked after a week of repairing the roof when a midwinter storm blew a tree onto the house, the fingernails darkened by black earth each spring when the garden goes in. Maybe this instinct to work with my hands is the connection that renders my mother's letter obsolete.

I look into my palms, see them surrounding one of my pigeons, which isn't difficult, but takes an entirely different kind of touch, not the grip of a hand on a tool, but the soft and confident hold of restraining a living thing, a creature with hollow bones that my hands could break with hardly any effort. It is that power, the harnessed energy between my hands, that most scares me, the hands that feed and cage and free. Acts of a tangible god with no more purpose than watching wing and wind, and who no longer imagines his hand holding someone else's.

41

*The father and son arrive in the village;
they pay tribute to an ancestor.*

My father's village looks like an exposed coral reef, bleached white and jagged. A man with a bamboo pole and skin the color of burned chicken stands waiting for us just before the road enters the village.

"Zhang?" my father says, and Yi Po confirms this. "He used to try to get us to pray to Jesus."

"He goes to church here?" I ask as we come to a stop. Zhang steps close to the van, so close I can see the pupils in his thin eyes. His leathery skin is tight around his jaw and cheeks.

"People do not," my father says, getting out of the van as I follow. "It was just him." With that, he pats Zhang on the shoulder and the two begin a conversation in which Zhang becomes quickly earnest and animated, his eyes widening at each high syllable. My father nods in a series of shorter and shorter movements. "Who is he to us?" I say, extending my hand.

"Village elder," my father says. "But no relation."

Zhang takes my hand and gives it a vigorous shake. His palm is rough and meaty—surprisingly so, for the little balding curve of a man he is. He speaks to me much more happily than to my father.

"He says you look like you eat well."

"Plateful of *long sut* every day," I say, patting my stomach. To my surprise, my father translates.

Zhang tilts his head and I look at him straight in the eyes until he laughs, which he does, wagging a brown finger at me. Then he turns to Yi Po and my cousin and greets them with gentle nods, running his hand through thinning white hair.

The air-conditioning from the van has worn off and I'm aware of exactly how hot and humid it is. My body feels wrapped, as if in wet muslin. My father's skin is already glowing with perspiration, and he pulls a white handkerchief from his pocket, dabbing his forehead as he and Yi Po speak to Zhang. The group of us walk into the village. This road runs between block-length rows of white buildings and drying pads for rice. A woman in a tattered straw hat, pants drawn up to her knees, shuffles in sandals through a patch of yellow grain. The wake of her feet leaves nearly perfect lines that circle back in paper-clip curves. On a separate pad, a woman uses a crude straw broom to sweep the chaff as another woman sifts it through a straw basket. Next to them is a large pile of yellow rice.

"So this is where you're from?" I say.

"One of the places," my father says.

As we walk through the village, I search for a new feeling, something that will confirm that part of me is from here too. But nothing. Nothing yet. Zhang calls out and a few people start gathering around us, mostly the very old and very young. Next to us are bundles of graying bamboo and thin sticks gathered together with wire. They look like captured whales, dried and peeled, revealing the interstices of bone and vein. A girl grabs my hand. She can't be more than six or seven. She has a pink birthmark in the shape of Florida on the side of her face. I squeeze her hand. "I'm Westen," I tell her, pointing to my chest.

"Wes-ton," she says slowly, and it sounds like a Chinese word. And then she points to herself. "Ming."

"She's a cousin," my father says. A dozen people are walking with us, and we're almost at the end of the village already. Before us stands the largest building, two stories, mossy, ceramic dragons and pheasants in faded shades of yellow and red crowning the roofline, which is accented by a green tile border. In front is a gravel square, maybe twenty by twenty feet. Two heart-shaped groups of harvested peanuts sit curing in the sun, spread out in a single layer four feet wide. The villagers rush ahead of us and stand in front of the building, smiling. I look at my father, who is nearly in tears. Ming lets go of my hand and disappears into the crowd.

"What's going on?" I ask, disappointed that I cannot innately share in whatever has overwhelmed my father.

"This is the building dedicated to our family name," he says. Beyond him, people start rushing in from the fields until we are surrounded with smiling Chinese faces. Almost all of them are middle-aged or older. My father does a slow spin and says hello, gesturing toward me in introduction. I wonder how many of these people might be my relatives. It's possible I'm one generation removed from working in a rice field. I look at the naked and sandaled feet, almost all of them grayish white with dried mud. One woman has long pink scars across both shins.

"What are we doing now?" I say, half waving at these people.

"They're here for *lai cee,* lucky money." He reaches into the plastic bag and pulls out the first of the red envelopes. The villagers surge forward. They remind me of when I was a child at the park. Aunt Catherine and I would buy two loaves of white bread to feed the waterfowl. In seconds we'd be surrounded, flotillas of ducks and geese speeding across the lake, some flying in like awkward squadrons, all of them clamoring and quacking for the tiniest piece of bread.

My father does his best to hand out the lucky money, one envelope per person, but I don't know how he can do it. All I see are extended hands, children's arms reaching upward like hungry baby birds, each one disappearing when it's fed a red envelope. Amazingly, the envelopes hold out. Most of the people disperse. I assume the few that stay are somehow related to us. "I feel like an ATM," my father says.

"Can you hear someone singing?" I ask compulsively. I can't place the location of the vague, high-pitched voice I suddenly hear.

"Singing?" My father looks west for a moment and then puts his hand on my cheek. "That's the sun. You better get inside." I turn and look at the building in front of us closely this time. On either side of the door are vertically aligned, orange ceramic carp attached to the walls, with spent incense sticks in their mouths. Above is a foot-wide yellow and orange lotus circled by bands of blue, red, yellow, green, orange, and white. And hidden in the eaves, perfectly preserved wall paintings of carp and lake scenes stretch the length of the building.

Inside, the building is dark and open, one large room, half of which has a twenty-foot ceiling. It's surprisingly cool here and the worn stone floors mute the conversation, all in Chinese, as we enter. There are no chairs, just stools, inches high, which we're invited to sit on. Zhang crouches on one, knees spread apart on either side of his body like a grasshopper. I do the same, but my father does not. In the back are three black-and-white photographs of men, two in suits, one I vaguely recognize as a very young Yeh Yeh. The third wears a silk cap and sports a long, thin mustache and beard. Below these men is a small shrine with ceramic incense burners and artificial flowers and fruit.

Zhang begins talking, pointing around the room, at the narrow stairway, the doorways, the floor, and finally at the photographs. I keep looking to my father for translation, but he seems lost in thought. His photo could be on the wall as well, except that he doesn't have the look of superiority. The *lai cee* bag pokes out of one pants pocket and the handkerchief out of the other. He looks rumpled and tired and a bit sad. I realize this is his home and he knew these men on the walls. It is an entirely different experience for him. It is a history I wish I felt connected to, even if some of his memories aren't pleasant.

As Zhang continues to talk, people wander in and out of the building. A woman brings in a small, unpainted wood table and sets it in the center of the room. On it she places a steamed chicken, three red teacups and a teapot, apples in a green bowl, a dish of bean sprouts, and finally a pair of chopsticks. When she is done, Zhang quiets and rises. He walks to the table and stands in front of it, bolt upright. Then he bows from the waist three times, arms hanging loosely from start to finish. A line forms behind him, and each person bows in exactly the same way. There seems to be an order, oldest to youngest.

My father taps me on the shoulder and signals with his hand for me to follow him in line. "This is out of respect to your *yeh yeh*," he says. A little start goes through me, something almost electric, and I immediately feel shaky. The singing only I seem to hear returns. To the others the room is silent. Those who have gone before us stand and watch. My father's bowing looks like a carbon copy of everyone else's, and that's a good thing, I decide. I watch him carefully, the way there's no movement below the waist, straight legs. The arms do not swing, but follow the torso's controlled momentum.

It is my turn, and I step before the table. I feel light-headed. I try to keep my knees from buckling under me. I hold them firm as I make my first slow bow. My hands tremble, and at the bottom of my bow everything goes black.

42

The father considers his place in the village;
he recalls naming his son.

They never seemed as happy to see me as to see my money. I had returned a few times already. That trip with Westen was not any better. No, the minute we got out of the van, Zhang informed me of my responsibilities. By responsibilities, he meant how much money I should be giving the village.

Not much had changed since I was a boy. There was a new row of buildings. They were not as nice as the ones we once lived in. I told Zhang I did not have extra money. But they never believed that. I told him I did not think they spent their money wisely.

"*Women yijing jieshou jiaoxun,*" he said. "We have learned our lesson."

"*Wo bu tongyi,*" I told him, but he would not let me disagree. I had a duty, he said.

He tried to calm me because I was upset. Zhang was always good at that. Whenever there was a dispute in the village, he was called in. He seemed wise even in his younger years. "*Bu yao fannao,*" he said. I did not want to have an argument in front of Westen, even if he could not understand us. I simply nodded. *Would he have understood you, even if you had been speaking English?*

I knew what my function was that day. There was a price for bringing Westen to the village. I had prepared dozens of *lai cee*. I might have given them one lump sum, but this way was less crass. I knew they would pool it together for something. Perhaps the bridge they were talking about.

There was no romance in this trip for me. It was not my village anymore. It was always hard for me not to think that had my family stayed, the Communists would likely have killed us. Yi Po remained there for many years. She told stories of landowners being tied up and led into the hills. Many did not come back. Her life was not easy. The villagers could not be kind to her for fear of reprisal. She lived alone and worked alone. *You ended up with the same life.*

But the villagers continued to honor our family name. Papá would not be pleased if I did not represent us with dignity, no matter the cost. Each year I sent money. Each visit I brought money. I did not complain to them. In a way, I felt that this was how the Communists might have wanted it. The landowners returning money to the villagers. My work was part of their collective effort.

One thing I learned as an American was that it was acceptable to be outwardly angry. Protest in almost any situation was respected. Even if it was an annoyance. Returning to the village required that I throw a switch. When I handed out *lai cee* to people I mostly did not know, I had to remind myself not to be angry. They pushed and shoved. Some of them called out my name. Some of them called out Papá's, as if my hands were his. The only one I was happy to help was young Du. I knew his father's father well. He was a good man. The last time I saw him was just after the accident. He was four months old. His father was doing repairs to the roof of their home, and a rafter broke loose and struck Du in the head. They said he never cried. Just gazed into the air for days.

When I saw Du in his parents' bed, his expression was fixed.

He looked stunned. His mother said he had hardly eaten. Some of the villagers suggested they give him to an orphanage. But his parents refused. Du obviously didn't have much potential. But love is not linked to productivity. *Then what is it linked to? Why don't you have the answer to that?*

I could never have given Westen up when he was born. Even under the circumstances of Celia's rape. They kept him in the hospital for three days. His breathing was abnormal. There was no rhythm to it. But his lungs strengthened and we brought him home. Oh, Westen was beautiful. He was born with a thick head of hair. His skin was smooth and olive. When his tiny fingers grabbed mine, they gave off a surprising warmth.

We sat in the living room for hours that first day. Celia lay on the used green couch her parents gave us because we could afford so little then. I knelt on the floor next to her. She wore a blue terry-cloth robe. Westen was swaddled in a pink blanket. Only he was not Westen at that point. We had not yet named him. For some reason we expected a girl. Her name would have been Renée Ling Chan. For a son we were not so certain. Sitting on the couch, holding her son's hand, Celia halfheartedly offered Wesley, her father's name.

"Close," I said. We both looked at our tiny baby. He was beautiful, if thin. He looked a bit hurt, even. It made me think of a passage by Remarque I had to learn at the boys' school in Hong Kong. "How about Westen," I said.

Celia looked up in thought. "That's nice." Then she spelled it out loud "W-E-S-T-O-N?"

"No," I corrected her. "It comes from *Im Westen Nichts Neues. All Quiet on the Western Front.*"

"You're so smart," she said. She kissed me on the forehead.

I didn't tell Celia about how Westen reminded me of the passage I had to recite for my class when we were trying to perfect our English:

Monotonously the lorries sway, monotonously come the calls, monotonously falls the rain. It falls on our heads and on the heads of the dead up the line, on the body of the little recruit with the wound that is so much too big for his hip; it falls on Kemmerich's grave; it falls in our hearts.

43

The father revives the son;
he translates honor.

Westen fainted. I turned him over and put his head in my lap. He came to quickly. Someone brought one of our bottles of water. "What happened?" he asked.

"*Ni yinggai daoqian,*" I said to him. He did not respond. Then I realized I had spoken Chinese to him. "You should apologize."

"Tell them the heat got to me," he said, sitting up. "But the truth is I'm nervous as hell."

I was glad to hear this. Westen always seemed so calm and detached. "Yes. Yes," I said. I stood up and told everyone that my son was overcome by the moment of meeting all of them. Also that he just now realized his lineage.

"What did they say?" he asked me as everyone nodded.

"Drink plenty of water."

44

The son notices an absence of female children;
he visits a home with his father.

Ming walks to me and reaches out for my hand. Her white
dress with red trim is surprisingly clean, almost as if she's pro-
tected in a bubble. "Go ahead and look around," my father says.
"They want to talk to me. But stay cool if you can." I take
Ming's hand and she leads me outside, where it is much brighter
than I remember. My eyes adjust. The air smells of burning
straw, buttery, and somewhere I hear a baby crying. Ming lets go
of my hand and keeps walking. Behind us, a group of children
about her age follow. We are headed to a pair of trees about fifty
feet away, where the road dead-ends.

As we get closer, Ming points to a concrete slab with a
rounded center defined by an inch-high lip. The two trees soon
fill with clamoring children. Ming motions me forward. At first
it looks like an uncapped hole. But it's a well, the concrete walls
quiet and green. The water itself is perfectly clear. Ming hands
me an aluminum saucepan. We brought bottled water to avoid
getting sick, but I don't want to offend these children, so I dip
into the well and drink. "Thank you," I say to Ming. The children in the trees cheer their approval. Some of them are eating
fruit from the closest tree, guava.

I look at Ming in her bright little dress and then back to the trees—seven boys, all wearing cartoon-print shirts with Chinese writing. Ming is the only girl, and I can't think of any other girls I've seen since we arrived. I've watched the reports on television about the one-child policy, the baby girls left on sidewalks for someone to find, the orphanages bulging with girl children. I wonder if that's at work here.

I notice the heat creeping up on me again, so I dip the pan into the water and pour it over my head. The boys in the tree laugh. "Does anyone here speak English?" I ask. One boy who looks the oldest, maybe twelve, jumps out of the tree. His black hair sticks up in all directions, and he rubs his hands across the ridiculous figure of a dog on his shirt. "Do you speak English?" I ask again.

"English," he says with a slight *r* sound to the *l*.

"Where are all the little girls?"

"Nixon," he says. "Ford. Reagan. Carter." He counts on his fingers.

I join. "Carter. Reagan."

Ming takes me by the hand again as if she's my designated tour guide, and the group of us walk back toward the family building. A trio of orange chickens passes in front, all of them with their head feathers dyed a curious shade of pink. The women have resumed sifting the rice on the drying pads, scooting about in it as the various chickens peck at the grains. I try to imagine my father living here, working in the fields. I think of him as one of these little boys with the cartoon shirts. But I can't see him beyond who he is today.

I stand still and look again out at the fields. In just a few places the rice is completely harvested, leaving behind brown, soggy plots of mud. They stand out like revealed secrets. This is the problem with my father and me; we show each other how we've ripened, but not where our roots lie. It's as if delay and disclosure are the same thing, and I'm exhausted by the process.

The remedy isn't as simple as a trip to a village. We have failed to show ourselves, as if our pasts are sealed tight from one another and all we really represent is missing history.

My father eventually meets me and the children at the door of the family building. "Feel better?" he asks. I nod. But he is the one who does not look good. His skin is pale and his eyes are red, not from tears, I think, but stress. "Would you like to see inside a house?"

"I suppose," I say.

He puts his arm across my shoulder. "Overwhelmed?"

"By a few things." I shrug him off, indicating that I'm hot. "By the way, where are all the girls?"

My father looks around us as we walk. I know he can't help noticing what I see. "At school?"

"They don't educate boys here?"

"It's not our business, Westen." With that, he changes the subject by pointing at a white paper lantern in the doorway of one of the buildings. "That means they are in mourning." He speaks to Zhang, who shakes his head. "Their oldest son died."

Waiting at one of the houses is a woman in her thirties and a man about the same age. Ming runs to them and hugs the woman—her mother, I guess. All three have bright white smiles set in wide faces. I'm introduced. "These are your cousins," my father says, but he offers no individual introductions.

"So many cousins, no names," I say.

"No. No. It's just easier to explain that way. Besides, you won't remember them anyway."

45

The son discovers photos of himself;
he compares his life with the village.

Another pair of young chickens crosses our paths, one stained with red, the other not. I try to come up with the meaning. Red-dyed chickens are yin and the others are yang. Or maybe these dyed chickens were part of a fertility ceremony to ensure good egg laying. The red symbolizes the blood of a healthy hen. I ask my father, "What kind of ceremony do those red-headed chickens go through?"

He chuckles and translates to our relatives and they join him in laughter. "No. No," he says. "They do that to figure out who owns which chicken."

The house we enter, identical to many along a row in the village, has two levels. The bottom level has a stone floor, single beds pushed to the walls, and a washbasin with a metal pitcher beside it. Next to that is a built-in woodstove, the once brightly painted brick in reds and greens. There are round cutouts on the blackened tile stovetop for a large wok and two pans. In the loft is a small shrine with a red light. My father pats his forehead with a handkerchief and our hostess immediately turns on the overhead fan. No one is sweating but my father and me, and the vague circulation is small relief. I follow the single exposed wire from the fan to the switch and then out through a back window, where I'm surprised to see miles of high-tension power lines, something I'd somehow missed when we drove in. Maybe because I was looking for "primitive" China, trying to re-create my father's childhood.

"How did you stand all this heat when you lived here?" I ask.

My father shakes his head. "I don't know. Of course, we stayed in the city a great deal. Your *yeh yeh* had business there, so we kept an apartment above a sewing store."

I spot something on the wall over my father's shoulder: a collage of photos, some in color and some in black and white. Two of them are distinctly me as a child, one I've seen before, the one with the blue jumper pajamas and the Santa hat. I point subtly, and my father looks. I cannot see his expression, but when he turns back to me he nods softly, matter-of-factly, as if of course my photo would be on that wall.

Yi Po is talking, sounding gruff like she is giving orders, pointing to different items in the house. There's an old television and a radio and a single clear lightbulb hanging from a cord wrapped around a wood beam. Everyone is nodding and I can't tell if they're interested or just being polite.

"In case you're wondering," my father whispers, "Yi Po is telling everyone how easy it is in the village compared to when she was a little girl."

"Of course," I say, looking around. "They're practically rich."

A man I haven't met steps behind my father and whispers something in his ear, making my father squint as his glasses slip down his nose.

"What did he say?" I ask.

"He says, '*Ta ke yi huo dao yibai sui.*' Which means she'll live to be a hundred. But it's the way he said it."

I feel a bit uncomfortable gawking at someone's home. It's not a garden or a temple. There are no vendors outside with

T-shirts or trinkets. People live here, people who may be related to me. Fortunately, Zhang grabs a wood chair and drags it across the floor to a side entrance. He talks to my father, motioning him to watch. Zhang holds a very broad piece of bamboo about three feet long. Half of a plastic bottle is attached to its side, with a thin tube rising out of the center. Zhang strikes a long match and lights this pipe.

"Water pipe," my father says. Zhang puffs on the end of the bamboo, his mouth pressed into the wide opening, cheeks tight, as if he were a jazz musician. Clean white smoke billows from the pipe and Zhang looks up, eyes glassy from effort. The smoke smells like a grass fire, a dry sweetness like the brush piles Uncle Cane and I burned every year in late summer.

I step outside and walk beyond the buildings while Zhang performs. My excursion takes me next to the drying pads, where some of the boys are chasing each other, running over the rice the women have spread out so neatly. Beyond them is the small reservoir, the surface faceted by a southern breeze. Behind me are the buildings. This is a place that begins and ends with water. The air is thick with it. Everything is wet, even the buildings are crumbling from the elements. The once-ornate trim has dulled and fallen away in many places.

The setting sun casts the eroding buildings in a brittle yellow. I hear my father and the others coming out of the house, talking loudly. They lead Yi Po and my cousin toward the van, and I follow. "Are we leaving?" I ask.

My father turns and shakes his head. "We're going to stay the night, and Yi Po will meet us in the city tomorrow morning. They're giving us a dinner in our honor tonight."

"Why doesn't Yi Po just stay here too? She's so pushy."

"Come here," my father says. He takes me by the arm as Yi Po and the others stand at the van, talking. "They're arguing about money." He leads me behind the family building. The foliage here is surprisingly dense and tropical, wild. Attached to the back of the building is a brick shack with a crooked tile roof and a wood door. "They made Yi Po live there for twenty years," my father says.

"By herself?" I walk closer to the building, weeds slapping at my legs. The building is probably ten by fifteen feet and without windows.

"The villagers were afraid to treat her too well for fear they might call attention to the fact she was part of a landowning family."

"So they ostracized her?"

"No. No. It was either this or maybe being killed."

For some reason it occurs to me just now that Yi Po is related to me in the same way as Great-Aunt Catherine. I try to imagine the woman who raised me living in this shack, try to imagine her without peach-colored gladiolus in spring, or without a pitchfork and pine-needle mulch in late fall. I can only think of her moving in a space of her own choice, even with Uncle Cane on his worst days. I recall, in this Canton heat, the warm summer week when I was fifteen. Aunt Catherine and I had tea each morning under the dying apple tree and we traded off reading aloud from *To Kill a Mockingbird*. I recall the luxury of it, time standing still for us.

My father behind me, we walk back toward the van, which is ready to leave. "Be careful about judging people without knowing all their history," he says.

46

The father and son spend a night in the village;
they decide to talk to each other.

After a long dinner, my father and I lie in beds on opposite sides of the room. Even though it is close to midnight, the air is still warm and sticky, and I lie on my wood bed in my underwear. "They must've spent a load of money on us tonight," I say into the darkness.

"They're not dumb," my father replies, and I hear him rustling in his bed. "It's an investment."

"Are you giving them anything for the bridge?"

"Yes. Yes. But not as much as they want." I hear my father sit up and pad across the floor. He pulls the chain for the light hanging in the center of the room. At first the light is startlingly bright, a clear, intense bulb. Then I realize my father is standing naked, the skin of his torso nearly flawless, yellowish brown, the nipples distinctly dark with three- or four-inch-long black hairs sprouting from each one. His abdomen is surprisingly flat, almost muscular, and his penis and testicles hang loose and darkly nested in pubic hair.

"You want me to walk on your back?" I joke, but he does not react.

"No, no. In the morning I am taking you on a boat into the

city and then we will take the hydrofoil to Hong Kong and this will all be over."

I sit up. "What are you talking about?"

My father walks to the single chair in the room, where he's placed his clothes, and puts on his gray boxers. He sits back on his bed. I can tell that without his glasses he can't see me well. His eyes look unfocused and bare. "I've been thinking this was all a mistake. I was ignorant to think that this trip would mean something to you." He winces as if he's in pain and lies down on his bed. "You haven't made a family. I should have taken that as a sign."

Now it's my turn to get up. I set his clothes on the floor and place the chair next to him, sitting. My shadow covers his small body and his eyes shine with reflected light. I think of all the years I spent wanting my father to be desperate for me, wanting to feel him want me. For how long did I imagine him taking me back, in Blue Falls or San Diego? How many days did I walk out of school and look at all the children being picked up by their parents and think that maybe my father might be one of them? And here he is wanting something from me, wanting me back after I've learned not to expect anything from him. "You did leave me," I say, touching his arm. It is warm and trembling. "It's not easy."

"I don't know what to tell you, Westen. I only have my own experience. Your *yeh yeh* and I were as close as a Chinese father and son can be. But he did not want me to marry your mother."

"But you did anyway," I say.

"He all but cut me off because of it. When he died I was not sad that my father was gone, but that we had wasted all that time harboring old wounds. That kind of sadness does not leave you."

I don't know what to say. I can't lie and say all is forgiven. "I'm grateful for this trip," I say carefully. "But it's also brought up a lot more questions than answers. For one thing, I came here thinking that I was half Chinese, and I don't even know if that's true now." As I say this, I understand there's a simple solution, the thing we're not saying, the thing we're both afraid of.

"You know," my father says, "on this entire trip you haven't seriously addressed me as 'Dad' or 'Father' or even said my name."

"I hadn't noticed," I say, but he's right.

"You used to call me 'Daddy.' "

"You used to be my dad." And this is the problem, I realize. It *is* spite.

"So what am I now?"

This is not the man I want to be angry with. It's the same body, but of course he's changed. And I understand that I'm largely upset because I'll never have the satisfaction of confronting the version of my father I remember all those years back. "I have no idea."

"Yes, yes. You have the right to take that away from me. But I will tell you this. I've never given up on the idea that you are my son. Even when I had every reason to question it."

"This is silly," I say. "I don't want to fight with you. I just want you to understand."

My father watches me for a clearer explanation. He is half-naked and vulnerable-looking.

I form the words slowly. "I want you to understand that living with Great-Aunt Catherine and Uncle Cane was wonderful. I had a good life. But I also want you to know that I was always aware things were not the same as they would have been. I waited for you to come back for a long time. Years. Maybe I've never stopped waiting."

My father's lips are closed and his head nods almost imperceptibly. "If this were one of my businesses, I would cut a check. Settle. I know I am twenty-five years too late, and I am sorry for that. I loved your mother. I loved you. No amount of money I have made has fixed the mistakes I made with my family." My father pauses, beginning to cry, smiling in embarrassment. But I'm right behind him, crying as well. "But if you take anything away from this trip," he begins again, "please understand that I never forgot you and it's been a constant punishment that I gave you up."

We are not loud, but the tears come from both us. I am thinking of all these wasted years. All the anger. And for some reason I am thinking of the people I've kept at arm's length, afraid to get too close, even Gideon, whom I cared for so much. I think of this and Aunt Catherine's advice that I dismissed. There have been a lot of wrong turns and I am wondering now just how to fix it all.

I stand and go to my bed. It's obvious my father and I are not going to be able to say anything more to each other tonight. The only sound is the palpable buzz of the lightbulb, which my father approaches one more time. "Good night, son," he says, pulling on the chain, plunging both of us into darkness once again.

The father says good-bye to the village a final time;
he decides on a name for the bridge he will pay for.

I hardly slept. Yes, but it was a good thing.

I knew when Westen and I left that it would be my last visit to the village. It was not my home any longer. The morning was dark. A thin fog hung over the river. The three of us sat in the boat, Zhang, Westen, and I. Without a van to return to the city, this was the surest, fastest mode of transportation. Yes, and maybe better to allow the village to fade away as the current separates us. Zhang handed me a silver flask. *"Qu hanqi de donxi,"* he said. He was a good negotiator. I understood he was only riding with us to make sure he secured a promise of money from me. *Is there a price for legacy, for family?*

"No. No. It isn't cold at all," I told him, and handed the flask back. He tapped Westen on the shoulder, making a drinking signal. "To take the cold off," I said.

Westen took a drink, and gasped. "Whoa," he said.

"What did you expect, milk?"

"You zhouyoue chenjiu de yi nian," Zhang said, taking a drink himself and screwing the cap on. I told him every year is a vintage year when you make the stuff yourself. The boatman hopped back onto shore for his cigarettes and disappeared into the gray. As a child, I swam in this river many times, but never

took a boat ride. Papá told us not to trust anyone who offered us passage. And above all, to never tell a stranger we were the children of a landowner.

The boatman returned. His cigarette was lit. The smoke was hardly distinguishable from the fog. We pushed off and the engine chugged to life. The boat was flat and wide. It was mostly used for loads of vegetables and rice. "How far?" Westen asked.

"Not far at all," I said. I looked back at the shore. No, I would never be that close to the village again. The physical pain inside me told me this was it. I was never one to be sentimental, but I imagined Papá and Ma on the shore waving good-bye. Westen and Zhang could not see me. I let myself cry, yes. When my life started, everything seemed so certain. I came from a good family. We were good landlords. Papá made sure we received a fine education and there was always food on the table. Every night we ate together, Papá's large blue bowl practically overflowing with rice. Even when the Communists came and we lost nearly everything, Papá kept us in good Hong Kong schools. I assumed we were a family destined always to be successful. *These are the memories you stole from your son.*

Somewhere along the line I did not hold up to the promise. I ignored Papá and married an American. *She died and you gave up your son.* I ended up with nothing that mattered except an apartment and enough cash to maybe build a bridge. Even at that, I knew my photo would never hang in the building dedicated to our family name.

I looked at Westen. His arms were crossed and his eyes closed. The morning sun barely cast light on his face. I could see his mother there. Celia was so beautiful when she was sleeping. Yes, yes, when the tension of the hospital slipped away and she dreamed. The boat rocked slightly and Westen swayed with it. He was a handsome young man. There was little I could give him, now, I thought. But I had promised Celia I would treat him like my son no matter what.

I thought of that promise sitting with Zhang, who wanted a bridge, and Westen, who wanted a father and a history. We floated down the river in silence. The only sounds were our engine and the hellos from other boats that passed us. As we approached Sun Cheung, I turned to Zhang, who had fallen asleep on Westen's shoulder. Somehow they made a good pair. I shook Zhang, trying not to wake Westen too. He yawned and complained about being stiff. "*Wo hunshen jiang yin,*" he said. I shushed him and explained what I planned to do for the village. Yes, I would send the money for the bridge. I only had one stipulation. They had to name it after Westen.

But also with that decision, I understood something important about Westen and me. I was like an investor wanting to buy stock in a company about which I knew nothing. Certainly I could see the outside, the hurt surface. But regret and resentment are masks. This is the defense men are taught. It seemed as true about him as it was of me—or anyone. To get past that, you have to *want* to know, to learn not just what he volunteers, not only what is easy for him to say. In order to fully understand, you first have to know what a man harbors.

The father and son leave the mainland;
they say good-bye to a relative.

Yi Po has a surprise for us: our stolen luggage, which is sitting
at her feet. The hotel did not explain the circumstances of its return, relayed no apology. Yi Po tells my father she simply got a
call from a hotel in Guangzhou that the luggage had been for-
warded to them. She arranged for a relative to drive it to Sun
Cheung. My father's bandages and over-the-counter medicines
appear untouched. "Is it there?" my father asks. I know what he
is asking and I nod. Mrs. Cheung's box.

Yi Po is confused by our search, but she is surprisingly misty-
eyed. She is handsome today in the oddly bright morning. There
is fog, but it has nearly burned away. Her gray hair shines; a few
strands have escaped from her low, tight bun. They flutter about
her face in the breeze, her age-spotted but delicate hands pushing
them aside. As she speaks to my father, she runs down a list, ticking off the items on her fingers. With each one, my father offers
an affirmative grunt. He takes out his curse pad and flips to the
only blank page left. As he writes, Yi Po reaches into her pocket
and produces a money clip, counting out several yuan. But my father waves it off and there is a brief ballet between them of offer
and refusal until she finally puts her money away.

My father taps my shoulder and points to a storefront with

large Chinese characters painted on the glass windows. "Last chance," he says.

"For what?"

"They serve dog."

"If only I'd known," I say. "I started the no-canine diet yesterday."

Yi Po turns to see what we are talking about. She shakes her head and speaks to my father very firmly, as if she doesn't approve.

My father translates reluctantly. "She knows a better place."

Yi Po picks up one of our heavier bags and walks inside the hydrofoil terminal. My father and I take the remainder and catch up. Then she sets the bag at the end of the passport line and turns. Grabbing my father's hands, she looks directly into his eyes and speaks more softly than anyone I've heard in China. Her voice is oddly powdery, yet purposeful. This time my father responds at length. It appears as if he's holding her hands as much as she's holding his. Tears form in both their eyes and I turn around while they finish their good-bye. When they are done, Yi Po pats me on the back and squeezes my hand, but she does not look at me. I can tell she is crying. My father, too, is flushed with tears. "What is all that about?" I ask.

"When you get older," my father says, his voice high and sniffling, "every time you say good-bye seems like the final time."

The father and son begin a game of cards;
the son recounts a moment of crisis.

It is a day of boats, first the trip this morning, and now the hydrofoil. It will take four hours to get to Hong Kong. My father and I take table seats next to a window in the galley area. On busier days, I imagine this would not be possible, but today there are probably fewer than fifty people on the hydrofoil. My father sits across from me, wet-eyed but calming down. He looks out the window, eyes fixed. A single rogue strand of black hair is pasted to his temple and across his eyebrow. He takes an immensely deep breath and sits back in his seat, looking straight at me with a big, relieved expression. "We're alone, Westen."

"We've been alone before," I say.

"No. No. We are not part of a tour. We are not being dragged around by family. We are on our own." His voice matches his words; it sounds relieved and liberated.

"So what now?" I say.

"Maybe we should just be honest now. Fill in some history," my father says.

"That sounds right," I say, though I'm really thinking we are so close to the finish line, and is this really the time and place to begin? "Can we handle a heavy conversation in front of all these strangers?"

"Yes, yes. But let's promise no hard feelings. We'll make a game out of it. A little gambling. Something to fill our time while we're waiting. Break the ice." He pulls out a brand-new deck of cards and slaps the sepia-colored, cellophane-wrapped package on the table. "Hi-Lo," he says.

"What are the stakes?"

"Winner gets to ask the loser anything."

"We're playing for memories?"

"We're playing for everything. Let's get all the old mess out of the way," my father says, taking the cards out of the package. "I apologize for these. Someone gave them to me." He shows me that each card has the face of a movie star. The cards shudder in soft undulation as they rainbow together in the shuffle. He sets the cards in front of me and I cut about a third off the top and turn them over. King of diamonds, Laurence Olivier. "Hamlet. Very good," my father says taking the next card. "King of spades. Charles Laughton."

"*Mutiny on the Bounty,*" I say. He shuffles again. I turn over Eleanor Powell, three of clubs.

"Too bad. Errol Flynn, jack of hearts." He waves the card at me. It's a young Flynn as Robin Hood, green tunic, feathered arrows peeking over his shoulder. "First question: How old were you when you decided to hate me?"

I'm a little startled by the frankness of the question and the relative calm with which it is asked. "This is a stupid game. I didn't even know the bet before we played. Anyway, I don't hate you," I say.

"We'll go again," my father says, picking up the cards and shuffling. Outside, the shoreline passes quickly. A group of barely clothed children stands in the shallows and wave as we go by. "What's your bet?"

"Okay," I say. "I want to know how your life would have been different if you'd decided to keep me." He sets the cards in front of me, and I cut to George Raft in a dark fedora, four of diamonds. He shows the eight of diamonds, Ginger Rogers.

Thinking of what I could say, I pause to consider whether there is any one moment I can pinpoint. I look at my father. He looks serious, his dark eyes focused and still. There are lots of things I could say. I recall being at the drugstore when I was young, watching a boy point to a spool of kite string and his father paying for it. I did not have a kite, nor did I want one. But I do remember being jealous because that boy had a father. I consider whether I should tell this, whether such a simple thing will make sense to my father. I'm not sure I can explain how many small moments like this kept adding up. "It wasn't one big incident or any specific time," I finally say. I take a breath because I'm understanding this myself just as I say it, and the simplicity feels awkward. "The problem is, you just weren't there."

The father continues a streak;
he thinks of his wife and a lie.

No, I did not think the card game through before I suggested it. But we were into it and I was not going to back out. Westen had resented me for a lot longer than I thought. I was not sure I could ever compensate for what I had done to him as a boy. But I think he was saying I was too late.

We played another round of Hi-Lo. I was embarrassed to use those cards. I had not known they had the faces of movie stars before we started. Westen's bet stood. He wanted me to tell him what I thought life would have been like if I had kept him. I tried to think of something less confrontational. "Tell me about your best day with your aunt," I said.

We cut the cards. Westen took the eight of spades. It was Sylvia Sidney. "I've never heard of her," Westen said.

"I think she was in *An American Tragedy*," I said. "In the thirties." My card was the ace of diamonds.

"That one I know," Westen said. "Olivia de Havilland. *Gone With the Wind*."

I waited. Westen put his hand on his chin. "My best day," he said. "It was the year before Uncle Cane died, and I was back from Los Angeles. It was early summer and Blue Falls was beautiful that year. Somehow Aunt Catherine persuaded Uncle Cane to go on a picnic, and the three of us found a place just above the river. By then he wasn't drinking anymore, and the two of them were getting along pretty well.

"I remember we had cold fried chicken and Aunt Catherine's special iced tea flavored with wild raspberry. It turned out they'd invited me for a reason. 'You've been a son to us,' Aunt Catherine said, and Uncle Cane patted me on the back. 'We want you to have the property when we're gone.'

"Both of them were teary-eyed, and I was flat-out crying. It wasn't the idea that I was inheriting something, it's just that for the first time in all those years I knew I had a family. I wasn't just some castoff. And it wasn't their fault it took so long, it was mine." He nodded and looked straight at me. "Yeah. I'd have to say that was my best day."

I wanted to tell him right then about the bridge. I was leaving him something too. But it seemed like a poor time, a facsimile. I shuffled. As long as we were in it that deep, I threw another hard bet. "So what was your worst time?" His stood. Three of hearts for him. Jeanette MacDonald. It appeared as if I was going to win again, but I turned over Joan Bennett, the two of hearts. *The time for games was when he was a boy.*

"Finally I win," he said, and paused. "What would your life have been like if you'd kept me?"

"Yes. Yes. I've thought about this a great deal," I said. "It would have been hard for both of us. We would have stayed in Los Angeles. I would have had to find a different job so I could be home when you were finished with school. We wouldn't have had much money. Maybe you would have been one of those latchkey kids they used to talk about.

"That's all the hard part. The other side of the coin is that we would have been together. We would have made it." I took a breath. Outside, the shore was green with bamboo. "You wouldn't have needed a picnic and an inheritance to know you belonged to a family." I looked at Westen. "I'm sorry."

Yes, if he had said he forgave me right then, the trip would have been worth it. But he simply grabbed the cards. "My turn," he said. "Same bet as yours. What was your worst time?" I cut the cards and showed Douglas Fairbanks in a pirate costume. Jack of clubs. Westen turned over the queen of hearts. Bette Davis.

I knew the answer, but I did not know whether I should tell him. I took a deep breath and tried to explain. Things were tense between me and his mother. It was after she found out she was pregnant. We were back together. We did not know for sure if it was my baby, no. We took a trip up the coast to Morro Bay to try to relax and figure things out. Dusty Springfield was on the radio when we arrived. Morro Rock stood unchanged and solid. Six hundred feet of solitary rock. It was almost sunset, so we decided to climb out on the jetty before going to the motel.

Westen's mother was a natural athlete. She scrambled over the rocks like a professional. She got to the end well before I did, and found a flat place for us to sit. I have never been a poetic man, but I remember everything about that moment. The waves crashed a few feet below us. The sea spray was cold and salty. The sky was orange. Behind us was the town and the power plant with its three huge smokestacks. "It's a child's game," Celia said, looking at the plant. She had mentioned before how awful she thought it was that they'd put the power plant next to the rock, as if it could compete in stature. "Someday they'll find out it's like Paper, Rock, Scissors. Rock beats Smokestacks, Ocean beats Rock."

Celia let her hair down and the wind pushed it back. She put her arm around my waist and lay her head on my shoulder. "I know you're not sure about the baby," she said. "But I am. I want to have it."

"No. No," I said. "It's not that. I'm not sure about me. This is all my fault. I let you down."

Westen stopped me with his hand. "You two were actually having a conversation about whether or not to keep me?"

"We are being honest, right?" I said. "I am trying to tell you everything. Your mother was very strong. There was never any doubt she was going to have you. The only doubt was whether I was going to be there." *You are a man of doubt still.*

I began telling the story again. When Celia saw I was nervous, she straightened up. "Xin," she said. "You do not get to have my pain. Those men raped me, not you."

"I failed," I said.

"I didn't marry you for protection."

"But a husband should be strong."

She cut me off. The sun was full in her face. "A husband should be what he is. Now, I want this baby. Do you?"

A heron flapped past us. The sun was misshapen and just then hitting the ocean. "Yes," I said. It was the biggest lie I've ever told. I did not know if I could love a baby that wasn't mine. This is not easy to admit even now, but it's true. We leaned against the rocks behind us. A few brown pelicans flew low over the waves. "I'll always be here for you and our baby," I said. That was the second biggest lie I've ever told.

When I finished the story, Westen was silent, setting the cards he held on the table before standing up. "I need a break," he said, and started to go. Then he turned around. "We should have played this game a long time ago. Here's a freebie. My worst day was years ago at a bookstore in L.A. I saw you there.

"It was a late afternoon on Sunset Boulevard. That place with bookshelves that go all the way to the ceiling." I knew the one he spoke of.

"I stepped up a few rungs on a ladder to look at a book on racing pigeons. A man came around the corner and stood below me, running his finger along the base of the books. It was you. I was paralyzed on that ladder. The book on pigeons slipped out of my hands. You picked it up and handed it to me. 'Good thing I wasn't a foot closer,' you said. Then you turned and went back around the corner. I stayed on the ladder. I couldn't believe you didn't recognize me."

"I vaguely remember this," I said. "But you were an adult by then. How could I know?"

"I'm not finished. So then you came back. 'I'm sorry,' you said. 'I'm looking for a book of T'ang poems. Do you have anything like that?' I remember how upset I was, but all I could manage was 'I don't work here.' With that, I jumped off the ladder and ran out the door."

After his story, Westen walked away. I didn't have a precise recollection what he was talking about but I remembered such an exchange in a hazy kind of way. To me he had been just an odd young man in a bookstore.

No, I was not a good father after I left him. Even at the proximity he described in the bookstore, I was a failure. *You never thought in all those years to ask Catherine for photographs, no.*

We were over halfway to Hong Kong. My body and mind were holding out but giving in. That old man who examined me in Chinatown, who lay his hands on my shoulder and told me to bring Westen with me to China, was wrong. We were opening old wounds, not healing them.

51

The son questions a reconciliation;
he recognizes his confusion.

I stand on the deck of the hydrofoil, hanging on to a centered railing, my back to the wind. I've this odd feeling of relief, having told my father something even I didn't realize was such an important part of my list of resentments. At the time, for sure, it was an event that spurred Gideon to lecture me on contacting my father. Still, I thought I'd packed it away.

The river is wide and wrinkled-looking, like a span of greenish brown cloth. Our wake cuts through it as if we are the tab of an endless zipper. I'm glad to be outside. This trip reminds me of coming home through Blue Falls one winter and seeing Mildred Pogue's white Cadillac turned over and half collapsed. I drove by slowly, without even thinking about it, just to catch a glimpse of tragedy. I feel this way now, as if my father and I are moving in slow motion, as if I'm looking at the two of us from the outside, as if I am the first on the scene, no ambulances, no police cars, only me gawking, hoping for a little blood and at the same time hoping for nothing.

I sit down. The clouds are flung in unfamiliar patterns, yet each formation is precise and perfectly sunlit. It seems like the kind of day set aside for truth, a conjunction of elements that will allow nothing else. I hear footsteps and my father sits next to me. "I thought I would take a break too," he says. We are both quiet for a long time. "Westen," he says finally, "why don't you get it all out at once? Just tell me how awful you think I am and get it over with."

I hear age in his voice. I can't think of anything except a familiar theme, the one that's run in my head all these years like a tape on a loop. So I start. "At the very least you shouldn't have let them change my name."

"That was unavoidable," my father says, sounding like a surgeon after an unsuccessful operation.

The space between us is livid with brightness. "It was your name too."

"I think I've told you. Your aunt and I thought children would tease you with a Chinese last name. We were trying to minimize the damage." My father reaches into his breast pocket and I can tell he's looking for cigarettes. "Old habit," he says sheepishly.

"You didn't solve anything," I say.

"Your last name hardly seems like the most important issue between us, Westen." My father looks over the top of his glasses like a teacher giving a good student a disappointing test result.

"What about my Chinese name?" I offer before I go silent. I think of two names: Chan and Gray. On a white page the space is the same. What's the difference, really? How can I explain the personal nuance, the feeling that a signature isn't the whole truth? I look at my father harder as a cloud passes over the sun and he grows darker.

"I thought I was doing the right thing." My father zips his jacket against the wind. "I made sure you had a family. Which is more than I've had for the last twenty-five years." He stands and invites me downstairs with a gesture of his head.

"In a while," I say. Our ship passes a large boat with a trail of silver smoke whipping behind it like a silk scarf. The smell of cooking is surprisingly strong, something specifically sweet and almost stinging, like saffron and hot mustard. I notice we are at the mouth of the river—the green landscape is diminishing. Mainland China is behind us. I sit alone, listening to the gusts whistling over the ship until I feel I hear nothing. The brashness of this music runs over me like voices in a choir, voices I can't yet comprehend. It is a language, I think, and if you could decode the wind, you could understand the Earth. Offering a parting and understated wave to the mainland, I stand for the final glimpse of what may or may not be the home of my ancestors. Either way, the feeling is the same. Has China failed me, or have I failed it?

The father and son resume their card game;
the son recounts a love's last moments with him.

M y father has returned to our table and sits alone, shuffling the cards. His jacket remains zipped, like a piece of armor. He looks at me without changing his somber expression. "Another round? I think we're getting somewhere."

"Why don't we just talk to each other?" I ask.

"We tried that."

"What's the bet?" I concede, sitting down.

He places his hands flat on the table and remains close-mouthed and tight-lipped. He scratches the back of his head, looking resigned and sad. "Let's agree that I have been the worst possible father. I did all the wrong things. That's clear. So, if I really want to understand you, tell me something else. Besides all the things between us, what is the most painful experience you have ever gone through?"

The minute he asks the question, I know the answer without a doubt. "*My* bet isn't so complicated: What do you want from me?" And even as we begin, I realize how pathetic we are for doing this.

"Fair enough," my father says. The cards rest exactly between us like an empty stage waiting for a tiny performer. "Be my guest."

"Marion Davies," I say. It's the ten of hearts. He turns up the ten of spades. Joan Crawford, a middle-aged version but not quite *Mildred Pierce*.

"You know," my father says, "one of the first movies your mother and I ever saw together was *What Ever Happened to Baby Jane?*"

"Doesn't seem like much of a date movie."

"It was a matinee and it was raining. Your mother could do a great imitation of Bette Davis. Something about fastening seat belts."

I have distinct memories of my mother, and movie star impressionist is not one of them. "That doesn't sound like Mom," I say. "She never did anything like that around me."

"Well, it's true. I bet you didn't know your mother liked horse racing."

"No," I say, but as it comes out, I vaguely remember a Kentucky Derby on television and my mother and father exchanging money afterwards. I shuffle the cards and hand them to him.

"No cut," he says, and I motion for him to start. He pulls the nine of clubs, a barely recognizable Barbara Stanwyck. I get Deanna Durbin, four of clubs. We sit for a moment in silence. I know I've lost, but I'm not sure if I want to follow through. My father looks at me and dips his head as if he can coax an answer out of me against my will.

"I don't really want to tell you this," I say.

"Why not?"

"Because it's personal and I don't want you to take it out of context. I don't even know if there *is* a context."

"Then why did you come back down here?" my father says. "Why did you start playing again? I think you want to talk to me but you are afraid to admit it." I look at him. His eyes are intensely black and pleading. Most of all, I think he's right, I do want to talk to my father. But maybe I want to be that eight-year-old boy sitting on his lap, not really accountable for anything.

"Okay," I say, trying to figure out where to begin telling him about that final week with Gideon. I am looking at a man who lost his wife, and I understand the one thing we have in common is love and death in the same story.

BY THAT FINAL March, Gideon and I had lived together four years. In Los Angeles it is not the weather that indicates spring; it's a Saturday afternoon in certain neighborhoods when the nylon car covers are taken out of trunks and slipped over vehicles, leaving the impression of cultivated rows of giant mushrooms lining the streets. The jacaranda in front of our house had just started dropping their purple flowers and sticky acids. There was something I admired about the indelible marks left by the falling petals. "It's because you don't own a car," Gideon said. By then he had been in and out of the hospital several times. He was lying in bed and wanted me to cover his Mustang, even though we both knew he would not drive again.

Gideon squinted his blue eyes at me as he always did when trying to decipher my logic. I saw his thin facial muscles working beneath nearly translucent, spotted skin. "Cover the car or the window, Westen. I don't want to watch it get eaten away."

"You *would* think of your car right now."

"It's better than thinking about a fucking bedpan. You'd understand if you ever learned to drive."

"I never have anywhere to go," I said, wishing that statement weren't as accurate as it was. I walked to the door and looked back at what had become solely his room. The deep mahogany stain of the bed and armoire deadened the light coming from the two windows. Gideon seemed to float over the dull golden haze of the oak floor. I never told him the nurse almost persuaded me to replace the four-poster with a hospital bed. I didn't have the heart to go through with it.

Gideon had been a remarkable case, in the hospital with pneumonia twice, the second time near death, and then out and working. And then he was in again because his kidneys were close to failure, and back home after only a couple of weeks. But the wasting away was something progressive and inescapable, like the meeting of tectonic plates, one side resisting, grudgingly slipping under the other. And that last time, a surprisingly simple case of dehydration.

I took care of him for a few days until he got his strength back, not knowing in that time he had made a decision for both of us. One morning I brought in his breakfast, even though he'd started walking around the house again. He was already dressed in dark wool pants and a pressed white shirt that sagged on his thin body. "Very handsome," I said.

"I feel like a well-dressed hobo." He sat at the edge of the bed and patted the place next to him. The room was warm and already smelled of the bacon and eggs I'd set on his dresser. "Let's have a talk," he said. "I want to move to the Silver Lake house."

"I guess we can do that," I said.

He put his hand on mine. It was surprisingly warm and moist. I looked down at its skin, vein-streaked with the incoherent shade of blue that strikes living room curtains at 2:00 a.m.

"No. Just me. I'm going to call my mother and have her come up."

"But . . . ," I said, and I had nothing to follow. Gideon looked softly into my eyes. He smiled, his skin running over cheekbones like the spoked ridges of a rice-paper parasol. I knew he had thought this through. He had talked a great deal about his mother lately, especially after their big family reunion in San Diego before he got sick.

"Westen," he said, "I want you to know that I love you. These last four years have been the happiest of my life. If someone had told me five years ago that I would settle down with one person and never have sex with him, I would have said they were crazy."

"I'm sorry about that," I said.

"I guess it was safer."

I stood up and went to the dresser with its cherry-framed mirror. Gideon's breakfast was almost cold, the bacon taking on a dullish red as the fat congealed, the meaty smell softening in the room. I watched Gideon over my shoulder in the mirror. He really did look as though he was wearing a much larger man's clothes. I felt guilty about appearing healthy. When he started losing weight, I wished my hair wasn't so black and my eyes distinctly hazel, things Gideon loved about me. I never told him I stopped working out because I hated the comparison between us.

"So what are you going to do?" he asked. "Call your family?"

"You're already here," I said.

Gideon stood up and walked to my side. He picked up a piece of bacon and took a bite. "In some ways I haven't been very good for you." He popped the rest of the bacon in his mouth and picked up the fork, poking the egg, the yolk running out like lava. He gave me a sly look. "For one thing, you still don't know how to make these over hard."

"And for another thing?"

"You don't have this father crap figured out by a long shot."

"I've got it figured out all right. And I don't want to talk about it now."

Picking up the second slice of bacon, Gideon brought it to my mouth. I nibbled a piece off the end, sucking the salt out of the meat instead of chewing. "Just let me tell you one thing," he said. "The biggest mistake I've made in my life was losing track of my family. Look at me. I'm practically the invisible man and

I'm calling my mother so she can take care of me. Where were all the phone calls to take her to dinner? Or to one of those stupid premieres? It's a friggin' waste."

I turned back to the dresser. "Your mother didn't *leave you*," I say.

"That argument only works for so long. Then you have to start thinking about what *you're* doing."

"Wes," he continued when I didn't respond, walking back to the bed. "You need to give me some credit. There have to be some perks that come with dying."

"Don't talk like that," I said.

Gideon took me by the shoulders so I would face him. "Look at me," he said. "This is the homestretch. I'm in the quiet land."

"What are you talking about?"

"Perspective. My life is full of silences now where I can think. It's like when we were staying in the desert and I just walked off. There's a whole quiet landscape I've found in my head where everything is so clear."

I put my hand on Gideon's leg. "That's good," I said.

"No. You don't get it. You don't have to be dying to think this way. The world is not as complicated as you make it."

I nodded, hearing Gideon but not listening.

He wanted to move out right away. I think he knew he didn't have much time. We spent the next few days gathering the things he thought he'd need, arranging for furniture to be stored. The Silver Lake house was already well equipped. In fact, it contained most of his personal mementos. It was a getaway and often a temporary rental for friends. There wasn't a day that I didn't spend time crying. It seemed like the worst time for me to be leaving, but I also knew he needed to be alone with his mother.

The bed was the last thing to go. My room had been completely cleaned out; what little I owned, I shipped to Blue Falls or stuffed into the car I'd just learned to drive. With my room empty, Gideon and I spent that final night together. I tried not to be emotional. We lay together, no curtains on the window, an orange streetlight tattooing shapes across our bed and onto the wall. "Are you going to be okay?" Gideon asked. He touched my hand and I turned to him, half his face concealed by the pillow, one eye sidelit as if it were a partly open doorway.

"Aren't I supposed to be asking that?" I said.

"I don't want you to see me when it gets really bad. I hate that you saw me in the hospital. That's not how I want you to remember us." He squeezed my hand. "God knows you're fucked up enough as it is."

"Now there's a sweet moment for me to carry through the years."

"Well, babe," he started, which is how he always began when he was trying to be sincere, "I haven't been that good for you in terms of you figuring out your shit. In a lot of ways, you're still like a little boy. If I had a wish for you, it would be that you would get ahold of your dad and do whatever you need to do there. I think a lot of this other stuff would just fall into place after that."

I put my finger to his dry lips. "I've had Aunt Catherine and you. A guy couldn't be luckier."

Gideon kissed my finger and moved it away. "Babe, you know it's true. You're incomplete." We were never physically intimate in all those years, but that final kiss has always been enough.

Neither of us said anything after that. Gideon fell asleep, and for a long time I just watched and listened. He inhaled fast, with extended, soft whistling coming with each exhalation. His skin was mottled by the light coming from the window, and I stared at it long enough that I began to imagine the colors fluctuating, septic reds briefly invading and then retreating to black. After a while I slipped out of bed and went to the window. The security light above the driveway lit an old eucalyptus, out of place in this neighborhood, its bark peeling away, revealing the revived shades of green beneath. I thought about what Gideon had said. I knew he was right. But it's taken me until now to feel like I can do anything about it.

I walked back to the bed and looked down at Gideon. He was a dark spot in the white of the bed linens. But then he opened his eyes calmly and reached out for my hand as I took his. "I know," he said. "You love me."

I AM NOT looking at my father when I tell this story. I'm watching the approaching island that rises both rocky and green out of the ocean. I am looking for the harbor. When I am no longer speaking, I turn and wait for a response, but he says nothing, as if he expects more to the story, as if I haven't given him closure.

"He died about a month later," I say. "His mother said they had a good few weeks together." A couple of weeks after the funeral, I went back to the house one last time. From the living room I could see the FOR SALE sign on the lawn. It was odd walking through that empty space, especially without Gideon. A house is really a private museum, made that way by its occupants, who are both curators and exhibits. Walking through ours for the last time, I realized I had come to expect shadows in certain places that were now simply bright and hollow.

My heels echoed as I went, finally, to Gideon's room. It was quiet, stripped of everything that might offer a memory except the vague outline on the wall where his Pissarro print had hung. It wasn't our house anymore.

. . .

MY FATHER REMAINS quiet. I wonder what he is thinking, if he'll ask questions about Margaret first, or Gideon, or what's happened since. I'm not certain what answers I have. Margaret so cleanly left me, did not answer my phone calls. I have always wanted to create a narrative about the man who lied to her about his heart. But now thinking back to how detached we were, how programmed by her religious beliefs, I wonder if she thinks of me as a mysterious blip on her radar, a narrow miss, like a fishing boat mistaken for a destroyer.

All these things rumble in my mind as I anticipate the barrage of questions my father surely has. But he simply reaches out and touches my hand and speaks softly as if we are suddenly allied, saying, "So, you lost someone too."

53

The father and son arrive in Hong Kong;
the father asks for forgiveness.

*D*o *you see how you have recorded this? These pages are not*
written as the past. You relive them as the present.

I touch Westen's hand. He and I stand in the same space and
time. Yes, our accounts are almost square. I have not felt this
way about the two of us since he was a boy. There are more questions I am not sure I can ask. Is my son sick? What about the girl
he was engaged to? I have heard of this "coming out," but I am
not sure that's what happened here. "I don't want to pry," I say,
"but how is *your* health?"

Westen shakes his head. "Fine."

"You were safe always, right?"

Westen looks at me in a way that tells me the timing is wrong.
"The safest. I've never had sex. Ever. With anyone." He runs a
hand through his hair in frustration. I will not inquire further.

"Is that my fault too?" I ask in all honesty.

"Oh yes," Westen says. "And I've never smoked pot or seen
It's a Wonderful Life. All your fault."

I begin to put the deck of cards away. One card slips to the
floor and Westen picks it up. "What do you know," he says. He
holds up the card. It is the four of spades. Anna May Wong. Of

course she has pearl-white skin and a jade outfit. "What was she in?"

"I have never heard of her," I say. I sift through the rest of the deck. She is the only minority.

Westen thinks this is funny. "My Chinese father! You know practically every white person in that deck and you don't know who Anna May Wong is?"

Yes, I am glad for the interruption and for the levity. "Well, at least I know she's Asian. Your grandmother on your mother's side thought the actor who played Charlie Chan was really Chinese." Hong Kong will be easy; one day and night, and I put him on a plane. And I have decided, without optimism, I will stay behind an extra week for treatment. *You were operating on false hope. What else might you have done with that week?*

OUR TAXI IS cramped, but I am pleased to be here, yes. Not because I enjoy the city. Too many people in too little space. Too many cellular telephones. Too much neon. But this was my father's city. He rebuilt our wealth here. This is where I learned English. This is where I first kissed a girl. I do not even remember her name. It was during a heavy rain. We huddled in the bird district. A green tarp hung above us, water pouring from its bowed center. We were both teenagers. I told her she was beautiful. I had such courage then. *"Xie xie ni de zan yang,"* she said. She was happy with the compliment. She kissed me on the cheek and then on the lips. The finches around us chirped. The girl took her lips away from mine. She giggled and ran into the rain. I did not follow. The woman who ran the booth stood next to me and shook her head.

Now my son is here with me. It is almost time for us to return to our homes. But there is something more we have to accomplish.

We sit shoulder to shoulder in the small car. "You gave me a free answer," I say. "So I am going to answer your last question without a deck of cards." My son looks at me calmly and I tell him a story. "We were living in Hong Kong at the time. I wasn't doing very well in school. 'You have to protect the family honor,' Papá told me. We were having tea next to the harbor. This was where Papá said he liked to think things through.

" 'I try,' I told him.

" 'You think you try. If you are my son, you *do*.' Then Papá told me the story about yin, the shadow. Which is like talking about the soul. There was a very old man who married a young bride. On their wedding night they conceived a son. But the old man died the next morning. When the woman had the boy, people were suspicious. They thought maybe he was not the son of the old man. The woman was taken in front of a judge who listened very carefully to both sides. He ruled that the boy would have no shadow if he was the son of the old man.

"This is one of the stories your *yeh yeh* told me that I never fully understood. But it stays with me. I'm always sad for the woman because no one believed her. And I think about the old man who only had one day of happiness in marriage before he died. I don't know about the boy. Papá never said if he had a shadow or not. But some days, even now, I check the ground behind me to see if I have a shadow."

Yes, I have invested all I can in this moment, so I simply look at Westen. "I made a mess of things in my life. So many wrong decisions. I never really talked to Celia and my father about my mistakes, and I never got a sense they forgave me." Westen listens dispassionately. I cannot tell what he is thinking. "I did not want to wait with you until it was too late. Neither of us is the same person he was twenty-five years ago. But I am hoping you will forgive me."

My cards are on the table. I've said it like I mean it. Even though this is what I have been wanting all along, it feels good to say it outright. This trip will be successful for me if I can walk away with my son's forgiveness. That is all the return I require. And I cannot tell him I am dying, no. It cannot come from that sympathy.

Westen looks forward. He rocks a few nods. "I see," he says. And then we say nothing.

Your secrets were out then. But no cure?

54

The father and son sit at the harbor's edge;
the son recalls his great-aunt's advice.

We sit for nearly two hours watching the harbor, saying very little. The moon over Hong Kong is a smudge of light behind the clouds, as if the city has shrouded itself to enjoy its own bright show. The harbor is hemorrhaging with refraction, every part of it a shining diamond-cut.

Almost a year ago, I visited Aunt Catherine and we did nearly this same thing, an early dinner and then sitting at San Diego's embarcadero to watch the sunset. It was cast with unusually pink tones. Aunt Catherine pointed to some clouds that looked like a set of bright sashes. "Wouldn't it be lovely if we could duplicate that color?" she said. And then she ran her own scarf through her hands as if dissatisfied.

"I can't coordinate the ones we have already," I said, pointing to my blue shorts and brown shirt.

Aunt Catherine looked at me with silver-gray eyes and smiled. "Evidently." She took my hand, squeezed it, and winked. I remember she was wearing white, just as she always had when I was younger. Her crepe scarf held back hair turned the same quiet color as ash from rosewood.

Looking out over the water, the boats in the foreground, a

dissipating sun in the distance, I couldn't picture another side of the ocean. There was only that shore and its limited possibilities.

"We should have tea like we used to," Aunt Catherine said. It was as if no time had passed between us. She looked at her watch, and in just a few minutes a deliveryman in a white sweatshirt that said SAN DIEGO GO CHARGERS! brought her an insulated nylon picnic bag. She paid him with a wad of bills from her sleeve. All of it planned out perfectly. "One lump or two?" she said.

We drank our tea and twilight fell, boats rocking in their moorings, gulls settling down. "We've had a fine time, haven't we?" Aunt Catherine said.

"It's been a wonderful day."

"No, dear. I mean always."

It wasn't like Aunt Catherine to be terribly nostalgic. She was a "What's next?" type of person, so I was curious. "Yes, of course," I said. "Is something the matter?"

"No, dear." She patted my hand. Hers was surprisingly warm and soft. "But I thought you might want to think about it. This can't last forever."

"What are you talking about?"

"Who's going to be your family when I go?"

I took a sip of tea and let the cup stay at my lip to buy time. "This is ridiculous" is all I could come up with. "I'll be okay."

"Westen." Her tone was reproving, her quiet way of letting me know I was being unreasonable. She poured more tea for each of us, coils of steam rolling around her hand as she stirred in honey. The sound of her spoon against the cup during this act was primary in my childhood memories.

"Look," I said, "Gideon left me money and you asked me to accept your estate. So I'll be fine."

"I didn't say money, dear. I said *family*." It scared me how many "dears" she was using, something reserved for moments when she wanted to convey her experience. "I was really hoping that Mr. Cavanaugh would have worked out for you."

"Mr. Cavanaugh" was Aunt Catherine's way of reminding me I'd never bothered to introduce her to Gideon. She never talked about dying, and I never bothered to consider that being an octogenarian made one consider such things. I looked at her. One would never suspect her years—even in the dim light her skin retained a moist, pink tone.

"I guess I'll be alone," I said. The breeze came up a little and I slipped on a sweatshirt I brought with me. A small boat streaked across the water, its engine sounding like an irritated insect.

"What about your father?"

"Uncle Cane is dead."

Aunt Catherine shook her head. "Don't be smart, please." She set her cup on the ground and faced me fully. "When I'm gone, that leaves your father out there somewhere. That man who left you with me and Uncle Cane. The man who's the reason I don't think you've ever been entirely happy. He's the reason you're incomplete."

I was shaken. "Gideon told me that same thing."

"He was a smart man, then. If you expect to spend your life alone and be happy, it has to be your choice."

That has been part of this trip to China, I think. To make that choice. My father and I sit at the edge of the harbor. The moon is still hobbled behind the clouds, the sky marbleized, the harbor more like a treasure chest than water. I consider what would happen if I just leaped over the railing and plunged in. Who would care, really, about a momentary spot of darkness in the light-filled sea?

55

The father and son shop for special fruits;
they visit a Curse Lady.

Hong Kong in the day is hot and damp; I push through the humidity as if it's wet tissue paper. We're going to see the Curse Lady today, and I'm going to open Mrs. Cheung's box no matter what. Though our first mission is to find a fruit stand with variety. My father passes over several shops. "Not fresh," he keeps saying.

The street is clogged with people, heads bobbing before and behind us, so many cell phones appearing and disappearing at so many ears that I'm convinced every person in Hong Kong has one. Ahead of us is a girl of about fourteen. She's wearing a short pink skirt with a matching sleeveless blouse. She unclasps her pink vinyl purse and snaps her phone to her ear. The movement is so practiced and smooth, she could have had this phone for years. And I'm surprised anyone can hear anything anyway above all the noise, the din of car engines and honking, trolley buzz, and the general hum of millions of conversations.

My father's pace today is slow and the white handkerchief remains in his left hand, dabbing at his face every few minutes. "I go away for a few years and I miss it here," he says. "But I always forget about the weather." We walk away from the traffic, up a sloping alley where we see dozens of vendors, half of them selling fruit and vegetables. This is not gleaming Hong Kong. It is something more primitive, more stone-sharpened knives carving on meat than electronics. The concrete is deeply stained from years of exposure and wear, and the air smells something like turpentine and lavender. We mainly find old women shopping, baskets in hand. I notice the people cut their fish live here, too, but a different way, across the back.

My father stops at a large display of fruit. "This is it," he says. "This is just right." He orders a batch of purple fruit and hands me one. "*San zuk*. Mountain bamboo. Go ahead." The skin is dry and has the texture of old rubber. I follow my father's lead, squeezing the husk open for the fruit inside. It's slick and white like a grub. It comes in uneven wedges, and I pop one in my mouth, less interested in the sweetness than in the odd seed with its impenetrable gelatinous cover. We also buy star fruit and something my father calls *longan*.

"Looks like small cantaloupes," I say.

"Yes. Yes. Tastes like cantaloupe," my father says. He hands me one. The skin is stiff and dry as a peanut shell. He also orders a large spiny fruit that looks something like a brown medieval mace complete with handle. "This fruit is terrible," he says. "I can't stand it. It smells so bad. Stinks up the whole house."

"Then why are we buying it?"

"I guess Mrs. Lee likes it." My father finishes his order with oranges, tangerines, peaches, grapes, and cherries, and two sturdy bags with handles that he has to argue over and clearly pay a little extra for.

Between us, we carry the load of fruit down another street, where we catch a double-decker trolley. The downstairs is full of people who look like they live in their seats. We walk up the narrow stairs and take a seat in the very front, next to the windows. "Having fun?" my father asks, wiping his face and cleaning his glasses. He looks as hot and sweaty as me, but he's smiling, clearly excited.

The trolley moves surprisingly fast with a slight rocking, and from this height it feels like we're swinging on vines. There are so many signs, neon and otherwise, at the base of each building, they look like the shed skin of giant vertical reptiles. My father anticipates our stop and we head downstairs, where we pay as we exit. It didn't even occur to me that we didn't pay when we entered. We stand on the blackened concrete platform as my father takes out his notepad and gets his bearings. "This way," he says in a confident tone.

A few blocks away I see where we're headed. "Under the bridge?" I say, referring to his notepad.

"Yes. Yes."

"What exactly are we about to do?"

Pushing his glasses up, my father looks at me in a very teacherly way, crossing his arms and putting one hand to his chin. "Think of this as anthropology," he says. "We're finally going to visit a Curse Lady, *da sieu yun*. Literally translated, it means 'hit little people.' "

"Like voodoo?"

"No. No." He pauses for a moment and drops his hand. "Well, yes, actually."

I'm holding my bag of fruit in both arms. It smells like something's squished, maybe a tangerine, but I can't be sure anymore. I feel the paper for wetness. Nothing. I think back to all the people my father has talked to on this trip, jotting their curses down. I think of the blind man selling *wong pei* in Guangzhou and how it probably wouldn't hurt much for him to have a little more satisfaction in his life than having a successful day selling fruit he cannot see to customers he cannot see for money he cannot see.

UNDER THE BRIDGE, three women sit on stools with card-board boxes in front of them like plain brown shrines. It's obvi-ous which one is Mrs. Lee, I think. She has neat black hair, too black for her age, and she wears a long-sleeved nylon red and green floral blouse. And her posture is perfectly erect and calm. My father has the same guess because he approaches her and speaks. She responds affirmatively and we set the fruit next to her. My father also pulls out a large wad of yuan tied with a string—all the money, I suppose, he's collected along the way. He hands her the pad and she flips through it, laughing and say-ing something occasionally to him.

"What's so funny?" I ask.

"She thinks my Chinese writing is terrible. I have to read the requests for her." My father steps back with the pad and reads from the first page.

I am prepared for some sort of elaborate ceremony. I expect that the woman will lift her box to reveal a porcelain sculpture with previously offered fruits and flowers. But as I stand closer to my father, I see that the open side of the box is empty except for a few scraps of paper. The woman listens to my father until he is done. She takes a black and yellow circle of paper and places it inside the box. Then she slips the black sandal off her right foot and slaps it down on the paper. If this were real, I'd think she had just caused someone's death.

We repeat this process for forty-five minutes, my father read-ing and Mrs. Lee slapping the paper with her shoe. It's hard not to feel guilty, even though I understand there is no power at work. But, still, we're putting curses on people. I imagine someone not waking up from their sleep, or keeling over in the middle of a meeting, maybe running off the road or drowning in a bathtub.

When we are done, there is very little exchange between Mrs.

Lee and my father. They just nod and we walk away. "That was weird," I say.

"A bit," he says, as we head back for the trolley.

"Doesn't it make you feel odd that we're participating in vengeance?"

My father stops walking and shakes his head. "No. No. Westen. What do you think happens?"

"Nothing. But, like you say, people believe in it. They *believe* they're causing death to people."

Now my father is laughing outright, the sound more full and open than I've heard from him before. "No. No. You misunderstand. All they are asking for is a bad headache, maybe a cramp. Really."

"Why bother?" I say as we step onto the trolley platform.

"Think about it. What's more satisfying—carrying around the guilt of someone's death or the knowledge you gave them a little discomfort?" My father looks over the top of his glasses. "Think about us. If you wanted to get even with me for leaving you, could you live with having me killed? How about just a little nagging pain?"

"Neither," I say. "It's not my style. I'd rather hold a grudge for twenty-five years."

"Yes. Yes. That you do well." We step onto the trolley headed back toward the harbor. "And one more thing," my father continues. "If you believe in curses, every time you get a little pain, it makes you examine your life to see if you've wronged anyone."

"No pains here," I say.

"Plenty here," my father says. And then, quietly, "Yes, yes. I've one last thing to show you."

5 6

*The father and son end their vacation;
the son offers forgiveness.*

It is our last stop in Hong Kong before my father puts me on
the plane. Both of us are oddly nervous and I'm not sure why.
The taxi waits for us at the top of the hill as we walk to the edge
of the marina, an odd expense that I don't question. We are on
one of two ferries that dodge pleasure boats to cross the green
water. In front of us is a gigantic gilded barge, the Jumbo Floating Restaurant. It's every Chinese cliché, red paint and gold trim,
dragon columns with fierce, spiky heads and snakelike bodies
coiled and ready to strike. Gigantic red lanterns.

"I'm not hungry," I say.

"No. No," my father says. "We are not eating. I just want to
show you something."

We step off the ferry and onto the barge. It's so stable I can't
even feel the water below me. "What's the appeal of a floating
restaurant?" I ask.

"It's been here a long time. It used to be a novelty. This place
used to be packed, believe me." My father leads me past the entrance to the end of the barge, which is at least a city block long.
We walk to the very end, where all that stands before us are a few
anchored boats, the open water, and undeveloped dark-green hill-
sides that make up the shoreline. I cannot see the main harbor

from here and it is much quieter, the air still and cooler than in the city.

My father points to a wide, flat dock not far away on which there are large wooden crates, and orange boxcars with no wheels. "That's where I went after school," my father says.

"Hangout for you and your friends?" I say.

"No. No. Just me. I never had many friends. I liked it there because I could think, especially after Ma died. She had been in Canada with my brother. Papá flew us over. I'd never seen snow before. I remember standing in front of the hospital with him. The box hedges were heavy with new snow. Both of us had on black wool coats we had to buy before we left Hong Kong. Papá wore black gloves too. My cheeks itched from the cold. There was a statue of a young man looking upward. He had snow piled on his face and his outstretched hand. Papá said almost nothing the whole time. His breath just fired out in slabs. I asked Papá if Ma was okay. He looked down and said, 'Zhen you zhi.' Childish. Later I found out Ma died before we got to the hospital."

I'm not sure why my father is telling me all this. It is sad, though, and I don't stop him. He takes off his glasses and puts his handkerchief to his wet eyes. "That was really difficult," I say as softly as possible.

"Yes. Yes, it was." My father sighs softly and continues. "It was harder because I was never close with Ma. Papá and I started growing apart too. I let that happen. That dock is where I went to think about things like that. Away from our apartment and all the noise and business. I would sneak in. There was not much going on anyway. It was mostly for impounded items, cargo that people could not pay for or didn't want. I would find a little nook among the boxes where I could watch the water and think."

"That sounds lonely," I say.

"Yes." In front of us, a boat horn breaks through the air as a smaller, speedier boats zips in front of a larger boat and the water is churned up briefly. My father seems calmed and he stutters a sigh. "I just wanted to bring you here because it's where I came as a boy and I wanted you to know that I left you but you never left me because I thought of you every day. In some ways that was part of my punishment. I was such a failure in everything. I ignored my father, turned my back on his advice. I was determined to be American, so I went ahead and married your mother. Yes, I failed her from the very start. Westen, I didn't want to ruin your life too. I thought giving you to your greataunt was best. But it was just another act of cowardice."

My father's eyes fill with tears again. It's likely that after this trip we won't have anything to say to each other. But it has been too long for both of us to keep agonizing about things we can't fix. And at the same time, I think of the letter he has from my mother. I know I am giving up the possibility of that too.

I put my hand across my father's shoulder and we look toward the dock where he hid as a child. "I forgive you," I say. "You don't have to worry about us anymore. You can put that away." My father cries full on, turning away, trying to hold it back, but it comes and it does not stop for minutes. This feels right. I put my arms around him and pat his back. I hate to stop him, but I have to. "We should go or I'll be late," I say.

"Yes. Yes," my father says. "Just a minute, though." He reaches into his pocket and produces a thin, palm-sized silver camera I've not seen before. He takes a photo across the water to the dock and then one of me. Then he hands me the camera, standing in the shot, bleary-eyed, glasses off, a wisp of hair caught in the air like a black horn, the dock of his boyhood over his shoulder. He smiles, and as I take the picture I realize I am slightly jealous of his growing relief and happiness. My forgiveness feels abstract. The son he needs absolution from is eight years old, I think, and that boy is dead.

Turning to take a last look at the harbor, my father appears solitary, as if he's been waiting for someone to stand at his side for a very long time. This moment seems right. I take out Mrs. Cheung's blue box, untie the ribbon a final time, and pull off the lid. Beneath her note, under the white cloth, is a thin, ornate wirework. It is hinged, expanding into a wide frame centered by a circular mirror, which reduces my image, so that nearly my entire face is contained within it.

It's not clear to me what this is supposed to mean, until I understand it is because I'm looking at myself. Not until my father turns around and faces me do I get it, see what is actually framed inside the looping wire and mirror. I am reflected, yes, and my father is on the left. To the right is the harbor he loved. In this gift of Mrs. Cheung's I find myself in the same landscape as my father for the first time.

The son is flying home. He is feeding his pigeons. He is thinking about repainting his house in Blue Falls. The father is taking Chinese medicine. He is returning to Los Angeles. He is terminally ill.

No one knows the end of their own story. Not this son and father. Not a year later when they have spoken just twice, and then briefly, with excuses about why they cannot talk long. But here is their end and their beginning. The father will die, the son will bury him. This is their future.

AT FIRST WESTEN Gray thinks he will not go. He has not been to this city in years. He does not like it here. Memories of Los Angeles and Chinatown are what made the dream he had a few nights ago possible. In it, Westen sat in the small, taupe-colored room, watching his father's choreography as acquaintances came and went, some of them much older versions of people he had been introduced to as a child. There was no casket, just his father covered to the waist by a sheet and wearing a cream-colored, long-sleeved shirt and red bow tie. People mentioned how good he looked, but Westen did not think the coloring was right. Placed around his father were various plants and flower arrangements. There was a gently woven ivy wreath laced with white gardenias like garish stars, a spray of even whiter roses, and a mix of calla and Casablanca lilies. The air was still and lightly seasoned by a *ruan* and *yang chin* duet playing in the background. The only brilliance, Westen remembers, came from the words written in Chinese on the red satin ribbons.

Now he knows he will drive to the airport and call his father from there. He will cancel their appointment and go home to Blue Falls. This isn't so special. Most men become dying fathers, Westen thinks, all men become dying sons. But it is not that easy. So he decides to get to Los Angeles, which holds him. Heavy rain backs up flights at LAX for hours. Westen watches the storm break across the city, water falling from the sky in unbroken streams like steel bars. He thinks of his father, of gardenias and incarceration, and he realizes he is not done.

The August rains come from the south, leaving behind a city inflamed and still. An hour after the thunderstorm, Los Angeles recaptures its summer sky. The retreating clouds seem stained with orange iodine. "In case you need to know," his father told him over the phone in a weak voice, "I saved your mother's letter." From his hotel room Westen sees Chinatown, the community of his youth, resting next to the hills, wet and pulsing with refraction. Out there, his father is holding on, waiting for his son.

WESTEN STEPS FROM the cab. The sidewalk seems comprised of idle people and scraps of paper, as if there has just been a parade. Chinatown has ignored the rain. The smell of winter melon soup slices through the humidity from the steaming streets. This could be a port city, Westen thinks, and he is reminded, somehow, of the scrap-heap villages bordering the river as he and his father rode the hydrofoil to Hong Kong. Westen fumbles with his father's address in his pants pocket, but leaves it there. Chinatown is more familiar than he thought it would be.

When his father brought him here as a child, Westen was sure they had crossed a border as they turned off Sunset and onto Broadway. All the faces he now saw on the sidewalks were like his father's. The look of each block also changed. Gradually there was room for less and less vegetation. A few twisting junipers grew at the entrances of restaurants, as if a couple of square feet were all that could be spared. Westen remembers imagining his face transforming into Asian features, convincing himself that the sharp jaw and broad nose he inherited from his mother would immediately lose their shape and he would fit in this new territory, for the day at least.

Today, in front of Emperor's Kitchen and along the main strip are large concrete pots planted with geranium and asparagus fern, remnants of a community renewal that never got past the first phase. Westen walks down this street he hasn't visited since his mother died. He closes his eyes at this corner and hears his father teaching him how to cross the street. He again smells the boiled plumage of freshly plucked chickens. A little farther on is precisely where he first heard the word *cure* in Chinese, and where he listened to his father and mother as they ate dim sum, gently arguing over names for a daughter. He wonders now if perhaps his mother was pregnant before she died.

Westen keeps his eyes closed, imagining the streets. He realizes he can tell time by how many blocks away his destination is. He thinks of Paleolithic man chipping the first tools, progress clocked by the position of the sun. Today, Westen is reduced to a point on a grid, an inset on a map. Every move is a new coordinate, and he realizes it takes a hard rain to scour away time. He opens his eyes and the strip looks again, for a moment, as if it were expecting visitors.

The wet asphalt makes the air taste bitter. Westen is bumped by a pair of Chinese women carrying pink pastry boxes tied with string. They wear matching Mao suits and their gray collars disappear under wide round chins. One of the women eyes Westen as if she recognizes him, and the other says something in Chinese as they pass.

His father's apartment is just up the street, next to Dr. Lee's office, where his father used to take him regularly for his asthma. He remembers the doctor, who was old even then, listening to his lungs through his fingers. "I hear also with my hands," he said, placing his thumb over Westen's trachea and extending his little finger across his sternum. After a while he would write on a scrap of paper and tell Westen to button his shirt. His father took the note to Mrs. Lee, who presided over the front office where the herbs were stored. Invariably she corrected the prescription. "Too strong. Too strong," she always said in English and Chinese, making sure they knew she was doing them a favor.

WESTEN TURNS IN toward the former centerpiece of Chinatown: seventy-year-old buildings that were somebody's idea of authentic Asian architecture. He walks across the stone square, looking around him at the proliferation of green and red paint. On any other street in Los Angeles, this would mean Christmas was near. But here the semiology is different. Somehow this culturally legitimizes the businesses for tourists—Shing Fung and Sincere Imports, Gin Ling Gifts and R.G. Louie Co. with its red neon Buddha sitting atop the word ART. Westen walks to the display window. There are a half-dozen variations on Buddha staring happily out from the glass. Some have protruding foreheads with a peachy tint to accent extra cranial capacity. Others have gold nipples and belly buttons. Finally there are tall porcelain vases with oyster-blue dragons and carp twisting around their curves. Westen remembers the factories in China. These might have been painted by artists, he thinks, or people just working for their next meal.

Westen sits on one of the wire-mesh benches that have re-placed the thick, wood-slatted seating he remembers as a child. Dr. Lee does not expect him for another half hour. There is an el-derly Chinese man in a suit jacket and matching slacks, feeding a dozen bleak-looking pigeons. Westen watches their gray heads bob up and down, salvaging the crumbs the old man tosses at his feet. Half of them drag tattered wing feathers along the ground as if they have given up on flight in a city where their prospects are the same wherever they land.

At his right is a bronze plaque honoring Peter Soo Hoo and Herbert Lapham. Their bas-relief faces are almost comical. Their noses catch the light with a particularly bright metallic shine. But what attracts Westen the most are the words on the plaque.

DEDICATED TO MR. PETER SOO HOO AND MR. HERBERT LAPHAM, CO-FOUNDERS OF CHINATOWN, WHOSE FORE-SIGHT AND UNTIRING EFFORTS WERE LARGELY RESPONSI-BLE FOR THE DEVELOPMENT AND BUILDING OF A FINER CHINATOWN UPON WHICH WORK WAS STARTED FEBRU-ARY 1, 1937.

As he looks at the familiar plaque, something beyond the brass symbols feeds his memory. Westen finds the landmarks of his childhood chalked off in his mind. There is a façade with its huge octagonal window and red trim faded into a conspicuous pink. Familiar cracks reach out from its edges and stretch around the corners like tentacles. Westen stands and follows an old visual trail that clears for him as if he were preceded by machetes in a jungle. He remembers this place from his childhood and sees himself at three or four, perhaps, rubbing his hands across these same brass letters. He knew then that they were symbols that added up to something. Somehow adults could unlock the mystery, moving their lips as they scanned the lines with their eyes. This was magic, private incantations that almost always rewarded the magician. Westen remembers himself standing in front of the plaque, moving his lips, hoping the meaning would come to him.

Today he stands up and rubs his hands over the words he touched as a child. The brass is warm and smooth. Of all the possible combinations, he thinks, someone has left an array of letters here and I understand them.

The wall and opposite gallery of shops lead him to the Chinatown wishing well, a stone-and-concrete slope with tin pans anchored at strategic places. Its lava rock falls have been spray-painted orange, yellow, and an almost inconsequential blue. The water is not running in this fountain, but sits in its basin as a still and gelatinous green. Small box turtles float motionless at the top, as mosquito larvae wriggle around their shells.

At random points in the rock there are signs indicating where visitors are supposed to throw their coins to get certain wishes. The signs bear words found in fortune cookies and Charlie Chan movies. Resting above silver pans, the red block letters read VACATION, LOVE, PROMOTION, HAPPINESS, HEALTH, LUCK, WEALTH, LONG LIFE. Some of the pans do not have signs, leaving the possibilities open. One might wish for another season, Westen thinks, hope for a solstice and a revelation.

He feels someone at his side. At first he sees the woman's thin white hair parted neatly over her pink scalp. Then his eyes meet hers and he recognizes Mrs. Lee. Her skin is darker now, speckled with age spots, but her smile gives her away. "Westen," she says, as if there is no question in her mind who he is. "Dr. Lee want to see you. Your father say you coming."

"I was just thinking about him bringing me here when I was a kid," Westen says, surprised.

"Dying too young," she answers, shaking her head with implication and respect. "He won't go to hospital anymore." After a quiet moment, Mrs. Lee turns and begins walking, obviously used to being followed. She wears a gray silk blouse embroidered with yellow magnolias around the neck. Westen walks behind her. "That wishing well waste of money," she says, looking back briefly. "The only way to get your wish is hard work." Westen can smell the perfume she makes from brandy, maple bark, and orange blossom.

The Lee storefront is now in Chinatown West, across the street. Mrs. Lee walks against the light into traffic. She stretches out her arm to stop the oncoming cars and the drivers obey, slowing as she and Westen cross. They walk past a fountain where the ornamental carp are mere gold and white ovals in dark water. "We moved the business five years ago when I retired," Mrs. Lee says, taking Westen farther into the beige stucco complex. He notices the lights strung between the rooftops. There are hundreds of clear bulbs and the remains of paper lanterns. An awkward silence rests over everything like a veil, and Westen realizes most of the shops here have gone out of business. Mrs. Lee stops at a narrow wooden door with the gold-stenciled words DR. LEE 12 P.M. TO 5 P.M. DAILY. She guides Westen with her hand as they step inside, her brown eyes shining like two freshly polished beads.

Bells hanging from the door announce their entrance as Mrs. Lee and Westen enter the office. The room smells of vanilla, a light and anaesthetic scent. Dr. Lee stands behind his desk and greets them. Beside him a small radio plays a baseball game,

Dodgers at St. Louis, but he has obviously turned it down low. "Mrs. Lee can find anyone in Chinatown," he says to Westen as a greeting. "We're closing a little early to meet our granddaughter for dinner."

"I was just looking at some of the places my father used to take me. I kind of miss it."

"You never like it before," Mrs. Lee says, patting Westen on the shoulder. The three sit down around the desk.

"I didn't?"

"You cry every time your father bring you."

"I came back, didn't I?"

"Best customer," Mrs. Lee says. "Come every twenty-five years whether you need it or not."

Dr. Lee rubs his hand over his head as part of a silent satisfaction. A sparse rim of white hair is all that is left of the thick gray Westen remembers. But the face has not changed much. His skin is still bright and smooth and taut over his bones from a lifetime of vegetarianism. He wears a white button-down shirt rolled at the sleeves and a pink cardigan vest.

Without saying anything, he puts his hand inside Westen's shirt in the old way, and Westen is surprised at the familiar heat of the doctor's hand. "You sound fine," he says. Westen remembers the old office and its wall lined with rows of drawers, how Mrs. Lee measured her herbs onto brown sheets of paper, or, if they were not to be mixed, rolled them into individual parcels. There was a glass counter where people selected certain roots for specific shape and size and on top of that, a large jar like a fishbowl containing small, people-shaped roots soaking in yellow liquid. The combined odor left a carbonized sweetness like a freshly lit match. Westen remembers his father speaking in Chinese as he took the small brown packages from Mrs. Lee.

Dr. Lee sits at his desk, removing a panda-shaped key chain from his drawer. "This is for your father's apartment. He told me to hold it for you in case." He sets it on the desk, the panda's black and white coloring faded. "When was the last time you saw him?"

"Last year in China," Westen says. "We didn't talk much after we came back."

It is nearly five o'clock and Mrs. Lee hangs a small CLOSED sign in the window. It is time to go. Dr. Lee stands and shakes Westen's hand, and he and his wife walk him out the door, the tiny bell jingling just as it did when he came in. Dr. Lee points to a set of stairs. "The apartment is up there."

Westen remembers the Chinese words for "thank you," *doh zeh,* and offers them in return. He watches the Lees walk away, then he ascends the stairs where his father waits. He pauses at the door, feeling an odd form of guilt, not oppressive but thorough, like a child concealing stolen candy, afraid of the penetration of a parent's eyes.

After a tentative knock, Westen waits, then hears a progressive thump inside, nearing the door. The person who opens it is a new version of his father, a man unsteady behind a walker, gray, with long white whiskers thin as silk dangling from his chin. "I knew you would come," his father says softly, turning into the room.

"I almost didn't."

Westen's father stops and leans heavily on the walker. "Then I guess I know you better than you know yourself, son."

Westen is silenced by this final word, tries in a flash to recall how long since he's heard it applied to him. A kind of electricity fills his chest as he and his father slowly move forward.

Very little is left in the apartment, nothing extra in the living room or in the kitchen, sparse furniture and dishes. His father has planned well. The room is dark and smells like green tea. Westen lifts a shade as his father continues toward the back rooms. Outside, long shadows of copper light streak the opposite buildings. There are no colors like this in Blue Falls, he thinks. Los Angeles has its own sun, it seems to him, a city with a private orbit in a singularly orange sky.

"It feels strange to be back," Westen says, walking to the bedroom over the carpet, which bears the worn tracks of his father's walker. The sound of the city enters like a jumble of high-pitched thunder. There is a narrow bed in the room where his father sits, curved and weak but pointing to a mahogany-stained rolltop desk that Westen recognizes as his mother's. "Open it," his father says.

Inside, the desk is packed with spiral notebooks, folded papers and envelopes filling each slot. He sits in the desk chair. The letter from his mother lies in the center, paper-clipped to a note in his father's handwriting. Westen feels as if his mother is in the room, as if they have all come together to say good-bye. He reads his father's note written in shaky handwriting.

Dear Son,

I am sorry we did not get a chance to see each other again and I'm sorry I didn't tell you I was sick earlier. Maybe it was another of my mistakes, but I did not want you to feel sorry for me. So, here is your mother's desk and some of her papers. Nothing much, but it's all I have of her and now it's yours (I have even paid for the moving). And, of course, the letter that says if I'm your biological father. So many times I wanted to open it. But in the end, I know you are my son. Now it is in your hands. I've done many things wrong in my life. I don't have any parting wisdom for you. I just want you to know that I never forgot you in all the years we were apart. Never. And our village will never forget you, either. They completed the bridge and named it after you, Chan.

I guess I only want to say we have had a complicated
life together and apart, and you cannot let that deter-
mine how you live from now on. There need to be people
and loves in your life, and you have to hold them close.

Your Father

Westen sits back in the chair and looks at the man in front of him, who is curved and tired. He reads the letter again. This is the man I remember as my father, Westen thinks, the man who brought me sweet dates, the man who made me feel Chinese when I was a boy. And now he is offering me everything again in my mother's letter. Westen's hands shake and he puts his father's note down.

Taped to the inside of the desk is a pair of photographs. They record Westen and his father standing on the floating barge. In one, Westen sees himself standing almost childlike, harbor and boats above his right shoulder. In the other, the one Westen took, the dock where his father retreated as a boy rests in the background behind his father. The photos are taped together so that Westen and his father appear to be standing side by side, an echo of the view he saw through Mrs. Cheung's box. He peels the photos from the desk and puts them together with the envelope containing his mother's letter. "And what are all these notebooks?" Westen asks.

"An old man's ledger. Someday you should read them to see if I've balanced my books." He pats the space next to him, calling his son to the bed. They sit in silence, not speaking. He listens to their breathing, unsyncopated but somehow unified. "It's all right to go now," his father says. "That's all I have."

"It's more than enough," Westen says, running his finger across his mother's envelope resting on his lap. "I'm glad I came." And although it has been a short meeting, not even an hour, and so few words have passed between them, Westen understands that he is a son who has come home and at the same time he is headed home.

At the bedroom door, Westen sees that his father doesn't have the strength to follow. He closes his eyes and imagines again the man who brought him dates and told him stories. He sees his mother in her nurse's uniform and then himself as a boy flying a red box kite in a wide-open sky. He looks at his father, who is smiling, who is gray but not defeated.

"It doesn't have to be a happy one," his father says, "but a man must choose an ending."

Westen nods his head and turns slowly to leave.

"Westen," his father calls hoarsely. "Son, find someone to love. Find another Gideon."

Of all the permissions in the world, this is one Westen never imagined, but its arrival lights on him with the unexpected delicacy of need and release. Outside, he locks the door to the apartment, knowing he has seen his father for the final time. The panda given to him by Dr. Lee dangles at the end of its chain. He slides the tip of his father's key into the corner of the envelope that seals his mother's letter, pulling along the top. He keeps the open envelope in his hands, instead examining the merged photo of him and his father, whose life seemed built on so many subtractions: leaving China and his own father, losing his wife, giving up his son. It would take anyone a long time to recover from all that, Westen thinks.

Walking forward, one finger inside his mother's envelope, Westen takes the folded letter out and stares at it as if the concealed contents will tell him what to do. Typed lettering shows through the paper. His father held on to this unopened, not for himself, Westen understands, but for his son. Westen could unfold the letter right now. But there, he realizes, would be the answer to a question he does not have to ask. He steps out to the sidewalk, to a group of empty steel barrels, drops the envelope in, and then the letter. I know who my father is, he thinks. He is not the man who abandoned me. He is the man who returned.

Sensing how quiet the city is, how truly calm and noiseless, Westen recognizes the silence someone described to him long ago. A firm breeze pushes from behind. The air is complex. It is warm as an incision. Downtown Los Angeles looms to the west of the pagoda façades still dripping rainwater's temporary lacquer. There are possibilities even in abandoned regions, Westen thinks. He stands in an enormity of sunlight, in the russet of a healing bruise. Amber warmth swirls around him. There are no answers or perfect trajectories, no advance scouts returning with news of clear routes. What more could a father offer his son, Westen thinks, than the possibilities of an uncertain future, the permission and directive to find someone to love. He looks at the photo in his hand one more time, at the spot where as a boy his father sat and felt alone. There is another side to that ocean, Westen thinks, buoys in still water, rudders and pontoons where only fathers and sons meet, other harbors where they understand each other without question among obsolete moorings and docks with unclaimed cargo.

Acknowledgments

Grateful acknowledgment is made to California State University, Northridge; the University of Louisville; Indiana University; the Families Leung, DiTomaso, Peeples, and Nelson; and all the Doran branches. For their friendship and support, I would also like to thank Thomas Alvarez, Matthew Brim, Manuel Muñoz, Simeon Berry, Nikki Moustaki, Adam McComber, Richard Blanco, Roland Thompson, Ryan Downing, Alice Estes Davis, Loran Estes, Charles Solomon, Scott Johnston, Brook White, Yvette Melvin, Pres and Jeannine Romanillos, Kevin Koch, William Reiss, Sally Kim, and PJ Mark.

Questions for Discussion

1. What do you think of the dual voices—those of Westen and his father, Xin—the author uses to tell the story in *Lost Men*? Would the novel have been different if the story were told from only one point of view? Additionally, why do you think the author chose to begin and end the novel in the third person, and what is the effect?

2. Though the title is *Lost Men,* in what ways are the women in the novel equally important to the story?

3. "Each season offers a new identity. When you live here long enough, you learn to do the same" (page 11). Consider Westen's statement. Does it reveal anything about his personality? What do you think it means in the context of what happens in *Lost Men?*

4. Talk about the relationships Westen has with the men in his life: his father, his uncle Cain, Gideon. How are these relationships different from, and similar to, one another?

5. Did it surprise you that after their trip to China, the two men spoke only twice in the next year? What kept them apart in this way?

6. Why do you think Xin hides his illness from Westen, despite the many times on their trip to China when he bares his soul to his son?

7. When Westen reveals to his father his nearly neutral sexuality, Xin gives Westen his blessing to find love, regardless of the gender of the person. Were you surprised by Xin's reaction? How did you expect him to respond?

8. Xin communicates most intimately with Westen through letters; Westen writes heartfelt letters to his aunt Catherine from China; Westen's mother has written a letter that reveals who Westen's father really is. Consider the acts of letter-writing in *Lost Men* and the freedom they allow these characters.

9. Were you surprised by what happens after Westen receives his mother's letter?